"I remember seeing her there, still in her habit, standing like a lost waif next to her suitcase. In fact, her father drove up just a few minutes after she got back to the Mother House."

"Back from where?"

"She asked Hudson to hear a last confession."

"I see." It didn't sound like the act of a victim.

"I walked her back to the chapel myself and waited outside for her. Then we walked back together. She never said a word. I don't know where Hudson was. He must have stayed in the chapel."

"How do you know she didn't get medical care?"

Joseph came back to the long table and stood with her hands on the back of the chair she had left a few minutes earlier. "We heard afterward that she had stayed at home with her father after her mother died. And on Christmas"—she paused—"Julia hanged herself."

THE
CHRISTMAS
NIGHT
MURDER

Lee Harris

FAWCETT GOLD MEDAL • NEW YORK

A Fawcett Gold Medal Book
Published by Ballantine Books
Copyright © 1994 by Lee Harris

Library of Congress Catalog Card Number: 94-94401

ISBN 0-449-14922-6

Printed in Canada

First Edition: November 1994

10 9 8 7 6 5 4 3 2 1

The author wishes to thank
Ana M. Soler, James L. V. Wegman,
Camari Gaines, Marsha Kugelman, and Greg Pinto
for their much-needed information.

For Jenni and Bill
from whom I have learned so much

1

It was my first Christmas as a wife and I discovered pretty fast that fifteen years as a nun and a little more than a year as a single secular woman had not prepared me for the holiday as a married woman. As though a chemical change had occurred within me, I found it was not enough to put up a small tree and decorate it as I had the year before, my first Christmas out of the convent. From deep within me came the desire to do more, much more, so that Jack, my husband of four months, would feel both the memories of Christmas as a boy and the sense that we were starting our own traditions, our own way of celebrating, so that years from now, in the next century, I marveled, our progeny would describe Christmas in our house as wonderful and memorable and the only way to celebrate, an old-fashioned Christmas.

But I had a lot of obstacles. It was easy enough with a man in the house to acquire a larger tree, to decorate it extravagantly, to put lights outside and in hard-to-reach places. But Christmas is so much more than a tree and lights. It is smells, the smells of special, seasonal foods cooking and once-a-year cakes and cookies baking in your own oven. I was almost completely at a loss.

Having entered St. Stephen's earlier than the usual post-high-school age because of the loss of my parents and other family problems, I had never had the opportunity to learn to cook at my mother's side. At the convent, where baking began weeks before the holiday, I had never participated. The nuns displayed their individual talents to benefit everyone, and a handful of excellent cooks and artful bakers, each with a few specialties and the desire to produce and share them, saw to it that we ate well much of the time. My talents lay elsewhere. I eventually got a master's in English and taught at the convent college. The closest I ever came to a cookbook was descriptions of food in the books I read. Dickens's portrait of old Fezziwig's Christmas dinner was incorporated into my personal Christmas lore.

Thus at age thirty-one I could cook only to stave off hunger and I had never baked in my life. With a policeman husband who had made a more than respectable cook of himself and who had a palate I envied, I was still too shy after four months of marriage to try new dishes, while the thought of baking brought me to a near panic. I had more or less decided after I left St. Stephen's and moved into the house in Oakwood that my aunt had left me that I would survive without learning how to cook. So what if the newspaper of record devoted pages every week to this increasingly popular activity? Did I have to run with the crowd? It was enough that I ran—or walked—on the streets of Oakwood every morning that the weather allowed. If Jack wanted a good meal, he could have the pleasure and pride of making it for us.

And then one day, as though the calendar had kept a secret from me, it was less than a month till Christmas, then almost two weeks, and Jack, who had never had a tree in his tiny Brooklyn apartment, was talking about trees and decorations—and food. My panic was palpable. So I did what I had learned to do over the last eighteen months when a crisis loomed. I turned to Melanie Gross.

That I went for help to a Jewish friend is not an indication of desperation but of the affection I have for her and, above all, how much I admire her homey skills.

"You've never made Christmas cookies?" she said in apparent disbelief.

"Melanie, you know I've never made anything. Until I met you and Jack, I thought tuna fish sandwiches were gourmet food."

"Chris, I gave you everything you need as a wedding present. You promised you would use it. I believed you." She seemed almost devastated, betrayed by her friend.

"It's only been four months," I said lamely, wondering if my unkept promise constituted a lie at this early point.

"Nothing's lost," she said breezily. "We'll start with Christmas cookies."

"Have you ever made them?"

"No."

"Then how do you know you can?"

She gave me her wonderful smile. "How hard can they be?" she said, and I knew we would succeed.

Her wedding present had been all the necessary cooking utensils a new bride would need. Before selecting them, Mel had gone through my kitchen, which was still very much Aunt Meg's kitchen because I had done little to change it. She had oohed and aahed at Aunt Meg's cast-iron pot and assured me it was priceless, but much of the other stuff she felt needed replacing or updating. Cookie sheets were banged up and uneven; cake tins were rusting. A favorite frying pan of my aunt's had a bottom that had risen, caused, Mel informed me, by plunging it hot into cold water. I did not tell her that my aunt had probably not been responsible for the demise of the pan.

The day before our wedding she had come to the house with an enormous carton filled with cookie sheets, round and oblong cake pans, a rack to cool cakes on (I had to ask what that one was for), and a set of essential pots and pans. I loved every shiny new piece she gave me, especially because I love her, because I probably couldn't have arranged a wedding without her and her remarkable mother, but I had not used even one of the baking items. Now they would get their baptism by fire.

Like the excellent teacher she is, Melanie had supervised while I did nearly everything by myself. When my kitchen, where we did our baking while her children were minded by a teenage sitter in their own home, failed to have some necessary electrical appliance, she showed me how to work with my hands and manual utensils.

"Here's how you sift flour," she said, spreading a piece of waxed paper on my counter and dumping flour into an old sifter.

"Aren't you going to measure it?" I asked with concern.

"After we sift it. Want to know why?"

"I guess I do, Mel," I said, wondering whether I could stretch my mind to accommodate all this new information that I had lived without for thirty-one pretty successful years.

"Because sifting will lighten it. There'll be more than you started with. Always measure after you sift, not before. Want to know something else?"

I laughed. "Is this need to know or nice to know?"

"It's nice to know. In Europe, they measure by weight. In a typical kitchen you'll find a balance scale—"

"A *balance* scale?"

"It's much more exact than dry measure and you can weigh first and sift afterward. We inexact Americans have to be more careful. Now, put it into the measuring cup gently, Chris, and whatever you do, don't shake it down."

And so it went. My stove was neither as new nor as accurate as hers, but she was so clever, she made it work right. (First thing next year I'm going to get the gas company out to check the temperature settings, which I just know will give me all the professionalism I need to pass myself off as accomplished. Alas, the sin of pride is the hardest to conquer.)

When Jack came home that night, late because he went to his law-school classes, he stopped just inside the door and took an immensely deep breath. "Woman," he said, "I may marry you."

"Again?"

"Oh sweetheart, it'll seem like the first time. Did you really bake today?"

"With a lot of help from Mel."

He dropped his books and marched into the kitchen, where pyramids of decorated stars and angels and snowmen were stacked on plastic plates and covered with colored cellophane and tied with red ribbons (Mel never does anything by halves), and he stopped dead, speechless for the moment. "I didn't know how to ask you," he said, his voice a little boy's, almost breaking.

"I thought you'd like it," I said lamely.

"It's incredible." He looked at the wrapped plates lining the counter. "It must have been like losing your virginity."

I went over to him and wrapped my arms around him, my wonderful husband who had not asked for what he wanted, to spare me embarrassment. "Let me tell you the truth. Baking is fraught with a lot more terror and possibility of failure than first-time love."

"Oh baby," he said, "but just think how satisfying it is."

I wasn't sure which he meant, but in the spirit of Christmas I agreed with him.

2

"You'll just love him," I said to Jack. I was feeling giddy. It was Christmas Day and we were leaving momentarily for St. Stephen's Convent. We had spent Christmas Eve with Jack's family, and we were packing our suitcases in a cramped bedroom in Jack's parents' house in Brooklyn. We had come home from Christmas morning mass a little earlier and were heading upstate as soon as our bags were ready. I couldn't wait.

"Sure I will," he said. "With all the things you've told me about him, he must be quite a guy. Did you ever find that blue tie? I know I packed it and it just isn't here."

"Maybe it's on the floor or under the bed."

"Maybe it walked home."

"Did I tell you he's picked up some of the Indian languages? Joseph said he's been interviewing the old people to preserve their recollections."

"Twice."

"Twice what?"

"You told me twice."

"I must sound like an idiot. Christmas does that to me. Jack, your parents really went overboard with their presents."

"They love you."

"It's so good to have a family again."

The man I had been describing for the ninetieth time was Father Henry Hudson McCormick, better known as Hudson to his friends, although I tended to call him Father McCormick because I had been only fifteen when I met him. Named after his own father's favorite explorer, he had inherited the wanderlust of both his namesake and his father. After years of serving at St. Stephen's, he had left for a job that I imagined fulfilled every dream he had ever had. Instead of being attached to a diocese, he was posted for periods of one to two years at tiny parishes serving American Indians, mostly in the south and west. He wrote us wonderful though infrequent letters and sent gifts that his parishioners made, ceramic pots and wool rugs that we cherished and displayed.

Several weeks ago he had left his latest church in a town in Wyoming and begun his way east, a journey he would complete this afternoon at St. Stephen's. It was his first trip back in seven years and the convent had arranged a combined celebration of Hudson's return and Christmas, which Jack and I were attending.

We lingered over our good-byes. His parents wanted us to stay and Jack had had a hard time explaining that although I had no family that compared with his, I considered the nuns my family and I could not imagine a Christmas that I did not share with them. Finally, after many hugs and kisses, we were on our way.

St. Stephen's is up the Hudson River on the way to Albany. It's far enough north of New York that it gets snow, which I feel is a distinct advantage at Christmastime. In the days before the holiday, the nuns decorate the Mother House elaborately with a huge tree, a handmade crèche, and lots more. The diverse talents of the nuns are drawn upon at Christmas as on other occasions for the benefit of everyone. The bakers bake cookies, embroiderers create beautiful linens for the chapel, rhymsters put together birthday-and Christmas-card verses. But the ones who are most needed at this season are those whose eyes envision decorations and whose fingers make them happen. I could hardly wait to see what the mother house looked like for Hudson McCormick's return.

But even without the anticipation of seeing someone I loved and admired so much, Christmas was a holiday that excited the child in me, that brought back happy memories of when both my parents were alive and the house smelled for days on end of cookies baking, of evergreens and spice. And although my new mother-in-law's house had all of that, it was the convent I was longing to see, the nuns with whom I had spent so much of my life, the grounds that I had walked with such happiness in every season and finally during the long year that had ended with a decision to leave.

To make the day even more special, my friend Arnold Gold, the New York lawyer for whom I did part-time work, and his wife, Harriet, were joining us at St. Stephen's this afternoon, having extracted assurances from me that there would be no presents, expensive or otherwise, that they were coming for the company and nothing else. In fact, I had gone back on my promise. I had found a store that still sold old-fashioned long-playing records—Arnold was very scornful of the new compact discs—and I had bought him one of his favorite Beethoven piano sonatas played by Horowitz. I was sure he would forgive my indiscretion.

It was only the third time Jack had been to St. Stephen's. The first was when we had agreed to be married in their chapel. We had driven up on a weekend last spring so that he could meet Sister Joseph, my former spiritual director, who is now the general superior of the convent. They had both heard a great deal about each other, all good and all filtered through me, of course, and the meeting went as smoothly and happily as I had anticipated. On the same day we met Father Kramer, who served the convent and would marry us. Father Kramer had known me since Hudson had left and he was the right person to marry us, having counseled me during that difficult year and having known me so many years.

"We near the turnoff yet?"

The sound of Jack's voice brought me back to the present. I looked out the window, suddenly recognizing a landmark and realizing we were closer than I had thought. "Yes. Just up ahead. I'm glad you've got a head for routes."

He poked me with his elbow. "Someone has to, right? You were dozing with visions of sugarplums dancing in your head."

"More like the ghosts of Christmases past. Right up there, Jack."

He slowed as we came to the intersection. In fact, he had a terrific head for roads and landmarks. If he drove somewhere once, it fixed itself in his mind. He had been a member of the New York City Police Department since his early twenties and a detective sergeant for the last few years. Attached to the Sixty-fifth Precinct in Brooklyn, he had offered me help two summers ago when no one else would take the time after I had gotten myself roped into investigating a forty-year-old murder in that part of Brooklyn. He was the first man I had met after leaving the convent, and although I had promised myself a year at least of living without men in my life, his sweet nature and gentle persistence had changed my mind, happily for me. He was now in his second year of evening law school, and because of his intensely packed schedule, this Christmas holiday was the first time in months we had been able to spend time with each other. For several days we had actually eaten dinners together, walked through the still-undeveloped areas of Oakwood, the little town in Westchester where I had inherited my aunt's house shortly before I left St. Stephen's. It was a happy time, free of the pressures of reading, studying for tests, and of course, the job. My own teaching, a single course at a college not far from Oakwood, was also over until mid-January, making it a real vacation.

"There it is," I said.

St. Stephen's rises out of the distance with a kind of medieval beauty. One sees a cross, a spire, a tower, bare winter branches, snow, roofs. My heart, as always, quickened. This was the home I had left and where I would always be welcome.

"Here we are." We had reached the gate. "There isn't a footprint anywhere. Isn't it beautiful?"

"Looks like a picture book." He drove along the curving road lighted with candles in paper bags toward the buildings. "Shall I park over by the Mother House?"

"Yes. Jack, *look!*"

The Mother House, the oldest building on the grounds, a large, square, heavy stone structure that always reminded me of a fort, had the largest wreath I had ever seen lying on its sloped roof.

"I can't believe it. How did they get something so big and how did they get it up there?"

"I bet they can't wait to tell you." He turned into the small parking lot.

"Do you see Arnold's car? Or one with a Wyoming license plate?"

"Negative twice. I think we beat everybody."

"Good. That'll give us time to say hello. Jack, that wreath is fantastic."

There were a few cars in the lot and I recognized one as belonging to Joseph. As General Superior, she often needed to travel, sometimes to New York to visit the chancery, sometimes to other places that were nearer by. I, too, had owned a car, which I paid for myself out of my dowry, in order to make a monthly trip to Oakwood to visit my aunt and her son, my cousin Gene, who lived in a residential community for retarded adults. I was still driving the same car, reluctant to give it up while it still had life in it, although Jack thought I should get a new one.

Jack took our suitcases out and a carton of gifts, which I carried. I had bought handmade gifts from a senior-citizens craft group that met in a church near Oakwood. The members of the group came from all religions, their common interest being their handiwork. I had picked up knitted gloves and mittens, hand-loomed scarves, slippers, monogrammed linen napkins, ceramic coffee mugs, and hand-carved napkin rings, things the nuns could use and enjoy.

We hadn't even reached the front door when it opened and my old friends poured out to greet us, hug and kiss us, and pull us into the warmth inside. It was absolutely beautiful. A fire was burning in the huge stone fireplace and I stopped to watch it. I find fires seductive, often more interesting than television. It isn't only the flames that bewitch; the smell of a wood fire has its own mystique.

I had the sense of everyone talking at once, of at least three nuns trying to make Jack comfortable—which was sure to make him uncomfortable. The suitcases were shunted off to a side—we would stay overnight in the college dormitory, a separate building—and someone took Jack's coat and led him to a long table laid with Christmas goodies and a full punch bowl.

The decorations were as accomplished and magical as I

had imagined. Elegant, ethereal, the indoors had become the outdoors. All around me were snow, sky, stars, *the* star, the crèche in one area, a fantasyland in another.

"You look like you're far away."

I turned to see Sister Angela standing next to me. "Angela, how good to see you. Merry Christmas." We hugged. "I'm not far away. I'm right here, just where I want to be. It's beautiful. It's wonderful. How on earth did you get that wreath on the roof?"

She laughed. "With a lot of difficulty. I thought Harold was really going to quit once and for all and leave us in the lurch over it."

Harold was the handyman who'd kept the convent buildings going forever. "But he didn't."

"It got to be a challenge he couldn't walk away from. Chris, you look *wonderful*. Come and have some punch."

We walked over to the table. "Have you heard from Hudson?"

"He called this morning. He went to mass in Buffalo, where he's been visiting with an old friend. He should be here very soon."

"Any minute," a familiar voice said. It was Joseph, looking happy and relaxed. "How's everything? How is your wonderful neighbor, Melanie?"

"She's fine. All the Grosses are fine. She sends her best and hopes you'll visit again."

"Hudson called about an hour ago from somewhere this side of Albany."

"You're right. He should be here any minute. How does he sound?"

"The same as always. I don't think he's changed since he turned sixteen."

"I can't wait to see him." I ladled a glass of punch into a cup and sipped it. "This is good," I said. "Mmm, really good."

"Put enough cinnamon and nutmeg in a punch bowl and anything you add tastes good," Angela said.

"Oh, there's Father Kramer." And I went off to say another hello.

We had hardly had time to say anything when I saw the door open. Harriet Gold was just entering, offering a gloved hand to the nearest nun. Behind her, Arnold came in, stamping snow off his shoes. A tall, wiry man with gray hair that doesn't always stay in place, he had a bright red scarf around his neck today.

I went over and hugged both of them. "Arnold, that scarf looks very flamboyant."

"Why do secretaries always think they have to give their bosses something for Christmas? I thought it was the other way around."

"It is the other way around," I said, laughing. "They do it because they love you."

"Just what I told him," Harriet said, taking her coat off. "What a great fire. Look at that, Arnold. Isn't a fire like that reason enough to have a little cabin somewhere that we could go to weekends?"

"If we had a little cabin, we'd close it up for winter and come back to Brooklyn. So your fireplace would just be for show."

"Hopeless," his wife said. "You look wonderful, Chris. Where's Jack?"

I had started to look for him when Arnold said, "Sister Joseph is the one I want to see. We were having an unusually intelligent conversation at your wedding when someone put some rose petals in my hand and that was the end of our talk. There she is." And he was off.

I took Harriet's hand and we walked over to the table where Jack was standing, talking to two of the nuns. As Harriet caught his eye I stepped back, feeling an enormous rush of emotion. This was my family: my husband, Jack; my friend and former spiritual director, Sister Joseph; Arnold Gold, who had given me away at my wedding; Father Kramer, who had married us; and all the nuns I had lived with for nearly half my life. It was warm in atmosphere and sentiment, and I felt both happy and fortunate.

Arnold was already engaged in an earnest discussion with Joseph, and Jack was now sitting with Father Kramer. Harriet Gold was talking to one of the older, retired nuns who lived in the villa, the home maintained by the convent for elderly sisters. I went through the group, stopping to talk to each nun. Many of them taught in the college that was part of the convent, where I, too, had taught for a number of years. It was good to hear about old students, how they were doing, what their plans were, what new courses were being offered.

I turned and saw Arnold standing alone. Joseph was bending over the chair where Jack was sitting as he was struggling to stand up and she was obviously telling him to stay where he was. I glanced at my watch and was surprised to find that an hour had passed since I had begun talking to the nuns.

Jack was standing now. I walked toward them, vaguely aware of an uneasiness in the air.

"Don't worry," I heard Jack say as he walked away. Joseph did indeed look worried.

"He should have been here by now," she said as I approached.

"Hudson?"

"It's a long time since he called, too long. Even allowing for traffic—and this is Christmas Day; there isn't much to speak of—he should have been here a long time ago."

"Is Jack checking with the state police?"

"He's calling them now. If there are any traffic tie-ups, the local troop will know about them and any other road conditions."

We stood around rather awkwardly, waiting for him to come back. Joseph looked at her watch. "We should be sitting down for Christmas dinner," she said. "It smells so good, it must be about done."

As she said it Sister Dolores came out of the dining room. "Is he here yet?" she said, looking at Joseph. "Everything's ready."

"Another few minutes." Joseph looked as worried as I had ever seen her. A woman whose face rarely showed any of the burdens she shouldered, today she could hide nothing. She looked at her watch again, as though another reading of the time would bring Hudson safely to the door. Then, abruptly, she walked away from us. Without a coat, she went out the front door.

"He's a good driver," Father Kramer said to me. "I don't believe he's had an accident. Knowing Hudson, he probably stopped to help someone else. We'll be hearing from him any minute."

I surveyed the large room. The Christmas cheer of earlier in the afternoon had been replaced by tense faces. The nuns, a Franciscan order, all wore the obligatory brown habit, the skirt at about midcalf, a simple brown veil with a plain white crown at the hairline. I looked from one to the other, then to Arnold and Harriet.

Joseph came in, a gust of cold air sweeping across the room. "It's very clear out," she said. "No snow. Maybe he lost his way. It's been a long time."

Jack came back and Joseph and I went to find out what he had learned.

"No report of any accidents on the thruway from Albany down almost to New York."

"What about secondary roads?" Joseph asked. "He might have taken those."

"Nothing reported. Road conditions everywhere are excellent. The weather's fine the length of the thruway. I left the phone number for them in case something turns up."

"Then I think we should have dinner," Joseph said decisively, and we all went into the dining room.

Like the room we had left, the dining room had been decorated festively. The guests were asked to spread out among the nuns and I watched Harriet go to one table and Arnold to another. I sat with Angela and Jack sat with Joseph. One nun at each table served us and the meal was splendid. It had been cooked by the nuns in the villa, the youngest of whom was past seventy. Father Kramer offered a prayer and included Hudson. I thought the amen was a little stronger than usual.

At my table we talked about everything except Hudson, and when dessert was finished, we sat around the tree and Joseph distributed the gifts. Arnold shook his finger at me when his name was called, but when he saw the shape of the package, he grinned with pleasure. As we all opened our gifts I glanced over at the tree. A group of beautifully wrapped packages was still there, awaiting the absent guest. I am generally a very up person, but the sight of those unclaimed packages made my heart sink. I had lost count of how long it had been since Hudson had telephoned from "this side of Albany." It was hours, long enough for him to have reached New York and turned back.

My gift was a whistling teakettle, something I had wanted for a long time but hadn't asked for. Not only would it boil water quickly for my frequent afternoon cup of tea, it would look smashing on my kitchen stove. I started around to thank everyone as everyone was also making the rounds.

Then the telephone rang.

3

Jack and Joseph got up and ran to answer it. I restrained myself from joining them. Since leaving St. Stephen's, I have relied less and less on prayer, but as I stood there, watching the doorway through which they would return, I found myself praying for Hudson's safe passage.

They were gone a long time. Arnold came over and put his arm around my shoulders. "Think positive," he said. "I've never believed in miracles, but I've seen some happen."

"How could he have driven all the way from Wyoming to Albany without a problem and then gotten into trouble a few miles from here?" I didn't expect an answer; I just needed to say it out loud.

"We don't know that he has."

Joseph appeared in the doorway and everyone turned to look at her. "Something's happened," she began. "No one seems to know what. A black clerical suit was found a little while ago near a rest stop along the thruway. There's no identification with it, his car isn't there, and there's no sign of Hudson. The state police are combing the area, looking for anything at all that can tell them what happened." She looked at Jack.

"That's about it," he said. "We don't know if that's where he called from or even if the clothing belongs to him, but the state police are taking this very seriously and they're not waiting the usual twenty-four hours to start a search for a missing person. Sister Joseph just called Buffalo and it's certain he was dressed in a clerical suit at Christmas mass this morning, but no one is sure whether he changed before he got into the car. We'll just have to wait and see what happens."

"I think it's time for evening prayers," Joseph said, and there was a murmur of agreement. Everyone went for a coat.

As Jack offered me mine, Arnold and Harriet joined us. "I don't like the sound of it," Arnold said.

"Me neither." Jack put his coat on and we followed the nuns to the door.

"Want to drive over to the scene and take a look? After prayers?"

"Good idea."

It gave me some comfort to know that Arnold was personally interested in Hudson's fate. We walked out into the darkness together, the nuns in a long line making their way to the chapel.

If anything brought back memories, that did. How many evening prayers does one attend in fifteen years? Thousands of them, and thousands of morning prayers. The nuns were singing now, their voices drifting back to us on the cold breeze as the line curved along the path, a gracefully moving silhouette. It was Christmas Night and the joy of the day had been rent from us, torn from our hands and hearts. The sharp cold of the wind brought tears to my eyes; the anguish of the situation clutched at my throat.

We entered the chapel and I heard Harriet say softly, "How lovely." The four of us sat in the last row, Harriet beside me. She patted my hand and told me not to worry. Then I listened to the service, once again becoming part of the convent family.

The nuns filed out first, looking peaceful, but I knew they felt as unsettled as I. We drove in Jack's car, getting on the thruway at the first opportunity. The rest stop, when we reached it, looked like any other with a large gas station at one end and a low building with food and other conveniences alongside a parking lot at the other end. What made this one different was the police presence. There were several marked state-police cars and numerous tall state-police officers wearing the distinctive campaign hats. Jack introduced himself to one of them and there was a brief exchange of confidences, Jack opening the scuffed leather case, a flash of the gold badge, and the trooper responded by leading us to the place where the clothing had been found. It was behind the buildings and over a small rise. A dog walker had found the jacket and collar.

A state policeman was standing guard at the taped-off area, but inside the yellow plastic tape there was nothing to see except trampled snow. The small, roughly square space was illuminated by four hand lanterns at the corners.

"Any sign of a struggle?" Jack asked.

"Nothing we could see. Maybe a little dancing around in the snow back here."

"Find his car in the parking lot?"

" 'Fraid not. We were told to look for Wyoming plates and there weren't any. Checked with the gas station, too. No one from Wyoming charged gas today and none of the attendants remember any Wyoming plates."

"You mind if we look around?"

"Don't mind at all. I don't think you'll find anything. We've had so many boots over the area, if anything dropped you'll have to wait for the spring thaw to find it."

"Any estimate on the size of the man from the suit of clothes?"

"Tall," the officer said. "Thin. Got a waist smaller'n mine, I can tell you that.'" He grinned. He was in great shape.

The sketchy description fitted Hudson to a tee. Tall and lanky, he had never shown an ounce of fat during the years I knew him.

"I guess you guys have been all over the area," Jack said.

"Up and down the hill, up the road, down the road. We were told his name and we've called it hundreds of times. Even used the car's loudspeaker system. If he's alive and out there, he heard us."

"Thanks, Officer."

"From the look of the snow," Arnold said as we walked away, "they've covered every inch."

"I agree," Jack said. "I don't think we'd gain anything from sliding over the snow ourselves. I want to look at the license plates in the parking lot."

We walked back and started going down rows. "What are you looking for?" I asked.

"I don't know. Something that doesn't fit. When I see it, I'll know. Any chance he was driving a spanking-new car that a car jacker would want to get his hands on?"

"Very little. It would have luggage in it, though."

"They've all got luggage. Tons of it."

He was right. In one car it was piled so high I couldn't imagine how the driver could see out the rear window.

The license plates were mostly from New York. There were a few from Ohio, Ontario, Massachusetts, and Michigan, and one each from Illinois and Vermont. There wasn't a single car from the west.

We looked at every car and I sensed that Jack hadn't found anything remarkable. We walked toward the building and found the Golds talking to two state policemen. When Arnold saw us, he said, "They're bringing bloodhounds in. Since they've got the suit, they're going to try to follow the scent while it's still fresh—if there's anything left in the snow to go on."

"Here they are," the officer said.

A state-police van had just pulled into the lot. Two police officers got out of the front and came around to the back, where they let out two large, beautiful dark-haired dogs. Jack went over and talked to the handlers and then waved the Golds and me over. I watched with fascination as the articles of Hudson's clothing were produced for the dogs to sniff. They were then taken to the taped-off area in the snow, where they sniffed the ground, then moved out from under the tape, looking for a lead.

They found it almost immediately and bounded toward the parking lot, their handlers running along to keep up with them. It didn't take long for the chase to end. They ran down the aisle between the second and third rows of cars, now pausing, now barking as they picked up the scent again. Then both dogs stopped at a parked car, barked, pawed the ground, and sat down.

The car had a Pennsylvania license plate and was empty. As we stood there a family with two young children came toward us.

"Is anything wrong?" the woman said. She was short and a little plump. An unhappy child was hanging on to her hand, telling her he was hungry.

"No, ma'am," the officer in charge said. "Can you tell me when you parked here?"

Her husband looked at his watch. "Fifteen minutes ago. We just stopped to take the kids to the bathroom. We're late for Christmas dinner."

The officer asked to see his driver's license and registration, then wrote something in his notebook. "Merry Christmas," he said. "Drive safely."

The man unlocked the car and they piled in. Just as the motor turned over, the dog nearer the front of the car started yelping and pulling away. I watched as man and dog started toward the building with the restaurant. But before the dog reached the building, he turned right and headed back toward the snowy area where the clothing had been found.

The Pennsylvania car drove out of its slot and the handler of the second dog gave him a piece of Hudson's clothing to sniff again. The dog sniffed the ground, turning around, until suddenly he seemed to pick up the scent the other dog had. Revitalized, he barked once and took off toward the building, following the identical path. I watched him turn at the same point and make for the snowy rise behind the parking lot.

Jack had followed the first dog. Now he came back to where I stood with the Golds between the first row of parked cars and the building. "Looks like he got out of his car, walked toward the building, then back to the snow, then cut diagonally back to his car. The dogs can't seem to find any other direction that he moved. He probably never got into the building."

"Then he didn't call from here," I said. "There are no phones outside."

"He could have called from the rest stop north of here. It's also south of Albany. Maybe he wanted to wait till the last minute to change his clothes."

"So what we've got," Arnold said, "is that he walked over to the taped area—and we don't know which route he took there and which back—dropped some articles of clothing, and took the other route back to his car."

"With or without someone who was forcing him with a weapon," I said.

"And then they—or he—drove away." Jack summed it up.

"If it was the car they were after, they would've left Hudson behind."

"It couldn't have been the car, Arnold. He would never have spent a lot of money on a car. Even if he'd had the money, and he probably didn't, he would have given it away before he'd spend it on a car."

"It seems to me that leaves two possibilities. One is that someone was after him, for reasons currently unknown. The other is that something happened to make him decide not to keep his date with St. Stephen's."

"That's just what I've been thinking," Jack said.

We threw hypothetical scenarios at each other all the way back to St. Stephen's but came up with nothing workable. By the time we got to the convent, the state police had called Joseph and told her about as much as we knew. They assured her they would keep looking for Hudson, but she sensed a resignation in what the officer said. The blood-hounds, which had been led up and down the strip along the thruway after we left, had found nothing, and all the police were convinced of was that Hudson—or whoever the owner of the clothing was—had left his car, walked back to the snowy area, and returned to the car, completing a circle that was more like a triangle. The snow had been so trampled that any footprints Hudson might have left were completely obliterated.

Most of the nuns had gone off to bed. The fire had also gone to sleep, but we got it going again and Joseph and I made coffee and cut some cake that had been on the long table in the afternoon. Then the five of us sat around the fire and talked.

"Tell me what you feel, Sister Joseph," Arnold said.

Joseph put her cup down and sat with her hands in her lap. "I feel something terrible has happened to him. I *know* something terrible has happened. We've been corresponding for months to set this day up. You didn't have to read between the lines to sense his joy at coming back here. It was in every word."

"Do you have the letters?"

"All of them."

"Tell me why he left, Sister."

"It was something he always wanted to do, something he had to work out with church authorities because he would no longer be under the direction of one diocese. He wanted to go to communities where there weren't many Catholics and there wasn't a priest, except now and then. He wanted to become part of those communities, to make a difference, to bring the people together, give a religious meaning to their lives, so that when he left, they would remember, they would be stronger. He never moved on until he was sure there was leadership, till he knew they could make it without him."

"If I asked you to describe his personality, what kind of person he seemed to you, what would you say?"

"Carefree and serious," Joseph said without a pause. "He's a friendly, outgoing man, loves a party, laughs a lot. And he's deeply religious, deeply committed. He cares. He cares about everyone and everything. He listens; he has time for people." She turned to look at me.

"I second everything."

Arnold leaned forward. He was still looking at Joseph as though she were the only one there. "Assume someone wanted to harm him. You knew him well and you knew him a long time. Tell me who and tell me why."

She turned her face toward the fire. For a long time she sat looking at it, not a muscle in her face moving. Finally she turned back to face Arnold and shook her head.

Harriet stood up. "Tomorrow's a workday, dear."

"Right." It was one of those years when Christmas hit the middle of the week. For Arnold, Thursday and Friday would be spent in the office. He stood and shook hands.

We walked the Golds to the door and Jack went out to the parking lot with them while I collected cups and saucers and took them to the kitchen, where I made fast work of washing them up.

Joseph handed me a key and said, "This will let you into the dormitory. I've left the door of 102 open. The key is on the dresser. There's only enough heat to keep the pipes from freezing, so we've put a very adequate electric heater in the room. The water's hot, so your shower shouldn't be too bad."

"It'll be fine."

"Whenever you wake up, we'll have breakfast for you."

"We're going to find him, Joseph."

"I hope so."

"Go on up. We'll see you in the morning."

I watched her go, a tall woman who held herself proudly. Although we were all upset, I thought that Arnold's questions had rattled her even more, but I didn't know why. There was no reason I could think of for anyone to wish harm to Hudson and I had no idea who would want to do so.

Jack came in a few minutes after Joseph had gone upstairs. It struck me that he had been outside with the Golds for rather a long time. He put his arm around me and kissed me.

"Feels like a long time since we've been alone together anywhere."

"I'm so glad you're here today, you and Arnold. Your calm has really helped. I've never seen Joseph so upset, even though she's working hard at concealing it."

"We're all working hard. Let's find our room."

"It's not much of a walk. We can leave the car where it is."

"Lead the way."

4

I sat on the edge of the narrow bed that was mine for the night, wearing the rose-colored nightgown that Jack's sister had given me as an engagement present. It was the most elegant and luxurious piece of clothing I had ever owned, spaghetti straps down to a permanently pleated gown with yards of yummy fabric that looked more like an evening gown than something to sleep in. Knowing where I was going to spend the night, I would have been smarter to take along a flannel nightie, but I couldn't resist the appeal of wearing something so fine in a place so spare.

Jack opened the door, returning from the long trek to the shower room. "Gotta be forty in that hall, but it's nice in here. Boy, do you look gorgeous. You wore that on our wedding night, didn't you?"

"It's the one your sister gave me." I stood and turned a full circle, relishing the feel of the soft fabric as it swirled around my legs and ankles.

Jack took his bathrobe off and put his arms around me, lighting fires inside. "The bed's too narrow, and even thinking of sex in this place gives me the creeps, but that's all I can think of right now."

"Me, too."

"Your place or mine?"

"I don't think it makes any difference. We'll probably end up on the floor."

He laughed and sat me down on my bed, but I was right. A couple of minutes later, aided only by pillows, we made love on the wooden floor of a dormitory room that couldn't have witnessed such activity in all the years of its existence. I found that exciting and Jack must have, too, because it was very good, a good way to end Christmas.

* * *

"You think Sister Joseph is holding something back?"

We were sitting on my bed in the dark room, the only light the occasional red glow of the heater as the thermostat turned it on. "I know her very well, Jack. She didn't answer Arnold, and I think she wouldn't lie except perhaps to save a life. If there was something she wanted to avoid saying, saying nothing may have been the most honorable way out."

"So you tell me. You remember him well. You thought he was a wonderful person. Everybody irritates someone. Who had a gripe against him? Who didn't like the way he counseled the students? Who hated his sermons?"

"No one ever complained to me. He was well liked. He's a great person."

"What was it like when he left? Was it sudden? Were there whispers?"

"I don't know, Jack. I wasn't here that year."

"What do you mean, you weren't here? Where else could you have been?"

"It was the year I went for my master's. I stayed at school over Thanksgiving, I remember, and I asked permission to visit Aunt Meg at Christmas."

"Christmas is a long vacation. You spent the whole time in Oakwood?"

I thought about it. "No, I didn't. I stayed through the holiday and then I came up here. Hudson was gone, I'm sure of it."

"So he left before Christmas."

"He must have."

"Before you left for school in the fall, was he talking about going away?"

"Not to me, but there was no reason why he'd talk to me about something like that. He would have talked to Sister Clare Angela, the superior, or Joseph, maybe to some of the nuns that he was particularly friendly with, but I was kind of a kid. He might have told me after it was in the bag, but I wasn't around. Why do you think there's something funny about his leaving? It was something he always wanted to do, travel, work with poor communities."

"Because Arnold hit her with two questions that she refused to answer. If I'd asked you the same question—who would harm Hudson and why?—what would you say?"

"Nobody. He never gave anyone a reason not to like him."

"But she didn't say that. And it left both Arnold and me feeling uncomfortable. Why do you think she didn't answer the way you did?"

There was only one possible reason. "Because for her it wasn't true. You think something happened that year I was away, that first semester, probably."

"Right. Besides the convent, where else did he serve?"

"There's a small, old church in the village. He lived in the rectory there and that was officially his parish, although he had a lot of duties associated with St. Stephen's. He would offer mass for us at six A.M. and then one at the church later. Father Kramer took over as pastor of the church when Hudson left, and continued here, too."

"Do you know where he was before?"

"Father Kramer? Somewhere near Newburgh. I don't remember where."

"So he wouldn't remember anything firsthand about that year."

"No. Tell me what you're thinking, Jack."

"Nothing very substantial. It just seems possible that something happened at that little church in the village, someone got angry at Hudson for something, and it precipitated his leaving."

"And the person carried a grudge," I said. "But how would this unknown person even know that Hudson was coming back today?"

"How about this? Hudson gets to the rest stop near Albany and calls St. Stephen's. But this other thing is on his mind. So he makes a second call to someone who lives around here and says, 'Let's talk. I'll meet you at the next rest stop in an hour.'"

"And the meeting takes a bad turn."

"It means we've got to find the phone he called St. Stephen's from and see what the next call was."

I didn't like it, but it fit a lot of what we knew.

"There's another possibility," Jack went on. "He gets to the rest stop where he's going to change from his traveling clothes to his clerical suit and he just can't do it. He can't face the convent."

"But why?"

"Sister Joseph knows."

"Then where is he, Jack?"

"Who knows? In a hotel somewhere. On his way back to Buffalo. Sitting in his car at the side of a road trying to make sense out of his life."

"You're awfully melodramatic for a cop."

"I guess you're right." He sounded playful. "How can a cop from Brooklyn appreciate melodrama? I should leave that for poetry teachers."

"What I'm really afraid of is that what happened to Hudson was random violence, someone seeing a watch he was wearing and trying to get it away from him, threatening him with a gun. Maybe he did have a car someone wanted, one of those four-by-fours I always see in the supermarket parking lot. His parishes always covered a lot of territory. Maybe he needed that kind of car or truck to get around difficult terrain, to carry things to parishioners. Maybe this is a car jacking after all and somehow he ended up being taken with the car."

"Let's sleep on it."

I kissed him and he got off the bed, waited for me to get under the covers, and tucked me in. Then he turned the heater down a little and turned the light off.

The bed was narrow and not very comfortable. At home we had a brand-new one with a firm mattress and lots of room. This was the first time I was alone in bed since my marriage last August. Somehow I knew it wasn't going to be my last.

There was no news from the state police in the morning. The trail had dried up at the rest stop. All they could be sure of was that the owner of the clerical clothing—who might or might not be Hudson—had gotten out of his car, walked out of the parking lot to the snowy area in back, dropped some of his clothing, and gone back to the car. With the people using the parking lot such a transient group, it was impossible to find anyone who might remember a Wyoming car. But they now had a license plate number and a description of the vehicle Hudson had been driving. As it turned out, I was right. It was one of those all-terrain vehicles with heavy-duty tires, purchased used several years ago. Although the police were now fairly skeptical about the possibility of foul play, they promised they would keep a lookout for the vehicle.

After breakfast, we drove into town and found the Church of the Visitation. It had been built late in the nineteenth century and little about it had changed. The trees nearby were gnarled with age. Like many old churches, its entrance was flush with the street, the double doors thick wood with wrought-iron trim.

We went inside and I dipped my fingers in the font of holy water and crossed myself. The interior was beautiful, high windows all around letting in the daylight, polished old pews that had taken their knocks. I walked around to one of the side altars and lit my usual three candles, one each for my mother, my father, and my aunt Meg.

Jack had his wallet open, but I motioned him away. Perhaps when I've been married longer I'll feel different about it, but I've always felt I have to pay myself with money I have earned or money that would come out of my daily expenses. There was a statue of a very sweet Mary at the altar, and I smiled up at her as I walked away.

Jack took my hand and we walked to the sanctuary. No one was around. A side door to the outside was locked, so we went back to the front door and out to the street. The rectory, a newer red-brick building, was next door. I rang the bell and heard a woman calling that she was on her way.

"Good morning," she said brightly as she opened the door. "I'm afraid you've missed Father. He's gone to the hospital to visit a sick parishioner."

"You're Mrs. Pfeiffer, aren't you?" I said.

"Yes, I am. You look familiar, too, but I can't place the face."

"I was Sister Edward Frances at St. Stephen's."

"Oh, of course you were! Come on in, Sister. Well, it isn't Sister anymore now, is it?"

"No, I'm Chris Bennett, Chris Bennett Brooks. This is my husband, Jack."

She said how delighted she was to meet him and invited

us to sit down. When we turned her down on coffee, I was afraid we'd wounded her mortally.

"But you'll stay for lunch," she insisted. "I've just made the best turkey salad you'll get anywhere."

I looked at Jack and he agreed with a grin. It wasn't the kind of treatment he got when he went out with a partner to interview a possible witness about a crime.

"You're really the one I wanted to see, Mrs. Pfeiffer. You've been here for a long time, haven't you?"

"My goodness, yes. I lost my husband in my thirties and I needed a job, and I won't tell you how many years it's been since then."

"You were here when Father McCormick came."

"Yes indeed. A wonderful man. Father Kramer told me this morning that he didn't get to the convent last night. I hope you're not bringing me bad news."

"No, no news at all. We don't know anything more than you do. I just wanted to ask you about the years Father McCormick served in this parish."

"I was here the whole time," she said. "I was here when he came and here when he left. Are you trying to find him? Is that it?"

"We're trying to figure out whether someone in the parish might have wanted to harm him."

"Impossible." She looked shocked. "Who would harm a priest?"

"Do you remember any disagreements while he was here? Any person or people who might have been unhappy with him as pastor?"

"No one. Never." She was adamant. I was asking for something she could not conceive of.

"Just think for a minute. Parish politics can be the making or undoing of a priest. One person thinks another has been shown favoritism. Someone thinks he's gotten the wrong end of the stick." I sat back and let her get her thoughts together. Jack had walked away from us, leaving us to face each other across a scarred coffee table.

"Well, there was that business about refurbishing the rectory."

"Tell me about it."

"It was very silly, really. It had to be done. The wiring

was shot and the plumbing was lousy." She made a face over her choice of words. "It's not as if Father McCormick was putting velvet covers on the chairs. The fire department told him he'd better do something about the wiring, and then the plumbing gave out about the same time. But no one would harm a priest over something like that, and ten years later to boot."

I had to agree with her. "Were there people in the parish who objected to the work being done?"

"Oh, there was some nastiness. It didn't amount to much and a collection was taken and the job was done. I had a few days when I couldn't use the kitchen sink, but we were all better off when it was taken care of."

"Do you remember who made the fuss?"

"Oh, that nasty Mr. Abbott. I know I shouldn't say that. Father McCormick said he was a fine man with a lot of problems. But Father McCormick always saw the best in people. As Father Kramer does," she added, lest I think she favored one priest over the other.

"Anything else you remember, Mrs. Pfeiffer?"

She pursed her lips and looked thoughtful. "Well—no, I don't think so. Everything went smooth. I'm sure of it."

"Does he write to you?" I asked.

"Oh my, yes. He never forgets my birthday. He sends me a lovely card at Christmas. Sometimes they're made by the children or by some Indian artist or something. He's a thoughtful man, but you know that."

"Any letters?"

"Once in a while."

"Do you remember when he left?"

"Yes, I do. We had some party for him. It was really lovely."

"Do you remember when that was?"

"Let me see. It was cold and there was snow. It was before Christmas, I'm sure of that. Father Kramer was here for Christmas that year. I think Father McCormick wanted to have Christmas at his new parish. That was so nice of him, bringing Christmas to those poor people out there."

"Was it sudden when he left?" I asked.

"Well, for me it was. It came so out of the blue, but I expect he'd been thinking about something like that for a long time." She flashed a smile at me. "It was pretty sudden when you left, too, you know."

And I'd been planning it for a year and thinking about it even longer. "Thanks an awful lot, Mrs. Pfeiffer. You've really been very helpful."

"Anything I can do. You two young people go out and look at our pretty village. I'll have your lunch at noon. How's that?"

"Terrific," Jack said.

We buttoned up and went out into the cold.

The village really was something to look at. Houses were decorated, stores were decorated, the streets in the center of town looked fantastic. Children in colorful snowsuits ran alongside women in warm coats and boots, sporting yesterday's presents on an arm, around a neck, perched on a head. In fact, some of the boots looked pristine to me, as if they hadn't yet slogged through the inevitable slush.

We walked around, looking in a craft shop, a china shop, a little knitwear store, buying nothing but having a good time. When we found a pay phone on a corner, Jack called the state police and asked if there was news. There wasn't. Hudson and his ATV had vanished from the face of the earth.

"You want to hunt up this guy Abbott?" Jack said after he told me the nonnews.

"I don't know," I said. "It seems so unlikely, so far-fetched. Someone who complains you're spending too much money when you're repairing wiring and plumbing is just a tightfisted old guy who complains when his wife buys a new dress after five years. He isn't someone who kidnaps a priest. You know, when Mrs. Pfeiffer said that my leaving the convent came as a surprise to her, I realized I was very much in the same position as Hudson. I kept it all to myself except when I talked to Joseph or Father Kramer. I didn't sit around gossiping to the nuns and I don't think Hudson did either."

"Want a cup of coffee?"

"Sure."

We went inside a coffee shop we were passing and sat at

one of several empty tables. I ordered cocoa and Jack got his midmorning caffeine fix, something I teased him about.

"I think she was telling the truth," Jack said.

"Me, too."

"I'll get someone to check on those rest-stop phones, but it may take awhile, Chris. So let's take another look at the other possibility, that your friend, Father Hudson McCormick had a reason why he didn't want to show up at the convent yesterday, and when he got to the rest stop, whatever was bothering him got the better of him and he just couldn't push himself to complete his journey."

"So he dropped the clothing to let us know he'd gotten that far and that was it."

"Why not?"

"Because there's no reason for it. What could be so threatening about St. Stephen's?"

"That's what we have to ask Sister Joseph."

5

We didn't get back to the convent until almost two o'clock. Our lunch at the rectory stretched out, not unpleasantly, as Father Kramer joined us at twelve-thirty. It was clear he had no desire to discuss Hudson, but he was genuinely interested in Jack and me and wanted to know more about Arnold Gold, whom he had spoken to yesterday for the first time at any length.

I was happy to tell him how we had met during my first investigation. Arnold had been a very young attorney at the time the crime was committed forty years earlier and had represented one of the men charged with the murder. During my investigation and after, we had gotten to know each other quite well and become very fond of each other, so that last August he had given me away at my wedding. That he was an old-style liberal who would defend anyone who needed a lawyer only added to his appeal.

Finally we excused ourselves and drove back to St. Stephen's. With the college students away and the postulants, novices, and many nuns spending the holiday with their families, the grounds were even quieter than usual. We parked and walked over to the Mother House, where we were told that Joseph was upstairs in her office. A call to her was greeted with an invitation to join her and we went up the wide stone stairs, worn smooth by generations of women, to the office of the General Superior.

"I've heard nothing," Joseph said as we came in, "but I made a phone call this morning to the church in Buffalo that Hudson was visiting. The priest who answered—not Hudson's friend but a new curate who met him—is certain Hudson received at least one and possibly two phone calls while he was there. I said I had called yesterday when we

33

were waiting for him, but he said these calls came before Christmas."

"I don't suppose the caller left a name or a message," I said hopefully.

"He didn't need to. Hudson was there both times and took the calls."

"So they came from a man," Jack said.

"And that's about all I can tell you."

"But someone besides you knew he was there."

"So it seems. It isn't much to go on, and maybe it's meaningless. I don't know how long he was planning to spend in the east, but I'm sure he has friends besides us. Maybe someone wanted to know when he could come to dinner."

She had been sitting at the long table that took up most of the room, the remains of her lunch on a tray at one end, piles of papers nearby. Now she stood and walked to the window behind her desk. "If the police think that Father Hudson McCormick changed his mind at a rest stop a few miles from here and decided to go into hiding instead of visiting us, they are wrong."

"I agree with you," Jack said. "With your permission, I'd like to walk around for a while and talk to some of the nuns."

"Of course you may."

"I think Chris wants to talk to you, and you'll both be more comfortable with me somewhere else."

Joseph smiled. "Come back and join us for coffee."

"You don't need to ask twice. Detectives need at least two cups of strong coffee to kick-start their hearts each morning."

After he closed the door, Joseph sat down again. "I don't know how you managed it, but you found a wonderful man. He didn't have to leave, but you want to ask me questions that you think will be embarrassing."

"I think you're holding something back," I said honestly. "I wasn't here the year that Hudson left. I never said good-bye to him, except when I left for graduate school in the fall and then I was sure he was going to be here when I got back, either for Christmas or in the spring. I think he thought he'd be here, too."

"He did."

"But he left before Christmas." I stopped. I have known Joseph for sixteen years. She is intelligent, thoughtful, clever, and difficult to fool. She is not a person who needs things spelled out for her. All the things I didn't say were superfluous. She knew exactly what I was driving at, knew that I had watched her avoid telling a lie to Arnold Gold last night, knew that I wanted an answer because it was futile to try to solve a puzzle if you don't have all the pieces.

"You're right, I am holding things back. No year is uneventful, you know that. Looking back I can't recall a year without a crisis—a death in the villa, an automobile accident, a series of thefts—you remember that all as well as I do. They pass and we're smart enough not to dwell on them. We set them aside and they become memories, sometimes even humorous ones, if we're lucky. The year that you were in graduate school was no exception. We had our annual crisis and you were never told because there was no need for you to know." She made it sound as though the plumbing had failed once again or Harold, the handyman, had fallen off a ladder and been hospitalized.

I didn't think for one moment that it was something as simple as that. "Is there a need for me to know now?"

"Hudson wasn't involved, Chris. For years he wanted to go out west and do the kinds of things he's been doing for the last seven years. The opportunity came and he took it, as he should have. I don't think it's necessary to rehash events of a long time ago. What has happened to Hudson—if anything has—has happened now, yesterday. I don't know how to get the police to take his disappearance seriously, but I'm convinced that someone has done something to him. He's not a man to walk away from his friends without a phone call, certainly not an hour after he called to say he was on his way."

For the first time in all the years I had known her, I felt a chasm between us. There was something she knew that she would not tell me, but in spite of that she seemed to want me to try to find out what had happened to Hudson. "Was Sister Clare Angela superior that year?"

"Yes, she was. We lost her two years ago. You were still here then."

"I remember." A woman in her sixties, she had died of breast cancer. "Joseph, I'm as concerned as you are, but I'm at a standstill. I know what kind of car he was driving and what the license-plate number is, where he was roughly late afternoon on Christmas Day, but the trail ends there. I haven't the faintest idea how to proceed, where to look, whom to ask. A man disappears without a trace, leaving only a couple of pieces of clothing behind—and we don't even know for sure that it was his clothing, only that the owner of the clothing walked away from his car and back to it. A small circle is all we have and circles lead nowhere."

"You're right. There's nothing we can do." She sounded as though she had come to a decision. "It's best to leave it in the hands of the police, at least for the time being. Why don't we go downstairs and find that husband of yours and see if we can rustle up some coffee?"

I found that husband of mine over near the chapel talking to Sister Dolores, who had created our Christmas dinner. I stopped short and retreated. Sister Dolores lived in the villa with several other retired nuns. She would remember not only Hudson McCormick's last year at St. Stephen's, but all the years he served the convent.

I took a quick turn off the path to another that led to a college building so they could have a private conversation. As a member of the detective squad, Jack spends a lot of his time asking questions, and I didn't want to interrupt. Instead I took a circuitous route back to the Mother House and helped get our coffee things together.

Jack didn't get back for another fifteen minutes. He had probably walked Sister Dolores wherever she was going, to the villa most likely, and when he joined us for coffee, he didn't say a word about his conversation with her or with anyone else. Joseph, too, had dropped the subject of Hudson and talked to us about Jack's law-school classes, my teaching, Oakwood, and my friend Melanie Gross.

"How do you find the commuting?" she asked Jack as she poured second cups of coffee all around.

"Worse than before but not as bad as it could be. Since I've been working ten-to-sixes, I miss the worst of the rush hour in the morning, and at night I go right from the station house to school. I get home pretty late, but I have someone waiting up for me, which is nice."

Joseph smiled. "Yes, it is. I remember all those years when Chris made her monthly trip to Oakwood to visit her aunt and cousin, and I always looked at my watch a hundred times when I knew she was on her way home. Once in a while she didn't make it as planned." She smiled.

"One flat tire," I said, remembering, "one snowstorm that left me sitting in a gas station till the snowplow came through, one accident I witnessed and stayed to talk to the police." There had been so many years, so many trips. "And once I ran out of gas and found that prayer had its limitations." We all laughed.

After the second cup, we got ready to go. The day was nearly over, the winter sun setting. We said our good-byes and put our coats on. We were almost out the door when a somewhat breathless Angela found us.

"Telephone," she said urgently to Joseph. "Father Thomasevich from Buffalo."

"Don't go," Joseph said. She looked around, then dashed into the kitchen where the nearest phone was. She wasn't gone long. When she came back she looked ravaged. "He's the priest I spoke to earlier," she said, "the one who recalled one or two calls for Hudson. He just spoke to the other curate in the rectory. Apparently there was also a call when Hudson wasn't around to take it and the caller left a message. It was something like 'Don't expect the nuns of St. Stephen's to save you.' "

6

Jack did the driving. We weren't talking about it. There was nothing to talk about. Joseph would not give us another scrap of information about Hudson's last year at the convent. Jack phoned the state police before we left and told them about the telephoned threat in Buffalo. The police said they would look into it. There was still no trace of Hudson or his vehicle.

Lights were on everywhere and there was a sprinkling of snow on the windshield. I was trying to think of what I could throw together for dinner, considering that we would arrive home much later than I had anticipated.

"She didn't tell you anything, did she?" Jack said out of the blue.

"Nothing." I recounted what Joseph had said about annual crises. "What about you?'

"Boy, was my personal charm wasted on that bunch."

I laughed. "What did Sister Dolores say?"

"She told me how she came to St. Stephen's fifty-seven years ago and how she remembered the first time she saw you and how wonderful you were and how smart, and how bad she felt when you decided to leave but she knew it was for the best. I thought she was going to give me a rundown on everyone who'd ever lived in the convent. When I asked about Father McCormick, she didn't exactly clam up, but she said all the polite things and nothing else. I think if we're going to have any luck with this, we've got to get someone up there to open up and maybe let us read the letters he wrote."

"Can you find out if there's a police file on Hudson?"

"I can try, but I'm not going in till Monday and I don't want to ask anyone else to do the digging."

"Then it'll have to wait for Monday," I said.

The house was freezing and the refrigerator not very accommodating, but Melanie Gross had shoved a note under the door inviting us to potluck if we got home in time. What Mel calls potluck is my idea of a feast. A phone call assured us the invitation was still open. So while our house heated up we walked down the block to the Grosses' and shared a wonderful dinner of leftovers and a good evening of conversation.

With the Grosses' permission, I had given their children small Christmas presents when they came over before the holiday to see our tree. I had also visited one late afternoon when they were lighting the menorah for Hanukkah and had stayed for potato pancakes fresh from the pan and a gambling game that we all played on the floor with a dreidel, a four-sided spinning top with a different Hebrew letter on each side. You become a winner or loser depending on which face is up when it comes to rest. My Hanukkah present from the Gross children had been a solid chocolate dreidel, which hadn't lasted long in my house.

We talked about everything from a crazy case Hal was handling to the disappearance of Hudson McCormick, and finally, at ten o'clock, we went back to our warm little house and our big, comfortable bed. I promised to sleep late and Jack promised to make pancakes and we both promised to do nothing over the weekend but enjoy ourselves.

That was the one that got broken.

After my promised late rising and Jack's promised pancakes, I went out shopping to fill my refrigerator and pantry. I was still new enough at shopping for two that I took pleasure in buying larger sizes and quantities. Jack is a big eater, although he complains that the uniform he hasn't worn for several years except to official occasions is too tight on him. Besides being an accomplished cook himself, Jack has a sister who started a catering company a couple of years ago and often gave him gourmet leftovers and new products to sample. Although he no longer lived in Brooklyn, he still worked there and she managed to drop off goodies at the station house. As an only child who was or- phaned at fourteen, I think families are wonderful and I am thrilled to be part of one that is so warm and caring. Even if it puts calories into us.

Jack wrote a lot of the shopping list for me since he in- tended to cook over the weekend, but I did the shopping because I'm more careful and less impulsive than he is. When you've spent a large part of your life going out with fifty cents in your purse, you tend to think before you spend.

On my way back I made a stop at Greenwillow, where my cousin Gene lives in the residence for retarded adults. I hadn't seen him for some time because he was invited to spend Christmas with the parents of another resident and he found that much more appealing than coming to me. Still, he was delighted to see me and show me his Christmas presents. Most of all he wanted to tell me about Steve's house.

"I never saw a house so big," he said, moving his hands to show me. "They have this room and this room and this room—"

"It sounds enormous," I said. "Did you have your own bedroom?"

"Oh yeah, with a bathroom, too, with brown towels, nice, brown towels."

"You must have had a wonderful time, Gene."

"I did. I'm going again."

"What did you do while you were there?"

"We went in the car, we went to a restaurant, we had a lot to eat, and we played checkers."

"I'm glad you had a good time. Maybe you and Steve will come and visit Jack and me."

"OK." He sounded offhand about it. Now that he was a man of the world, visiting homes where he had a private bed and bath, his mother's old house had lost some of its charm.

We took a walk together and found Steve, who thought a visit to my house would be a lot more fun than another visit to his parents. Eventually, I left them together, happy that my cousin had a friend, that he had had a happy Christmas, that his life was fulfilling.

I drove home and put all my purchases away. Jack was out somewhere with his car, and a glance at the kitchen table gave me a clue. An open toolbox and an old lamp minus its socket lay on a sheet of newspaper. He had gotten the itch to fix something and was probably at the hardware store. By the time I was finished in the kitchen, he was back.

"Do you know you've been living in a house with a smoke detector without a battery for the last year and a half?"

"How can that be? I never took the battery out."

"Your aunt probably did. When the battery dies, they give off a sound that drives you straight to the hardware store to get a replacement."

"Or you throw it in the garbage to shut it up. She probably wasn't feeling well enough to go out and get a new one and she didn't want to bother me with it."

"Well, honey bunch, you're safe now." He kissed me. "I'll just go put it in."

When he was finished, we bundled up and went down to the "beach" that all the home owners in the area owned jointly. There's a little cove in the Long Island Sound with a sandy strip along its half circle. We walked along it, feeling the force of the wind, the salt spray of the sound. No one else was there. We were a comfortable drive from the heart of New York and here we were alone on a sandy beach. It seemed amazing, but then a lot of things that have happened to me have seemed amazing. That was a lovely afternoon, a day when we had nothing to do but enjoy each other. When we got home, Jack built a fire in the living-room fireplace and started cooking something with shrimp. When the phone rang, I was reading a magazine in front of the fire and I heard him pick it up.

He came into the living room a minute later, his face set in the working-detective mode. "It's Sister Joseph. I think something's happened."

I dropped the magazine and went to the kitchen, where pots and pans were on the stove and the aromas were gorgeous. "Joseph?"

"Chris." She stopped, as though deciding whether or not to continue. "They've found Hudson's car."

"And Hudson?"

"There's no sign of him anywhere."

"Where was the car?" From the corner of my eye I could see Jack stop what he was doing and turn to look at me.

"I'm afraid it's too complicated to explain over the phone. I know it's a lot to ask, but could you come up for a few days?"

I said, "Sure," although my heart really wasn't in it.

"I promise you I will tell you everything, everything that happened before Hudson left, and after. And you may have complete access to the letters and anything else you think will help you. I don't know if he's alive or dead, but it's pretty clear that his disappearance is related to what happened the year he left us."

I looked at Jack. "I'll drive up this evening," I said.

7

"In September of that year a new novice came to us. Her name was Julia Farragut and she had visited here several times, so perhaps you knew her."

"I may have seen her." But if I had, she had not made a strong impression. There were few enough girls interested in a religious career that it wasn't hard to recall most of them, but this one had probably started her novitiate after I had left for graduate school.

Joseph and I were sitting in her office with all the lights on. By the time I had arrived, after dinner and packing and apologizing a hundred times to Jack, most of the nuns had gone off to bed and the heat had turned itself down for the night. A small electric heater, like the one we had used in the dormitory on Christmas Night, whirred on and off a few feet from the table we sat at.

"I sensed from the first time I met her, before that September, that she was an unstable person, that she was looking for something at St. Stephen's that she wouldn't find here or at any other convent, and although I expressed my opinion when I was asked, I didn't do it as forcefully as I should have. Sister Clare Angela was sure Julia would work out well and make a contribution to the convent." She paused. "And her parents were generous."

Yes, of course, I thought, keeping it to myself. Even in a convent, generosity could influence decisions. "I understand," I said.

"Right from the beginning there were difficulties. One night she was found missing from her room and several of us were awakened to form a search party. We went through all the rooms in the convent and the college and finally found her huddled in a confessional in the chapel, pouring

43

out her sins to an absent confessor. She was in a terrible
state, distraught, frightened. Sister Clare Angela called her
parents—although Julia begged her not to—and they came
and picked her up. But a few days later she was back, looking fresh and happy and as normal as any of the girls in the
college."

"How did her parents feel about her returning?"

"They seemed all for it, her mother especially. They really seemed to believe that she would be all right here, that
our life was what she needed. Later, when I had a chance
to think about it, I came to realize that they were using us
in place of psychiatry, as a substitute for therapy and medical help."

"A convent is probably more acceptable than a sanitarium in most families."

"I'm afraid that's it in a nutshell. Anyway, there were
other problems, other outbursts, other indications that
Julia's life was far from normal."

"I suppose Hudson counseled her."

"It was part of his duties. The village parish, as you
know, is very small and their pastor has been our pastor for
generations. He celebrated mass with us, heard our confes-
sions, and counseled several students. True, this one was
different, but it was part of his work and I think he always
enjoyed counseling. He always liked young people, and
even though he was in his thirties at the time, he seemed
like such a boy himself. Students always felt he understood
them, and I know he did."

At that point I began to sense what was coming. My
stomach felt a little sick, my throat was too dry. Joseph was
going to tell me that a disturbed novice had nearly ruined
Hudson's sterling career. "Tell me what happened."

"It was terrible, Chris. Hudson recognized after a few
weeks of counseling that she needed professional secular
help. He talked to her parents, who were furious with him.
I know that Hudson gave the matter a great deal of thought,
because I was one of the people he talked to about it. We
agreed that if her parents had been the kind of people who
were open to medical help, sending her home would have
been the best course. But he was concerned—we were
concerned—that living at home would only make matters

worse. She was adamant about staying here. She seemed almost afraid to go home. And to be perfectly honest, I have to admit that when she was well, she was a lovely person. She was helpful, she had a smile for everyone."

"But something happened."

"I think it was just before Thanksgiving. We were sleeping. I remember that I woke to hear what sounded like a wail. I went out into the hall. Several nuns were already there. We didn't know where it was coming from or what was making the sound, but we knew we had to find the source. It was coming from Julia's room. She was lying in her bed, curled up, and emitting this terrible sound, this sound of doom—that's the only way I can describe it."

"What had happened?"

Joseph moved her hands. "Nothing, as far as we could see. She had no temperature, she wasn't ill, she was just in a terrible state. When she calmed down enough to speak, she said something like, 'He was here and we have known each other.'

"Someone said, 'Who was here?' and she said, 'Father McCormick.' "

Joseph stopped. It was clear how painful it was for her to tell the story, to relive that awful night. "The first thing Sister Clare Angela did was clear the room. She kept Sister Mary Teresa with her—you remember her; she was in her sixties then and in good health. She's been in the villa for the last few years and her health has unfortunately deteriorated."

"I remember. They were always good friends."

"I think Sister Clare Angela wanted a witness, if nothing else, to anything that might be said in that room. I went downstairs and called the rectory. Father McCormick answered as though I had awakened him from a deep sleep, which I'm sure I had. I told him briefly what had happened. He offered to come to the convent, but I said he should wait to see if Sister Clare Angela wanted him."

I was following her logic. The Mother House, as well as the dormitory, was locked up tight in the evening, usually by nine o'clock, when most of the nuns went to bed. If someone tried to enter the Mother House, a doorbell would ring in Sister Clare Angela's room. And any man who managed to gain entry and tried to walk through the halls would be extremely foolhardy. At any moment a nun might get up and walk out of her room to go to the bathroom or, on a sleepless night, to walk, to sit downstairs with a book, or even to go out to the chapel to pray. Not that I believed for a moment that Hudson had entered the mother house in any way but the novice's fantasy.

"So Hudson was in the rectory," I said.

"And I am his witness, although he didn't need one. Sister Clare Angela spent some time calming Julia down, after which she fell asleep. In the morning Sister Clare Angela called the Farraguts and said Julia would have to leave St. Stephen's."

"I don't know how they could refuse."

"I suppose if things had been normal in their house, they wouldn't have. Sister Clare Angela talked to Mr. Farragut, who said his wife had recently been hospitalized and there was no way he could care for his daughter without her."

"What was wrong with her?"

"I gather he didn't say or she didn't ask, but we found out later that Mrs. Farragut had suffered from mental problems on and off over the years and she had recently been committed to an institution."

"What an ordeal," I said. "The poor man."

"It certainly seemed that way. Sister Clare Angela had a meeting of her council, of which I was a member, and we agreed reluctantly that we would have to keep Julia at the convent until Mr. Farragut could make arrangements for her, which he promised to do. Hudson came to St. Stephen's the next day and spent a lot of time with her. He reported to our group that she was confused about a number of things, that she had denied to him that she had said what several of us had heard her say the night before. He said he would try to see Mr. Farragut to talk to him about Julia's situation, but I really don't know if any meeting or conversation ever took place. Later that day Sister Clare Angela got a phone call from Mr. Farragut. He was outraged and nearly incoherent. His daughter had told him that Father McCormick had raped her and he was going to take the case to the bishop." Joseph paused, looking quite miserable.

"Joseph, did anyone take Julia to a doctor to be examined?"

"Of course, that would have been the correct thing to do. Why we didn't, I'm not sure, except that Julia had never used the word *rape* or indicated that anyone had assaulted her."

"I'm wondering," I said, "how her father got his information."

"Remember, everything I know came to me secondhand. I assume Julia telephoned him during the day."

"Either before or after she spent time with Hudson."

"Before or after, yes."

"How strange, but then, she wasn't exactly a rational person."

"No, she wasn't."

"And we can assume that Hudson knew a great deal more about her problems than he discussed with you."

"It's fair to assume that, yes. But whatever he knows will be kept from us forever."

We were referring to the confessional. If Julia Farragut had had secrets, fantasies, desires that she could not or would not speak of outside the confessional, Father McCormick would never disclose any of it even if his life or his career depended on it. And it was also possible, although not required by the church, that he would consider the counseling sessions to be equally privileged, as such sessions with a psychiatrist would be.

"How did it all end?" I asked.

"Not happily. We kept Julia over Thanksgiving and had our annual feast, which she participated in very enthusiastically. But late that night Sister Clare Angela got a call from the sanitarium where Mrs. Farragut was a patient. Julia's mother had hanged herself a few hours earlier."

The shock that ran through me was violent. Joseph's description of Julia Farragut and the events of that year had been so clear and so moving that I felt as though I knew her, as though I had been there that semester instead of far away on a peaceful campus. "How terrible," I said. "No wonder she was disturbed, living with a disturbed mother."

"That's how all of us felt. But we were also concerned for Hudson. It turned out that before Mrs. Farragut's death,

her husband had spoken to the bishop and the bishop con-
tacted Hudson."

"And that's when the arrangements were made."

"Quite rapidly, as I remember. All this happened before
the current wave of stories about abuse in the church, and
I thank God for that. If such a thing happened today, it
would probably be made public and the priest's reputation
would be ruined before he had a chance to defend himself.
Not that I think everyone charged is innocent. But Hudson
was innocent. Hudson never touched that girl, with or without her permission." She spoke firmly, passionately. Joseph
is the kind of friend who will stand by you forever.

"How much of this got out, Joseph?"

"I think we managed to contain it. The nuns, of course,
knew; at least many of them did. I am convinced the bishop
believed Hudson and wanted only to save his reputation by
getting him away as soon as possible. I have never discussed any of this with Father Kramer, but I assume the
bishop didn't leave him in the dark. But I believe that the
village parish was kept out of the rumor mill."

"So you gave him a big party and he went out west."

"Essentially that's it. But of course, there was still Julia."

"I hope she was given professional care."

"I wish she had been." Joseph pushed her chair away
from the table and stood up. She nudged her glasses a little
higher on her nose and walked to her desk. "Her father
came for her the next day. Sister Clare Angela had already
told her about her mother."

"How did she take it?"

"Strangely. As if she hadn't quite heard the news or it
had failed to penetrate. She became very quiet. Either Sister
Clare Angela or Sister Mary Teresa sat with her for a long
time that night and finally she fell asleep. In the morning
she went to prayers with the rest of us, and to mass, then
went back to her room and packed her bags. Her father
never called to say he was coming, but she seemed to know
that he would. She was downstairs waiting for him when he
arrived to take her home. I remember seeing her there, still
in her habit, standing like a lost waif next to her suitcase.
In fact, he drove up just a few minutes after she got back
to the Mother House."

"Back from where?"

"She asked Hudson to hear a last confession."

"I see." It didn't sound like the act of a victim.

"I walked her to the chapel myself and waited outside for her. Then we walked back together. She never said a word. I don't know where Hudson was. He must have stayed in the chapel."

"How do you know she didn't get medical care?"

Joseph came back to the long table and stood with her hands on the back of the chair she had left a few minutes earlier. "We heard afterward that she had stayed at home with her father after her mother died. And on Christmas"— she paused—"Julia hanged herself."

"Oh Joseph."

"It could not have ended more tragically. I cannot tell you how many times over the last seven years I have asked myself if we couldn't have done more for her, if we shouldn't have overridden her father's order and gotten a psychiatrist, if one of us could have helped her with the counseling." She looked as though she were putting herself through the agony once again. "When Sister Clare Angela was ill, she spoke to me of it again and again, as though her entire religious career hung on that poor child. It was devastating, Chris."

"I can imagine. How terrible for everyone. No wonder Hudson never came back to visit. The thought of all that must have been enough to keep him away."

"Which brings me to the end of the story." She sat down again. "Apparently Mr. Farragut dropped his charges when Hudson left the area and Julia died. I can't even tell you if she ever spoke to either the bishop or the police about what allegedly happened. If I had to guess, I would say she hadn't or that her story was so twisted it was worthless. We heard a few years ago that Mr. Farragut had moved away from the area, too—he had lived in a small town about twenty miles from here—and we never heard anything from him again. Until today."

My heart froze. "What happened?"

"The state police called and said that an all-terrain vehicle with Wyoming plates had been spotted parked at a curb in front of a house. The town had a restriction on overnight street parking, so it was noticed when a police car made its usual rounds. They checked the plate number and it was Hudson's car. There was some luggage inside but no blood or signs of a struggle."

"And no sign of Hudson."

"None. What was most remarkable, if that's the word, is where the car was parked. It was right in front of the house the Farraguts lived in when Julia was a novice."

8

I slept in an empty nun's room in the Mother House. It was two doors down from the room I had occupied for many of the years I had lived at St. Stephen's. It was as simple and bare as the others, even barer because it wasn't permanently occupied. I had brought my own sheets and towels, a bar of soap, and a mug in case I had afternoon or evening coffee with the nuns.

Jack had said not to worry; he had plenty of studying he could do in advance of the coming semester. I hated to leave him. We had planned for so long to have these days together when both of us were free of work and study. Now there was the rest of the winter ahead of us before we could manage a few carefree days together again.

But after hearing Joseph's tale, I was convinced that someone had to dedicate full time to finding Hudson, and although I hoped and prayed he was being held somewhere, I added "dead or alive" to my thoughts. The significance of the location of the car could not be denied. The same possibilities still existed, that someone who hated Hudson because of his alleged abuse of Julia Farragut had somehow learned he was coming east, followed him or met him by appointment at the rest stop, waylaid him there, and left his car in front of the Farragut house as a symbol, or that he himself, finally coming to terms with a terrible chapter in his life, had left the car there to indicate his remorse. I could not believe the latter. But I had to accept, difficult as it was, the possibility that he was already dead, that he had been dead since Christmas Night, his body buried where it might never be found.

As tired as I was, I lay awake for some time trying to plan a strategy. Jack always says investigations have a flow:

known facts, information gathering, analysis, conclusions, and results. I still didn't have all the facts. Joseph didn't know whether Julia Farragut's father was still alive or where he might be living. Someone near the old house might know, or perhaps he had had a lawyer who handled the sale of the house and who would have a forwarding address. If Julia had been eighteen seven years ago, her friends from high school would now be in their mid-twenties. Old friends might be married but still living in the area. After what had happened to Julia, it was unlikely any of them would have forgotten her. But there were possible sources of information much closer to home. Now that Joseph had released the nuns of St. Stephen's to discuss whatever they knew with me, one of them might remember a conversation with Julia, a rumor, a piece of gossip that she had kept secret. I would get started first thing in the morning with step two, information gathering.

I arose at five with the nuns and joined them for morning prayers, mass, and then breakfast. Joseph spoke to them in my presence, instructing them and encouraging them to be open with me. She didn't have to add the word *honest;* that went without saying.

Angela came over to me as I left breakfast. She and I had been friends—and still are—when I was at the convent. She had come as a novice when she was eighteen, the age at which I would have entered if my family situation had been more normal. We were about the same age—she might have been a year older than I—and we had liked each other from the start. Because convents discourage close friendships—that is, exclusively close friendships, between nuns, we were perhaps on less intimate terms than I was with Melanie Gross, but secular society has fewer fears of close female friendships than a religious one has.

"Talk to me first," she said as we walked into the large room that held the drawers assigned to each nun. Angela opened hers and dropped her napkin and ring into it. When she returned for her next meal, she would take them out again and perhaps find her mail waiting for her inside.

"Anyplace special?"

"In the switchboard room. I'm on bells as usual. It's pretty quiet this week, but just in case."

I followed her into the room with the old-fashioned switchboard, ancient front cords and back cords, jacks connecting the board with Joseph's office, the kitchen, the villa, and several other locations so that the nuns could receive and make calls. There was also a ringer allowing Angela to call any nun to the phone. If it was slow enough today, she would switch it so that all calls would go to one phone or another, which would make it difficult to reroute them.

She sat on her little operator's chair and I pulled an old rock-maple kitchen chair over so that we faced each other. "Do you know something I should know?"

"First, let me apologize to Jack for ducking his questions."

"He understands."

"I was in a very uncomfortable position. We were all told to say nothing about Julia Farragut but to answer any other question you and he asked. You understand that our loyalty—"

"I understand and you don't have to explain or apologize. We're friends, Angela. I've been there myself. But now that Joseph has released you, I need to know everything."

"I remember Julia very well. I was one of the younger nuns when she entered and she often came to me with questions, not serious religious questions but practical ones. She was studying the history of the community, as we all did our first year, and preparing for her vows. Her father had given her a large dowry and he also provided the nuns with a lot of personal necessities, so that we were spared a lot of expenses for a long time. Even after she was gone, we remembered him for that every time a tube of toothpaste ran out or we needed a new bar of soap. And you probably know, he gave the convent a large cash gift."

"Joseph said as much."

"But getting back to Julia. I knew about her mother, Chris. I don't know who else knew, if anyone, but she told me one day and asked me not to repeat it. One thing I know how to do is keep a secret."

I smiled. She wasn't the only one, but I would trust her with anything. "I know."

"She said her mother had been ill for many years, that it had started when she lost a baby maybe ten years before. It was a boy baby and Mr. Farragut had wanted a son very much. Julia said her father seemed unforgiving that her mother had lost his only son and could never have another one. Anyway, the mother was hospitalized for mental problems when Julia was a girl, not long after the loss of the baby, she thought."

"Were there other times?" I asked.

"Yes. She didn't know how many, but she knew there were others. It was part of the reason Julia decided she never wanted to marry, that she wanted to do something else with her life."

"Did you get the feeling that the 'something else' could as easily have been teaching school or practicing law?"

Angela thought a moment. "It might have been, but I don't think she was just casting about for a career and stopped when she thought about being a nun. She was deeply religious, as was her mother, and I think she would have come to us eventually even if she had looked elsewhere first, if she had already entered training for another career."

"Did she ever say anything to you about Hudson?"

"Never. His name never came up. You can be sure if I had heard something like that, I would have gone to Sister Clare Angela. Or I might have gone to Hudson himself. When I heard Julia's revelation, I was as shocked and stunned as anyone else. I still am. I absolutely don't believe it."

"So you feel as I do, that he hasn't disappeared of his own free will."

"Someone's done something to him, Kix," she said with emotion, using the nickname my cousin Gene gave me when we were children and that had stuck until fairly recently. "Who could it be besides her father?"

"I don't know. I'm going to have to find him—if he's still alive." If he wasn't, I had a very big problem on my hands. "Angela, Joseph told me the whole story last night, at least a great deal of it. Since Julia Farragut obviously liked you and confided in you, you should be a good judge of her behavior. The way Joseph described it, she went from erratic outbursts to appearing quite normal, so that a decision to send her away at night could easily be changed the next morning almost as though she'd had a bad dream that disappeared with the darkness."

"That's just the way it was. When we talked, we were two young women with common interests and goals. I knew a little more about the workings of the convent than she did, so I was a source of information. We even gossiped—I remember once confessing to Hudson that I had spoken maliciously about one of the nuns." She looked pained at the memory. "It was just one of those things that tumbled out in one of our conversations and I knew as I heard myself say it that I shouldn't have."

"We all do it, Angela. But what you're telling me is that to you Julia seemed a normal young person."

"Absolutely. If she was having problems, she kept them to herself. Perhaps I should have been more astute when she talked about her mother, but at the time I wasn't. No family is perfect. There's a skeleton in every family's closet, even mine. It wouldn't have been kind or fair of me to jump to conclusions when it was clear this girl needed a confidante."

"Your judgment was right, Angela. No one could have foreseen what was coming."

An insistent buzzer sounded and Angela swiveled toward the switchboard. "Good morning, St. Stephen's Convent." She turned to me and pointed. "She's right here, Jack. Hold on and I'll transfer you to another line."

"Thanks," I said, standing. "Where to?"

"Try the kitchen. It should be empty by now."

I ran off to get my call. The last nun in the cleanup squad was just leaving and waved as I came in.

"What's the story?" Jack asked as I answered.

"It's too long to go into, but I'll give you the relevant details." I told him briefly about Julia Farragut, finishing with her suicide and where Hudson's car had been found.

"Wow. That's some story. Look, I've got the phone number of the state-police officer that we talked to the other day. Let me give him a call and ask some questions. When did the Farragut girl kill herself?"

"It was Christmas, Jack."

"So it looks like someone with a long memory waited seven years to even a score."

"It does look that way. And I have nothing at all to go on except the father. I'm going to try to locate him through his sale of the house. Then I'll see if I can find someone to give me some names of Julia's friends. The schools are all closed, so it's not going to be easy."

"Nothing is when you start, honey. But I have to admit, there doesn't seem to be much to go on here."

We talked a little about other things and then Jack said, "If I come up with something and you're not around, can I trust the nuns to get a message to you?"

"Joseph told them to speak freely to me about everything. And I've just gotten an apology from Angela because she stonewalled you the day after Christmas. I think you can trust them all today."

"Then I'll talk to you later."

It was still early in the morning, but I wanted as early a start as possible. There was someone at St. Stephen's I needed to talk to, but that could wait. According to Joseph, the Farraguts' former home was about twenty miles from there, and I wanted to be present when the real-estate agents opened for business. I went back to the switchboard room and thanked Angela for her help. She had nothing to add except, she said, her prayers for Hudson. We all had those. We had offered them at the chapel this morning.

Then I found Joseph. She gave me the last known address of Walter Farragut in the little town of Riverview along the Hudson, south of St. Stephen's. By the time I was ready to leave, it was almost eight-thirty and it would take me at least half an hour to get there since I was using local roads. I promised Joseph I would be in touch with her during the day. Then I took off.

9

The house was a turn-of-the-century gem, three stories with cupolas and chimneys and shuttered windows everywhere, each one with a candle and wreath in the center. It was set back from the quiet street, a snow-covered lawn stretching perhaps seventy-five feet to the curb. The house was painted pale gray with soft rose accents, and I have to admit I loved it at first sight. It reminded me for a moment of my cousin Gene's description of the house he had spent Christmas in: *They have this room and this room and this room.* I couldn't imagine how many rooms this wonderful old house had, but I wouldn't have been surprised if some were still to be discovered by the present owners.

The flagstone walk from the front veranda was neatly shoveled, as was the sidewalk as far as I could see in both directions. The other houses on the street were also large and of the same vintage as this one, indicating a core of building early in the town's history. The trees were all mammoth and their leafless branches intertwined, a summer blessing. For as far as I could see, the snow around the house was still pristine. Neither Hudson nor anyone else could have tramped on it, because there hadn't been enough new snow since Christmas to cover tracks.

There was no movement anywhere around the house, and after a minute or two of unobtrusive looking, I drove away. It was only a few blocks to the center of town, and when I got there, I saw a real-estate office down the block from a bank. As I passed I looked in the front window and saw a woman at the first desk talking into a telephone. They were open for business.

She was still on the phone when I walked through the front door, so I went down the open aisle between two rows of desks, most of them empty, to the only other one that had an occupant. His name was Reg Fuller and he was all smiles as I sat down. I felt a little guilty. The housing market, from everything I'd heard, wasn't sparkling, and a new face might make a realtor think he had a prospective buyer.

"Good morning," he said, offering his hand. "What can I do for you on this nice Saturday morning?"

"I'm just here for some information," I said apologetically. "There's a house at 211 Hawthorne Street. It was owned by Walter Farragut until a few years ago."

"I know the one you mean. Great old Victorian, beautiful house. I don't think they'd consider selling."

"I don't blame them. It was Mr. Farragut, the former owner, that I was interested in. Do you have any idea where he went when he sold the house?"

"That's a toughie. Hold on, OK?"

"Sure."

He went to the woman at the front desk and talked to her. Then he went to a bank of file drawers and opened one. After searching for a minute, he came back. "Our office handled that sale, but we're not supposed to give out information. Mr. Farragut left Riverview when he sold the house on Hawthorne Street." He stopped as though that was as far as he was prepared to go.

"Do you know what town he moved to?"

He looked pained. "Come with me."

I followed him to the woman at the desk in the front window.

"Eileen, this lady has some questions. Maybe you can help her."

"Hi, I'm Chris Bennett," I said. I hadn't introduced myself to Reg Fuller and I needed this woman to trust me enough to tell me something she knew she shouldn't. "I've just come down from St. Stephen's Convent—"

"Oh, I know them. The Franciscans, right?"

"Yes, that's right."

"My friend's daughter is a student at the college."

"Oh, really? It's very small, but it's an awfully good school. I taught there for a long time."

"Yes, Patty's very happy there. What can I do for you?"

"It's about the house at 211 Hawthorne Street."

"The old Farragut house. That was a tough sell. A lot went on there and buyers may like history, but they don't like reminders of violence."

"Julia killed herself there."

"And managed to do it on Christmas. She was a very disturbed girl. Wasn't she a student at your college?"

"A novice in the convent."

"I see. There were other things, too."

"Her mother."

"Yes. You seem to know the whole story."

"Some of it. I'm trying to track down Mr. Farragut. I know he sold the house and moved a few years ago, but I don't know where."

"Well." She looked down at her perfectly polished long nails. "Can you tell me what this is for?"

Which meant she would give me the information if I could win her over. "Someone is missing," I confided, "a very remarkable man who knew Julia. Father Hudson McCormick. His car was—"

"Oh, I heard about it this morning. They found his car parked in front of the old Farragut house, didn't they?"

"That's right."

"Aren't the police looking for him?"

"I don't know what the police are doing," I said honestly. "They seem to have got it in their heads that he parked the car there and walked away. The nuns at St. Stephen's are afraid something's happened to him."

"Where would he go if he left the car there?"

"I don't know."

"Where would anyone who left the car there go?"

It was a question that nagged at me, too. "I don't know that, either. I'd like to find Mr. Farragut and see if he can shed some light on all of this." I was hoping she wouldn't ask me for a connection, since there didn't seem to be one.

"I could give you the name of Mr. Farragut's lawyer, but I know for a fact that he's in the Virgin Islands for the holiday. I tell you what. I haven't looked at the Farragut file, so I haven't taken any information out of it. My boss probably wouldn't want me to disclose the address, but I live here in town and I knew the Farraguts well enough that they gave me a forwarding address. So I'm speaking as a citizen, not a realtor."

"Understood," I said. "Thank you."

"I got a Christmas card from Mrs. Farragut last week and—"

"Mrs. Farragut?" I felt a chill as I heard the name.

"Walter's mother, Mrs. Cornelius Farragut. She lived with them. It was her house. Didn't you know?"

"No, I didn't. How old is she?"

"Pretty far along now. Late seventies anyway. Let me call my husband. He'll find the address for me." She picked up the phone and made a quick call, writing as she listened. From what I could tell, her husband was reading from an address book near the phone. "Here it is." She handed me the paper. "Good luck. I hope you find the missing priest."

"Thank you." I looked at the address. "Do she and her son still live together?"

"I don't know. She never writes about him, and I usually only hear from her at Christmas. As far as I know, she's in terrific health, both mentally and physically."

"I appreciate your help."

She assured me it was nothing, but it was a lot more than that. It was the first piece of solid information I had gotten.

I drove back to 211 Hawthorne Street and parked in front of the house next door. A man was walking a large dog across the street and didn't look my way at all. I got out and walked slowly toward 211. There was no distinct boundary between it and the property I had parked in front of. This was a friendly, fenceless street. One lawn ran into another and the land on this side of the street rose gracefully from the curb, so that all the houses were high and prominent.

I stopped in front of the old Farragut house. The slate walk had a step or two every five or ten feet to accommodate the rise. The door looked new, a natural dark brown with an oval window in the center, etched to make it thickly translucent. At the far end, the left side of the house as you faced it, there was a long gravel driveway that ran alongside the house and curved at the back. The driveway was plowed or blown so that it was clear. A side door opened onto it, probably the way the family came and went. In many communities, front doors have become obsolete, like the beautifully furnished living rooms that no one ever uses except for company, while the family spends all its time in a den or family room.

I kept walking, looking up the slope through trees until I was pretty sure I had reached the next homestead. Then I turned and started back. If it had been summer, with leaves on all the trees, I would not have been able to see it, but because of the bareness and the white of the snow, I could make out a structure at the end of the driveway. It looked more like an old barn than a garage. The doors were closed and there were no cars in sight. I kept walking, eventually stopping to admire the house I had parked in front of, a larger, fussier Victorian painted cream with blue trim. I got in my car and drove back to the center of town and found a telephone.

Joseph was surprised to hear of the elder Mrs. Farragut. She recognized the address as a town somewhat north of Riverview but still well south of St. Stephen's. I told her I was on my way there now and had nothing else to report.

Mrs. Farragut's new residence was an apartment in a complex built for senior citizens. Besides groups of garden apartments, there was a community building, from which I could hear music and singing. I wondered if Mrs. Farragut was a little old lady in a running suit who spent her days in structured activities. When I had left my car in a spot designated for visitors and rung her doorbell, I found I couldn't have been more wrong.

The woman who opened the door was tiny and dainty, dressed in a rose-pink suit with the ruffle of a white silk blouse showing at the collar. Her slender legs were fitted into elegant black leather shoes with a two-inch heel. I felt as though I had interrupted her on her way to a luncheon. By contrast, my skirt and sweater, comfortable shoes, and oversized shoulder bag, which I abused badly, made me wonder if my wardrobe needed some fine-tuning.

What was most distinctive about her was her scent. It was delicate and warm, faintly floral, and very light. There was nothing old-ladyish about it, nothing heavy, nothing to make me wrinkle my nose in distaste.

"Can I help you," she said, without making it a question.

"Mrs. Farragut, I'm Christine Bennett. I was a teacher at St. Stephen's College for several years and—"

"St. Stephen's." She said it as though those were the concluding words of the conversation.

"Yes."

"I'm not sure I have anything to say about St. Stephen's."

"Mrs. Farragut, a man's life may be in danger." I decided to be direct. What I had said was true.

"Someone's life is always in danger. Come inside, please. I don't need neighbors asking questions."

I stepped into a beautifully furnished living room with a thick Oriental rug in shades of blue that were picked up in the upholstery and the heavy draperies, which were opened to let in the sunlight.

"Thank you. You have a beautiful home."

"Take your coat off and leave it on the chair near the phone. I'm sure this won't take long."

I was starting to feel like a kindergartner, but I did as she said, sitting in a chair that faced the windows, holding my shoulderbag on my lap so that I could take out my pen and notebook if I learned anything important.

"What is it that you want?" She sat on the sofa and crossed her legs. She had an exquisite face, the face of a great beauty. The lines of age only added interesting details. I could imagine this woman entering a room and having all eyes turn to admire her. I could also imagine her accepting such admiration as her due.

"Father Hudson McCormick was on his way to St. Stephen's on Christmas Day. He never arrived. Yesterday his car was found in front of 211 Hawthorne Street in Riverview." I delivered it as a complete package. She had to know who Hudson was, just as the address was part of her permanent memory.

"What precisely do you expect me to say about that?"

"His disappearance has to be connected to what happened to your granddaughter seven years ago. If you know anything that might help us to find Father McCormick, I hope you'll tell me."

"The only thing I can tell you is what you apparently already know. During the time my granddaughter was at your convent, Father McCormick acted in a very unpriestly manner. If he went to our old home to apologize to us, he's a few years too late. We aren't there anymore."

"I don't think he went to apologize. I don't think he went there at all. I think someone has kidnapped him—or worse—and left the car on Hawthorne Street to indicate a connection with your family."

"Forgive me for being frank, but I think that's preposterous. With a little effort you could probably write potboilers. The man simply left his car and a lot of foolish people are reading silly things into it."

"Mrs. Farragut, were you living in the house on Hawthorne Street when Julia came home from St. Stephen's?"

She looked at me with her picture-perfect face tilted slightly as though she knew how to show it off to advantage. "I owned the house. Of course I lived there."

"Can you tell me about Julia during that period of time? Her mental state?"

"She was a wreck. What else would you expect? She had lost her mother, her confessor had abused her, her vocation was destroyed. The child was in pieces."

"Did you get help for her?"

"None of this is your business, Miss Bennett. None of this has anything to do with the car left on Hawthorne Street. It's Saturday morning and I have many things to accomplish today."

"Can you tell me about Julia's mother?" I said, ignoring her implied suggestion that I leave.

"She was a poor soul who found it hard to cope with the world."

"I understand her problems began when she lost a child."

"Her problems began when she was born." She seemed not to want to go on, but I waited, hoping she would resume. "My daughter-in-law was a lovely person. When she was well, she was a good wife to her husband and a good mother to her children."

"Did Julia have a sister?"

"She had a brother. Foster is now nearly thirty."

I hoped my shock didn't show. Angela had told a convincing story about Julia being an only child, about her mother losing a son and not being able to have another. Was nothing that Julia Farragut had said the truth?

"Where is Foster living now?" I asked.

Mrs. Farragut's lips moved into a half smile. "I'm sorry. I've said about all I can, more than I intended. I don't know how you found me, but you'll have to work a lot harder to find Foster. I have no intention of giving him up to you."

"What about your son?"

"I'm sorry."

"Has your son remarried?" I asked. I felt there might have been an event in his life that precipitated the move.

Mrs. Farragut stood. "I think it's time for you to leave, my dear. I hope you find your priest. I suggest you do what the police do and see if he took a train out of Riverview after leaving his car. He's probably playing games with you. Wherever he is, he deserves to be punished."

I got up and put my coat on. "Why didn't your family press charges against him if you were so convinced he'd done something terrible to Julia?"

"The victim died," she said tautly. "There was no witness and no case."

"Thank you for your time."

"Be careful on the front walk. It may be slippery." She shut the door.

10

What stayed with me was her scent. Far from being overpowering, its delicacy was haunting. For me it had special significance. While I had let my hair grow and had it styled when it was long enough, bought myself simple but fashionable clothes, and become a thoroughly secular person in the year and a half since I left the convent, I had never used perfume. More than clothes or jewelry or hairstyle, perfume seemed too confusing to allow me to make a selection. On several occasions I had sniffed some in cosmetics departments and brought home samples on cardboard or in tiny test vials, but I had never actually put any on my skin. Unlike a ring or a necklace, which I could remove easily, there seemed a permanence to perfume that kept me from trying it. What if I hated having it there and could not wash it off effectively? What if Jack hated it? What if it gave me a headache or made me ill?

Now, at the age of thirty-one, I was entranced by the scent of a woman more than twice my age. Although there was nothing distinctively old about Mrs. Farragut, it seemed odd to me that of all the scents I had experienced on other people, this one would make such an impression.

I drove into town, where I stopped at a coffee shop and found a telephone with a small, local directory hanging from a chain. The only Farragut listed was the one I had just visited. What I needed was a larger directory for the county or area, but there was none around. I decided to try something that had worked for me before, so I turned the car around and drove back to Riverview. The Catholic church was easy to find and I went to the rectory where the pastor was just on his way out. He glanced at his watch and agreed to hear my question. It didn't take long for him to give me an answer.

"I can tell you without looking at the records. Walter Farragut left Riverview without so much as a fare-thee-well. I can tell you I was surprised—I was hurt, if you want me to be honest—because Walter had been generous, had served on committees, had always been someone we could count on."

"You knew they were moving, didn't you, Father Grimes?"

"Everyone in Riverview knew they were moving. The house was up for sale for a long time. It was a weak market and they wanted a lot of money for it. But when the sale was made, Walter picked up and left. Only his mother came to me to have her records sent to her new parish."

"Father Grimes, I'm a friend of Father Hudson McCormick."

"Oh, good heavens, I know who you mean. Is there any word? Have they found him yet?"

"Not that I've heard since this morning. I feel somehow the Farragut family is the key to his disappearance."

"You may be right. That was a terrible ordeal they went through."

"Did you know Julia, Father?"

"Quite well. I came here before her confirmation and I knew her until her death." He set his lips and shook his head. "She and I talked about her entering St. Stephen's. I was all for it."

"And her family?"

"I believe they were, too, except for her mother. I think her mother would have liked her to stay home."

"Did you know her mother had problems?"

"I knew. I visited her at the hospital on several occasions. I never dreamed her life would end the way it did, or that her daughter's would."

I took a chance and asked a question that had been nagging at me. "Was anything going on in that family that might have contributed to the suicides of the two women?"

He looked at me for a long moment. He was a man in his fifties or sixties, balding, his face lined as though he carried the worries of his parish in his own soul.

"I wish I could answer that," he said, and I knew I had reached the end. Either he didn't know anything, or the privacy of the confessional prevented him from answering.

"Thank you," I said. I drove back to St. Stephen's.

I found some leftovers in the kitchen and made myself lunch. While I was eating, Angela stuck her head in.

"Jack's on the phone. I'll transfer the call."

"Thanks, Angela." The phone rang briefly and I picked it up.

"Get anything?" he asked.

"The runaround." I told him what I had and hadn't learned.

"The state police have nothing more on Father McCormick. The local police in Riverview have been through the vehicle and lifted prints. They'll do what they can with them, but I wouldn't hold out much hope. In cold weather people wear gloves for warmth, and it's been pretty cold. They've also been through the contents of the car. It sure looks like he intended to complete this trip. He had Christmas gifts for a lot of people with *Sister* in front of their names, and there's even one for you. The suitcases are full of his clothes, the clerical kind and pretty casual stuff. And there are envelopes of snapshots that I assume he was going to show around. There sure isn't any indication that he was planning a detour."

"I'm not surprised," I said.

"It looks like we've both drawn blanks. If someone's holding him for ransom, they're not too anxious to deal or we'd have heard from them by now. So it doesn't look good, Chris."

"I know. I've been sitting here trying to think where to go next. Is there any chance you can find out where Walter or Foster Farragut lives through the DMV?" They were sure to own cars and I couldn't think of any other way of locating them unless their old neighbors on Hawthorne Street knew where they had gone, and I felt that if they hadn't let their pastor know, they might not have let anyone else know.

"I'll give it a try. I think one of the guys here in Oakwood will do me a favor. Otherwise, I'll call Brooklyn and see who's working today."

"I'm scared, Jack. I'm scared for Hudson."

"I know, honey. I'll get on it right away."

I washed my dishes slowly, pushing myself to think of some other direction to move in. After what I had learned this morning, I no longer felt that talking to the nuns would be fruitful. If Julia had lied to Angela, who had been especially friendly toward her, what likelihood was there of learning anything useful from anyone else? Still, there was one I ought to talk to.

I left the mother house and walked to the villa. It was afternoon and many of the nuns there would be taking a nap, but I would try anyway. I had to find Hudson soon or it was all over.

One nun in the villa that I was particularly fond of was visiting family, and I would miss her. Two nuns were sitting on a sofa reading magazines. I asked for Sister Mary Teresa and they pointed me toward her room.

The names of the nuns were on the doors on white cards lettered by hand in an italic print, a talent I recalled one of the younger nuns had. When I found Sister Mary Teresa's room, I stood at the door and listened. There was no sound. I tapped lightly with my fingernail but got no response. Very quietly I turned the doorknob and looked inside.

The room was empty. I pulled the door closed again, stopped to chat with the nuns who were reading, and went back outside. It was too cold for anyone to be sitting in the sun, but I checked the patio anyway. The snow had been cleared, but no one was there. I backtracked and went down to the path to the chapel.

Even in the cold, even with the trees bare and the beautiful grounds covered with snow, I had no difficulty remembering the day in August when I had walked from the Mother House in my wedding dress, accompanied by the nuns of St. Stephen's, on a morning so bright and so beautiful that I could not have imagined anything more perfect. The chapel, a small structure in the traditional shape of a cross, had been decorated with white flowers so that it looked light and airy. Joseph led the nuns, carrying the crucifix. She was followed by two sisters carrying candles.

Then the rest of the Franciscan sisters followed down the aisle. When I entered, I had a fleeting sense of sadness that my parents had not lived for this happy occasion. Then I turned and saw Arnold Gold.

The people I met in the first weeks after I left St. Stephen's have become both friends and family to me. First there was Melanie Gross, then Jack, and a little later Arnold Gold. I could see Mel and Hal from the back of the chapel, Harriet Gold sitting beside Jack's parents, and here, to take me to my future husband, was Arnold, this tough old lawyer who had choked up when I asked him to give me away, this tireless advocate who never turned away a person in trouble, never asked if they could pay for his services, this wonderfully bighearted man who had once told me he had grown up hating cops but who had taken Jack into his family circle, saying, "I can always use another son-in-law." On my wedding day he looked improbably exquisite, his lanky frame in a well-tailored suit, his hair absolutely silver and almost in place, a man who was as close as anyone would ever come to being my father. We hugged and waited for our musical cue as I wiped away a tear and he squeezed my hand.

My friend from high school, Maddie Clark, who was my matron of honor, gave me a quick smile and started down the aisle on the arm of Jack's brother. I took a deep breath and grinned up at Arnold. Then the music changed and we started our walk.

On this cold, end-of-December day, I sat in the last row of pews, looking at the masses of red poinsettias and remembering the white roses of August, the moment, how I felt when I saw Jack at the far end of the white carpet, how Arnold and I kissed, my veil held high to accommodate, how I turned to Jack and we exchanged a smile. I had never felt more sure or less nervous than I felt at that moment. In some magical way I knew that we were meant for each other, that I was the last of his women as he was the first and the last of my men. I had an immensely powerful desire to be with him and make him happy, a feeling that persists to this day.

The altar was bare as we stood before it. To the right were three candles and we walked over to them and each of us lit one. Then together we lit the one in the middle, symbolizing our union. After that there were the readings we had chosen, and then the marriage ceremony. This was followed by the offertory.

Halfway down the length of the chapel there was a lateral aisle and in it, on the right, a table with the offerings and a magnificent altar cloth that had been commissioned by Jack's mother as a gift for the convent and made by Sister Gracia, who worked on it for months. Four nuns carried the cloth down the aisle, unfolded it, and laid it on the altar, the embroidery evoking gasps. Two of them then returned with the bread and wine so the mass could continue.

My wedding dress was the greatest extravagance of my life. I had gone shopping with Melanie Gross and her mother, Marilyn Margulies, determined to wear a street-length white dress or suit. But the moment I saw myself in yards of white lace and *peau de soie*, I changed my mind, with the agreement and encouragement of Mel and her mother. They showered me with compliments, delicious adjectives describing my physical attributes, how they would all be enhanced by a gown that flowed, a bodice that revealed, a train that lingered. I remember laughing at first, then realizing how much I had missed in not having a mother after my fifteenth year.

Except for me the chapel was empty, conducive to thought. What I wanted to do was get inside the house at 211 Hawthorne Street. Although it had surely been redecorated, I felt that just being there would inspire me, would evoke ideas, open new avenues. I wanted to see the room that poor Julia had lived in; I wanted to see where she had killed herself. Poor child, I thought, sitting in my pew. She wanted to join her mother. I wondered where the rest of the family had been that Christmas Night, why they had left her alone so long that she had been able to do that terrible thing.

There was a sound, almost a groan, and a figure in a brown habit rose from a pew near the front of the chapel. I had not been alone after all. Someone had been kneeling the whole time I had sat there, praying silently. The figure turned and I recognized Sister Mary Teresa.

I waited till she had acknowledged me and then passed

me before standing and following her outside. "I was looking for you," I said. "Would you like to have a cup of tea with me?"

She seemed almost dazed, as though kneeling for so long had affected her equilibrium or made her drowsy. "That would be nice. Sister Edward, isn't it?"

"Chris," I said. "I was Sister Edward when I was at St. Stephen's." I had taken the names of my parents, Edward and Frances.

"Oh, of course, of course. Silly of me. My head must be somewhere else."

We turned toward the Mother House. I kept my pace painfully slow to match hers. She walked as though she had to think about the process, this foot, then that foot. Joseph was right; she had deteriorated greatly since I had left.

"Wonderful weather," I said blandly.

"Good weather for Christmas, yes. Snow before and sun after. I like winter. I just don't like the cold."

"Winter's nice," I agreed, ignoring her contradiction.

"Where are you living now, Sister Edward?"

"In a small town called Oakwood. My aunt had a house there."

"You used to have a cousin there, didn't you? Some little fella you always visited?"

I marveled at her mind, its strengths and its lapses. "You have a good memory. He's not so little, but I used to visit him regularly. He's in a home for retarded adults. He's very happy there."

"Do they take him to mass?"

"Every Sunday. Sometimes I take him, and then we go somewhere for lunch. He enjoys that."

"Very important to take him to mass."

We had arrived at the Mother House. I held the door open for her and we went inside.

"Want a cup of tea?" she said.

"Good idea. I'll make it for us. Let me take your coat."

"I like to keep it on. Takes me awhile to warm up."

I picked up our mugs and we went back to the kitchen, where two nuns were preparing dinner. They had a kettle on the stove and the water came to a boil quickly. Sister Mary Teresa sat at a table away from them and I got a teapot and some tea together. The cooks were noisy, talking and banging things around, and I didn't want any distractions, especially with someone whose memory was so fragile. When the tea had steeped, I asked her if she'd rather go back to the community room, where it would be quieter.

"Lots of noises here," she said, pushing her chair back. "We can sit somewhere else."

When we were resettled, I poured the tea and we sipped it. I noticed how she held her hands around the hot mug. "Do your fingers hurt?" I asked.

She laughed. "Everything hurts sometimes. Fingers, toes, knees, legs. I don't have my teeth anymore, so they can't hurt, that's one good thing. You have your teeth?"

"All except a wisdom tooth."

"That's what we need, a little wisdom."

"Sister Mary Teresa, do you remember Julia Farragut?"

"That poor child. Of course I remember her. She would have made a wonderful nun. She was so dedicated, such a fine young person."

"Did you know her well?"

"She trusted me. There were problems in her home. She told me about them."

"Do you remember what those problems were?"

She put her hands around the mug and held it. Then she raised it and sipped and sipped again. "Her mother was ill. It was tragic. She killed herself, you know."

"I heard."

"Thanksgiving. Sister Clare Angela, God have mercy on her soul, got the phone call. It tore poor Julia apart."

"I can imagine."

"She had a good upbringing, that girl. They were a good family, even if the mother had some problems."

"Did you ever visit Julia at home?" I asked.

She put her mug down and looked at me. "I don't think so. Should I? I only knew her here. I never went to her home." She smiled and her eyes were suddenly clear and full of reason and intelligence, as though she had returned to her full self.

"I wondered because I drove by the Farragut house this morning."

"They don't live there anymore."

"How do you know?"

"Someone must have told me. I just remember hearing that they'd moved."

"You know that Father Hudson McCormick is missing."

"Everyone knows that. He didn't come on Christmas Day. I was praying for him in the chapel."

"Do you know the rumors about Father McCormick and Julia?" I asked hesitantly.

"I won't talk about that. Sister Clare Angela said we were never to discuss it. She was right. This convent has never had a scandal, and that's because we've always held our tongues and minded our business. I won't be the first one to break a promise—or the last."

It didn't surprise me that she gave Sister Clare Angela's admonition to keep quiet more weight than Joseph's instruction to speak freely to me. "Did Julia talk to you about it, Sister?"

She was still wearing her coat, although I had taken mine off in the kitchen. Now she opened the buttons, revealing the brown habit underneath. She had a lined face and thick glasses in rimless frames, an old woman who had spent half a century in this convent and could be counted on to protect its honor and the honor of the General Superior who had been her friend.

"We had enough to talk about without that. And she was too much of a lady."

"For what?"

"Christine, isn't it?"

"Yes."

"Don't believe everything you hear, Christine. Julia was a fine young lady, a dear girl." Two tears fell onto her cheeks, puddling at the rim of the lenses. She took a tissue out of her coat pocket and patted her face. "It's time for me to go. Thank you for the tea."

"I'll walk you back to the villa."

"Thank you, I like to walk alone. The air is good for me and I'm in no hurry. Fast or slow, I always get where I'm going. My memory fails me sometimes, but my legs never do. I'll let you clean up the tea things and put my mug back in my drawer."

I walked her to the door and stood outside in the cold,

watching as she made her way slowly along the clean path. She stopped now and then and looked up at the sky, or perhaps at a bird or a tree, then plodded along again.

I went inside and did as she had told me.

11

Angela came into the kitchen and told me Joseph was looking for me. I dried my hands and took the two mugs, dropping them off as I went. Joseph was in her office.

"I know you would have told me if there was anything new, but I thought you might just want to throw some ideas around."

I sat at the table. The depth of her anxiety was clear from her invitation, from her acknowledgment that she expected nothing new from me. What she wanted was the comfort of my company. Perhaps for the first time in the sixteen years we had known each other, she was allowing herself to communicate fear, admitting her own inability to cope. It made it that much harder for me as I realized a burden had subtly shifted to my shoulders. The pressure was terrible on both of us. We were not merely looking for a killer; we were trying to keep a man we loved from dying—if he was still alive.

"I've been to see Walter Farragut's mother."

Her face relaxed as though I had said I'd found Hudson safe and sound. "Oh Chris, that's wonderful. I was so afraid there was nothing, that there was nowhere to turn. Tell me about it."

"There isn't much to tell. She's Mrs. Cornelius Farragut, in her seventies, I'd guess, and lives in a retirement community halfway between Riverview and here. She won't say where her son lives. I found out, too, that Julia had a brother. She told Angela there were no brothers, but she had one and he's alive somewhere, but Mrs. Farragut won't give an inch. Jack is trying to find the two men through Motor Vehicles. If they own cars in New York State, we may be able to track them down."

75

"Go on." She had sat across from me and taken a pencil and a sheet of blank paper, but she had written nothing.

"Let's start with the little we know. Hudson's car was found outside the Farraguts' old house yesterday morning. That means it was left there either the night of Thursday the twenty-sixth or the early morning of the twenty-seventh. Let's say—and I don't believe this—that Hudson left it there himself to send us a message of remorse. That means he had no transportation. He would have had to take the train out of Riverview. I think we should find out what the schedule is and see if anyone at the station remembers him. Do you have any photos of him?"

"I can find one."

"Now let's look at the other possibility. A kidnapper or killer, someone who knew and loved Julia Farragut, met Hudson at the rest stop on Christmas Day and forced him to drive somewhere. It's possible"—I looked across the table at her—"that Hudson has been dead since Christmas Night."

"I know that."

"He gets rid of the body—or he's holding Hudson somewhere for reasons that I can't imagine—and decides to leave the car in front of the Farragut house to send a message of vengeance. But he has the same problem. He has to go back to wherever he started from."

"And that means the train."

"So it seems to me I'd better talk to the people in the station, find out if anyone saw Hudson or if they saw anyone waiting for a train besides the regulars."

"Let me find a picture of Hudson." She went to a cabinet and pulled out a box of pictures. She went through them quickly, finally handing me one. It was a color snapshot of Hudson with two of the nuns in front of the chapel.

"This is fine," I said.

"Are you going now?"

"After I make a phone call."

Joseph looked at her watch. "We'll put your dinner away. We've just been given a microwave oven as a gift. When it came, I couldn't think what we'd do with it, but I'm told they're great reheaters. You can be the first to try it."

I was about to get up, but I changed my mind. "That house. Were you ever in the Farragut house?"

"No. It's possible Sister Clare Angela was. I think Mr. Farragut visited here with Julia, but I never really knew where they lived."

"It's an amazing house. I can see that the new owners have given it a new paint job and probably replaced some windows. It looks new and sparkling. I can't quite explain it, but it does something to me. I feel that I want to get in there."

"Why? To see what?" She said it urgently, as though I were holding something important back.

"I don't know. I just want to see where Julia Farragut lived. And died," I added. "It was very quiet when I was there this morning and I didn't want to ring in case they were all sleeping. Maybe after I go to the train station, I'll see if anyone's home."

"Would you like someone to go with you?"

"Thanks, Joseph, I think I have to do this alone."

"We'll see you later."

I started out. "Leave the instruction manual for the microwave in plain sight. I'm all thumbs when it comes to technology."

The train station was a disappointment. They had closed down before midnight on Thursday and not reopened till early Friday morning. The ticket agent shook his head when he saw the picture of Hudson.

"Are there any trains after midnight?" I asked.

"We got a few in both directions. You can get your ticket on board. Don't need to keep this place open for a couple of passengers."

I went out to the parking lot and walked around. A sign announced in no uncertain terms that cars without a permit would be ticketed and towed at the owner's expense. It was a long commute to New York, but there were probably people who did it daily. They would come here early, park their cars, hop a train for the city. Or perhaps they went north to Albany or some town between. I looked at the cars, not knowing what I was looking for. Then I got into my own car and drove to Hawthorne Street.

* * *

Number 211 was as quiet as when I had parked there this morning, but I walked up the flagstone path, up the stairs to the wide veranda, and rang the bell. A lamp in a front window was lighted and I could just make out the sound of music from inside. But no one answered my ring, and after a few futile minutes I decided no one was home and a timer was turning on lights at dusk and perhaps a radio or television set.

I went back to the street and walked to the house next door. It was even larger than 211 and also set back. This one was painted cream with blue shutters and trim and a blue double door as well. I rang the bell and a woman opened it almost immediately.

"Yes?" She said it with the restrained hostility of one who suspects you are selling something.

"My name is Christine Bennett and I'm looking for the people next door at number 211. I wondered if you knew where they were."

"They won't be back till after New Year's. They're in St. Croix for the holiday."

"I see. I wonder—were you friends of the Farraguts?"

"Is this about the Jeep they found yesterday?"

"In a way it is. I used to teach at St. Stephen's, the convent where Julia Farragut was a novice."

"Why don't you come in. It's cold out there."

"Thank you."

She was a tall, slender woman in her fifties, her hair not quite gold and professionally arranged, dressed in the kind of flowing pants outfit you see in fashion magazines. I followed her through a spectacular living room with a grand piano almost lost in one corner and into a smaller room that was comfortably overstuffed.

"Please sit down. You're . . . ?"

"Chris Bennett."

"I'm Marilyn Belvedere. Can you tell me what's going on? One of our neighbors saw that car when he was walking his dog yesterday and he said there'd been something in the local paper about it. The police were all over it, but they wouldn't say anything. I'm afraid I'm just not up on the local news."

"Father Hudson McCormick was on his way from Buffalo to St. Stephen's on Christmas Day. He called in the afternoon from Albany and that was the last we heard from him. He was our priest when Julia Farragut was at the convent."

"Then he's the one who—"

"There were charges made against him, Mrs. Belvedere. I knew him and I don't believe there was any truth to them."

"I don't know what to believe about that whole situation."

"Did you know the Farraguts?"

"I thought I did." She reached out and switched on a lamp next to the chair she was sitting in. The walls were covered with a fabric that matched the upholstery and the thick rug. Along the edges of the room a beautiful old wooden floor gleamed with polish. "We've lived here a long time and the Farraguts moved in a few years after we did. Serena and I became friends."

"Is that Walter's wife?"

"Yes. They had the little boy and Julia was a few years old when they got here. They were a very nice family, I thought."

"Was Walter's mother with them when they moved in?"

"She was already here. She and her husband, Cornelius, had owned the house for years. When she was widowed, she invited Walter to live with her. But it was always her house. And she let you know it if you got it wrong."

The characterization didn't surprise me. There was nothing reticent about old Mrs. Farragut. "I understand Serena was hospitalized," I said, turning back to the unlucky wife.

"She had a nervous breakdown at one point. I could see it coming."

"In what way, Mrs. Belvedere?"

She folded her hands and unfolded them. "She was a poor soul who found life hard to handle. Maybe it was a genetic defect. The daughter, after all . . ." She left it hanging.

"Was there anything you knew about that she couldn't cope with?"

"Mother?" It was a man's voice and we both turned toward the door we had entered. A young man, thirtyish, was standing there in his bathrobe.

"Tom, you're up. Dad was looking for you."

"I'm going out for a while. I'll get myself dinner."

"Have a good time, dear." Marilyn Belvedere turned back to me as her son walked away. "They turn the clock around, don't they?" she said with a smile. "At least during vacations. I always look forward to having him, and then I only see him for a few minutes at a time. He lives in his own apartment now."

"That's nice," I said, wanting to get back to more important things. "We were talking about Serena Farragut."

"Why is this important?"

"Because someone has kidnapped or killed Father McCormick."

"I don't see what Serena Farragut's nervous breakdown can possibly have to do with that priest."

"I don't either," I admitted, "but there's some connection between Father McCormick's disappearance and the Farraguts. That's why his car was left in front of the house."

"I suppose you're right." She looked pained, as though she knew what I was after but didn't want to talk about it, as though her son's interruption had reminded her to keep quiet. "I wish I could help you."

"I think you can."

She pressed her lips together and crossed her legs, tossing silky fabric. "It wasn't a happy family," she said finally. "I don't know what else I can say. They certainty had enough money, but that isn't everything. Maybe it was the presence of Walter's mother, the friction between the women, maybe it was something else. These things happen, even in the best of families."

"What things?"

"Unhappiness," she said vaguely.

"You mentioned a son."

"Foster, yes."

"Do you know anything about him?"

"He was a problem. That's all I can tell you. Foster was always in trouble."

I took a chance. "Was your son friendly with him?"

"Not at all. They didn't get along. Tom had nothing to do with him."

"Do you know where Walter Farragut is now?"

That was the question that disturbed her more than any of my others. "Miss Bennett, after all the years we were friendly with that family, all the misery and tears I shared with Serena, including standing at her grave seven years ago, they left without a word. I haven't seen Walter Farragut since the day he moved out of that house. Even his mother didn't give me a forwarding address. I haven't gotten so much as a Christmas card from her. They left this town and the waters came together over their lives. There's nothing left of them, nothing left of my friend Serena, not a tree planted in her memory or a plaque in the school. She gave to this town, and when the women's club decided to hold a lunch in her memory, Walter refused to attend. They were a strange family."

"What about the new people? Do you know them?"

"The Corcorans? They're wonderful. I couldn't ask for better neighbors."

"Do you have the key to their house?"

"Why do you ask?"

"I thought they might have left it with you while they're away. I could see they have lovely plants inside. I would hope someone would water them."

"I water them."

"I'd like to get a look at the house, especially where Julia lived."

"I couldn't let you in. And they've changed a lot of things."

"Did the Corcorans know about Julia's suicide when they moved in?"

"They weren't told. I understand there's a law now; they have to tell you things like that before you buy. But at that time it wasn't law yet, and the house had been on the market for some time with people afraid to live in it. The realtor just kept her mouth shut and the Corcorans didn't find out till they'd moved in. I can tell you they weren't happy about it."

"Were you aware that Julia was seriously depressed?"

"I'm not a professional and I'm not sure I can tell the

difference between extreme unhappiness and depression. Her mother's death had a terrible effect on her, which didn't surprise me. She was only eighteen or so when it happened. I assumed she would get over it, but she didn't live long enough."

"Were you here when she committed suicide?"

"We were here. I remember hearing the sirens and seeing the lights. I even remember seeing them carry that poor girl out in a plastic bag." A chill seemed to go through her body as she said it.

"I wonder that they left her alone on Christmas after she had suffered such a loss."

"She wasn't alone. It's a big house. You could probably have a party in one part of it and not hear it in another."

I wrote down my name and the phone number at St. Stephen's. "If you change your mind, I'd like to come with you on your watering visit. I wouldn't leave your sight."

She looked at the piece of paper. "I'll think about it," she said. Then she walked me to the front door.

12

There was a dinner plate full of food in the refrigerator and handwritten instructions telling me what to do with it. I put the plastic-wrapped dish in the new microwave, punched some buttons, and watched. A light went on, a digital clock counted down, a bell rang, and lo and behold! I had a hot meal.

Jack used to live in a small apartment in Brooklyn Heights where he had miniaturized appliances, including a half dishwasher and a small microwave. He didn't use it much when I was there because he always enjoyed cooking, but the few times he stuck something cold inside and pulled it out steaming, I must admit I marveled. As I did tonight. I sat by myself, my notebook open, and ate slices of roast beef, beets, mashed potatoes, and a nice salad that had also been left for me in the refrigerator.

Everything I had heard about the Farraguts indicated an unhappy family with a lot of problems, but I had nothing specific to work with. The phrases in my book left no room for interpretation. *Extreme unhappiness and depression. They were a strange family. Misery and tears. Foster was always in trouble. It wasn't a happy family. Friction between the women. There were problems in her home. She was a poor soul who found it hard to cope with the world. The child was in pieces.* I was back at old Mrs. Farragut's comments now. Even Joseph had told me that Julia was an unstable person. But there was a big difference between being unstable and taking your life, and if she was unstable when she arrived at St. Stephen's, if *there were problems in her home* when she was growing up, Hudson McCormick was in no way responsible for the troubles she brought with her to the convent.

83

The phone in the kitchen rang as I was finishing my salad. I got up and answered it.

"Chris? It's Angela."

"Hi. I'm just finishing dinner."

"Jack called while you were out. He asked to talk to Joseph and she said she'd like to see you when you have a minute."

"Thanks, Angela."

"I don't suppose you've found him."

"No. I'm just picking up a trail of misery that goes back years. But it doesn't seem to be pointing anywhere."

"See you later then."

I washed my dishes and carried my notes upstairs to Joseph's office. "Did Jack locate those addresses?" I asked as I went inside.

"One of them, yes. The one for the father, Walter Farragut. He's living a little farther downstate now, closer to New York. Jack is pretty sure this is the Walter Farragut you're looking for. The age fits. He said there were a number of Farraguts."

"Good. I'll try to see him tomorrow. Maybe I can get Jack to meet me there. I'm not sure he's a man I look forward to speaking to alone."

"There's more, and this is something of a shocker. Jack couldn't find a current license for the son, Foster, and he did some additional checking. Foster's in jail, Chris. He's been there for almost two years."

Maybe I shouldn't have been surprised, but just as there was a huge chasm between *troubled* and *suicidal*, there was at least as great a gap between *in trouble* and *in jail*. Still, the news effectively ruled out my likeliest suspect in the kidnapping of Hudson McCormick. Someone daring enough to have been in trouble was just the kind of person who could have waylaid an unsuspecting priest and taken him somewhere to exact revenge.

I called Jack, who said he would contact the prison to see if he could find out anything else about Foster Farragut. What he had learned from a police file was that Foster had used an unregistered handgun to pistol-whip an old friend, whom he then robbed. It was an ugly crime committed by a man from a family wealthy enough to keep him financially content. Unless his father had chosen not to.

In the meantime there was no word from any source on Hudson. We agreed to speak again in the morning and decide how to approach Walter Farragut.

I checked the nuns watching television downstairs, then got my coat and went outside. It was a clear, moonlit night. The huge wreath on the roof of the mother house almost glowed in the celestial light. The cold had eased off thanks to a warm front coming up from the south. I wondered where Hudson was, how he was spending his night, if he was still alive.

I went to the villa to talk to Sister Mary Teresa again if she was of clear mind. She was sitting with a group of elderly nuns who were chatting and laughing.

"Sister Dolores," I said, spotting the Christmas-dinner cook. "I haven't thanked you for the wonderful meal you made."

"I'm sure you did," she said. "I've lost count of the thank-you's. Maybe I should spend more time in the kitchen in my old age. I had an awfully good time fixing that meal."

"I was at a convent in northern Pennsylvania last year where the sisters put up jams and jellies and sell them in a tiny store. People from all around come and buy them."

"That sounds like fun." She had a face that looked like fun, with full cheeks and sparkling eyes, and a body that showed her enjoyment of food. She had once told me that her father had been a baker and she had grown up with floury hands. "What do you say, Sisters?"

There was some agreement along with some good-natured calls for her to enjoy her retirement. They were a nice group of elderly women, women I had known for sixteen years. At that time many of them had been vigorous, active people. Now they were plagued with physical ailments or worse. A couple of them sat silently, barely aware of their surroundings. Others needed help getting around. They had outlived their parents and many of their siblings, and now the convent was truly their family. I spoke to a few of them, then found Sister Mary Teresa.

"Could we talk for a few minutes?" I asked.

"Of course," she said brightly. "Didn't we talk this afternoon?"

"Yes, but something's come up." I held out my hand and she used it for leverage as she rose with difficulty. Then we walked to the far side of the large room and sat in two adjacent seats.

"I'd like to ask you about Julia Farragut again."

"I told you this afternoon. She was a lovely girl, would have made a good nun."

"Did you know she had a brother?"

She looked at me through the thick lenses. "I never heard about a brother."

"His name is Foster."

"Foster." She looked at her hands as they rested in her lap. "I don't know that name, Foster."

"She never talked to you about him?"

"It's all so long ago. It's hard to remember." But she was disturbed. The name—or the mention of a brother—had stirred something in her, reminded her of something, made her uncomfortable. "My memory isn't what it used to be." She opened and closed her hands as though to get the circulation going.

"When Julia died, did you and Sister Clare Angela go to the funeral?"

"Yes, we did. I remember that. It was very cold. Sister Clare Angela drove."

"Did the whole convent go?"

She shook her head. "They didn't want it."

"Who didn't?"

"The family. Julia's father. It was a suicide, you know. Of course I've always been convinced she had a change of heart at the end, when it was too late. So it wasn't really a suicide. It was an accident. She had a Catholic burial. The priest—I've forgotten his name—"

"Father Grimes?"

Her face broke into a smile. "Yes, Father Grimes. How did you know?"

"I met him."

"I think Father Grimes thought so, too, that it was an accident. I know she went to heaven, poor soul."

"I'm sure she did. Then you and Sister Clare Angela were the only nuns at the funeral?"

"The only ones. Just Sister Clare Angela and me." She looked at the watch she wore, a large round white face with clear Arabic numbers. "I should go now, Christine. Thank you for coming."

I said good night and watched her go. As she passed the group of nuns she waved to them. When she was gone, I left the villa.

Outside, I turned away from the Mother House and started walking. With the bright moon and the milder weather, it was a good night to make up for the morning walks I had missed in Oakwood. Nothing would make up for my lost days and nights with Jack, but we would have other times together and Hudson would have nothing if we didn't find him.

Sister Mary Teresa's clever manipulation of Julia's suicide into an unfortunate accident intrigued me. It was a theological point I had heard argued many times. Catholicism does not condone suicide. There was a time when a person who committed suicide could not be buried in hallowed ground. There were priests who would not officiate at the funeral. But Catholicism is not unbending, not without understanding and sympathy. After all, how are we, the survivors, to know whether the poor soul, in his last moment of life, after he has taken the irrevocable step, did not regret his act? How can any of the living be certain that after the trigger was pulled or the poison swallowed or the stool kicked out from under, the dying victim did not instantly repent and wish he could undo his last act? Because we feel merciful toward people who have erred, it is usually assumed nowadays that the victim was sorry, that given the time and the opportunity, he would undo or reconsider.

That was how Mary Teresa felt, that Julia had had a change of heart when it was tragically too late to do anything about it. It was a kindness from a kind woman and I felt a warmth toward her. I felt glad that Julia had had someone like Mary Teresa to talk to and to comfort her. St. Stephen's was an institution, a place on a map, a collection of buildings and trees and lawns and statues, but most of all it was a group of women who were good and kind. I was not only happy to have spent fifteen years here; I was proud of it.

13

There was noise everywhere, the screams of women, the sound of running. My first thought was that there was a fire, but there had been no alarm, no knock on my door, no official warning, no telltale smell of smoke.

I got out of bed and pulled my robe out of the closet. Out in the hall a group of nuns stood in robes and nightcaps, some crying. I ran over to them, putting my robe on as I went.

"What happened?"

Sister Gracia turned to me. "It's Sister Mary Teresa."

"Oh no."

"She dead, Chris."

"Oh how awful. Was it a heart attack?"

"She's been murdered!" one of the other nuns said shrilly, her voice out of control. "Murdered. They left her lying in the cold near the chapel."

My heart was pounding. "Have you seen Joseph?"

"She's going there now. To the chapel."

I ran back to my room and threw on a pair of jeans and a sweater, sneakers, and wool socks. I took my coat and bag and flew out of the room. The group was still standing there, but I didn't stop to say anything. I had forgotten my watch, but it was still dark and the nuns had not yet gotten up for morning prayers, so I assumed it was earlier than five.

It was freezing outside, but I was moving so fast I didn't mind it. The occasional floodlights that were turned on from dusk to dawn were still lighted and helped me find my way.

A small group of nuns in coats over their nightgowns

were huddled outside the chapel. I recognized Joseph as I approached and I called to her.

She turned to face me. "Chris. We've had a tragedy."

"Tell me."

"It's Sister Mary Teresa. Harold found her a little while ago. I think she's been strangled. Angela's gone to call Father Kramer. Did Sister Mary Elizabeth find you?"

"No. I woke up when I heard the commotion in the hall. She must have missed me."

"Listen to me, Chris. We don't have time to talk now. I want to stay with Mary Teresa. I will have someone call the police when I think to do it. They will not enter the villa until I have personally walked through it to make certain no one is there. I want you to go to Mary Teresa's room right now and go through it. Somehow this has to be connected to Hudson's disappearance."

"I'm on my way."

"Do you have gloves?"

"I'm wearing them."

"Good. We're a law-abiding convent and we will cooperate with the police in every way, but they have refused to cooperate with us in the disappearance of Hudson. We have begged them to do something, anything, to find him, and they have done little or nothing. I think it's up to us to find out whatever we can before they get here and shut us out of their investigation."

"Do you think she was killed in the chapel?" I asked. This was very important for the convent, as it would indicate a desecration and the chapel could not be used until it had been resanctified.

"I don't think so. The door was closed and the lights were off. It probably happened out here. We don't have time to talk now. I'll see you later."

She turned back to the group in front of the chapel and I took off for the villa, my mind reconstructing my last talk with Mary Teresa only a few hours before. I had mentioned the name Foster and she had become disturbed, her face screwing up, her hands opening and closing. She had not known Julia had a brother, but the name Foster meant something to her. It was she who had broken off the conversation, looking at her watch and saying she had to go.

Where had she gone? Not to join the sisters. She had walked past them. Had she gone to meet someone? Had someone called her earlier in the day and arranged to meet her that evening?

I pushed open the villa door. Inside, the nuns were gathered, old women in nightgowns and robes, their heads covered with little nightcaps the older nuns wore to bed. In case they died in their sleep, the cap was "God's holy habit," which would protect them.

I dashed up the stairs as they watched me, remembering approximately where Mary Teresa's room was. Inside, I turned on the light and pulled down the window shade. The bed was made. She had not slept in it tonight or else she had gotten up, dressed, made her bed, and gone out, and that seemed very unlikely. It isn't easy to get up at four in the morning, even if you're used to five. An autopsy would tell us the time of death, but I was pretty sure Mary Teresa had agreed to meet someone after she and I had had our conversation last night.

Her missal and a black handbag were on top of her dresser. The missal had a few pages marked with ribbons but was otherwise empty. I sat on the easy chair and opened the bag, laying the contents on the night table next to me, piece by piece. There was no wallet. Sister Mary Teresa had probably never walked out with more than a dollar on her person, and that could fit easily in a change purse. There was a thick wad of tissues, folded twice, three remembrance cards from funerals she had attended this year, two of them for St. Stephen's nuns, one for a man named Joseph J. Morgan, and a change purse on a cord anchored to the lining. Something was inside, but when I opened it, all I found was a penny and a marble. I was not surprised. Most of the time life at St. Stephen's required no money.

I pulled out two letters and read them quickly. One was from a young niece or grandniece, a child who wrote in carefully shaped printed letters on lightly ruled pencil lines and described school and a baby brother. The other was from an adult named Ann-Marie who was obviously reiterating an invitation to visit and sounded genuinely sincere.

The return address was Syracuse. I jotted down the name and address in my own notebook.

A piece of newsprint turned out to be a clipping from a local newspaper announcing the end of the first semester at St. Stephen's College and the nuns' plans for Christmas.

> *General Superior Sister Joseph is looking forward to the visit of Father Hudson McCormick who has been, most recently, serving a parish in Wyoming. It will be Father McCormick's first visit to the area since leaving for the west seven years ago.*

So it wasn't exactly a secret that he was coming back.

There were several safety pins of different sizes along the bottom of the bag, a loose black hook without an eye, a small tube of Vaseline, half-used, a pair of glasses in a case, and a very worn address book.

She must have had the book for decades. I opened it to the *A* page and saw the name Gladys Arnold with an address and phone number and the notation *Died Jan. 3, 1972.* I turned to the *F*s and went down the page. There were no Farraguts, no Fosters. Then I went back to the *A*s and went through the whole book.

They must have been largely friends and relatives, many of them living in New York State with zip codes close to the Syracuse one of the letter from Ann-Marie. An awful lot of the people listed had died, and each one had a date of death added. Whoever they were, she had kept up with them till the end.

I put everything back and left the bag where I had found it on top of the dresser. Then I went through the drawers, feeling like a voyeur, a sad one who got no pleasure out of seeing an old woman's underclothes, warm cotton underpants, sturdy brassieres, heavy gauge stockings, some of them carefully repaired to stop the inevitable runs.

The drawers yielded no secrets. There were medications in the top drawer from a pharmacy in town, prescribed by a doctor who was commonly called when a nun fell ill. Sister Mary Teresa took a number of pills every day for a variety of ailments including high blood pressure and arthritis. In a lower drawer a beautifully knit brown Shetland cardigan lay wrapped in tissue paper. The label sewn into the ribbing around the neck read *From the Knitting Needles of Ann-Marie Jenkins*. Ann-Marie would truly mourn her aunt's loss.

But there were no papers, no notes, no phone numbers or names in the dresser, and when I finished, I went to the closet. A nun's closet is monochromatic. The hanging habits were all the same shade of brown. A bathrobe in a beige washable velour was the only piece of clothing that was distinctly different. I put my hand in each of the pockets but turned up only a used tissue. No other pocket on any of the other garments yielded any more. On the floor were a pair of warm slippers and a second pair of comfortable oxford shoes. There was also a pair of warm boots that she had not needed last night because Harold had done such a good job of cleaning the paths, good enough that her killer would have left no footprints. All the shoes were empty, as I found out when I shook them.

I closed the closet door and went over to the desk, which was standard in a nun's room. Inside the large, shallow drawer across the top were the usual contents of desks: pencils, ballpoint pens, a box of inexpensive stationery, three stamps, a ruler from a local hardware store, a couple of buttons, and a small pencil sharpener. The only other drawer, along the right side, contained mostly snapshots of children, each with a date, and some sepia-toned photographs of people who were probably Mary Teresa's parents and siblings, of whom there were many.

So there was nothing. I was sure that by now Joseph would have called the police and they would be here momentarily. I stood with my back to the door, looking at the neat bed, the handbag atop the dresser, the clean desktop, the night table with the lamp on top. The night table. I ran back and pulled open the only drawer. Inside was Mary Teresa's New Testament, some tissues, a paperback mystery with a bookmark at page 227, and another tube of Vaseline. The Bible had several remembrance cards stuck in it like bookmarks. The first one I looked at said, *May Jesus have mercy on the soul of Julia Farragut*. As I started to look at the card more carefully, there was a knock on the door and Joseph walked in.

"They're here, Chris. Have you found anything?"

"Nothing. I was just looking at her Bible. The remembrance card for Julia Farragut is here along with a lot of others."

"Give it to me. I can carry it out more easily than you can."

"I'm not sure there's anything in it that we're interested in."

"No, but you've just begun to look at it and you're not sure there isn't. Round up the nuns downstairs and walk out with them. I'll go around turning off lights in case anyone downstairs is looking up."

"See you later."

The nuns downstairs had dressed and I helped them on with their coats and let one lean on my arm as we walked outside and turned toward the mother house. "Sister Joseph will be out in a minute," I said to the nearest police officer.

"Thank you, ma'am."

I escorted the group slowly to the Mother House.

14

It was a terrible morning. I kept the villa nuns in the Mother House so they would not have to see the body and the investigation around it. Father Kramer, who was certain the murder had not taken place in the chapel, thereby desecrating it, insisted that the police allow the community to attend mass there. To avoid seeing either the body or the tape marking the crime scene, we entered the chapel through a rear door.

I have never seen a group so torn apart, so filled with misery, as those nuns that Sunday morning. This was not a natural death, which would be equally mourned but could be accepted; it was an unnatural, unholy act committed against a holy community, upon a woman who had been kind and decent and given her life to the church.

There was also fear. St. Stephen's stood high on a hill on a large campus, separate from the surrounding towns and villages. We had always walked in peace there, believing we were safe. Although we locked building doors at night, we did not fear. Now we would. Now we had joined the other world that knew intruders as part of life.

Father Kramer did a masterful job that morning, speaking to both the grief and the fears. I watched the faces and could see the attentiveness. The nuns were listening, reaching out for comfort and reassurance.

Breakfast was a somber and tearful affair. The police waited until it was over to question the residents of the villa and anyone else who might know anything. Eventually, it was my turn. I sat with a detective in a corner of the community room minutes after I had had a chance to wash and change my clothes.

"I'm Detective Lake," the policeman said, introducing

himself. He was a veteran officer with graying hair, a tall, heavily built man with huge hands that delivered a firm handshake. "I understand you were one of the last people to talk to Sister Mary Teresa last night."

"I went over to the villa after I ate. I'm sorry I can't remember the time, but I was late for dinner and I ate alone. I washed my dishes and walked over there."

"What did you talk to her about?"

"The Julia Farragut suicide."

He made a face that indicated I was way off base. "That happened a long time ago in another town. What would she know about it?"

"She was friends with Julia, kind of a mentor. Julia confided in her. Sister Mary Teresa and Sister Clair Angela, who has passed on, were the only two nuns from St. Stephen's to attend Julia's funeral."

"May I ask what your interest is at this point in Julia Farragut's suicide?"

"I think there's a connection between the Farraguts and the disappearance of Father Hudson McCormick."

He made the face again. "It's likely that a common criminal killed Sister Mary Teresa last night."

"It's possible."

"But you don't think so."

"No."

"Did she say anything to connect the two events?"

"She didn't say much. I asked her if she knew that Julia had a brother and she said she didn't know. I mentioned the name Foster and she became agitated. She looked at her watch and said she had to go. That was about it. It wasn't a very long conversation."

"Where did she go?"

"Out of the community room."

"Out of the building?"

"Not that I saw."

"But you think she went to meet someone?"

"I think it's possible."

"Do you have any idea who this person would be that she might have met?"

"Frankly, no."

"Was Sister Mary Teresa the kind of person who might just have taken a walk at night?"

"Yes, she was," I admitted. "Earlier in the day we talked in the Mother House and she wouldn't let me walk her back to the villa. She said her mind failed her sometimes, but her legs never did." I smiled, remembering the moment. "I had seen her in the chapel just before that. She'd gone there to pray for Father McCormick."

"So last night she might have gone back to the chapel to pray for him again."

"Yes, she might. And I should tell you, Detective Lake, when a nun can't sleep, and it happens, she's likely to go to the chapel at any time of the night."

He handed me his card. Detective Barry Lake. "If you think of anything, I'd appreciate a call. The McCormick case isn't ours, you know. The car was found in Riverview. But we're in touch with their police department, and if he turns up, we'll know it. I think you ought to let us all do our jobs."

"I never interfere with the police, Detective Lake."

"Thank you for your time."

I found a telephone and called Jack. When we got past the news, he said, "OK, I'll meet you at Walter Farragut's house. How's two this afternoon?"

"Fine."

"And Chris, what the detective said to you, that it could be a common criminal who hit on a nun going to chapel, is a strong possibility. I think you ought to watch your rear and stay inside after dark. That goes for everyone."

"I heard they're leaving a couple of cops on the grounds tonight. They're borrowing them from the state police because the village force is so small. We'll be safe."

"I've heard that before. See you at two. I miss you."

"Me, too."

By the time I got to the chapel, the crime-scene people were finishing up. From the look of the area, the crime scene almost didn't exist anymore. The snow all around the chapel had been trampled, although I assumed it had been photographed from all angles before the trampling began. Whatever it had looked like when Sister Mary Teresa had died, it looked nothing like that now. Jack had often lamented the fact that crime scenes were destroyed more by the police than by any other means, and it was true enough here. I got some polite hellos from the departing men as they tucked their gear in the station wagon. The body had been removed and thankfully the coroner's van was gone. I waited till the crime-scene wagon was on its way and then went into the chapel.

I remembered that yesterday, when I had sat here and seen Sister Mary Teresa suddenly rise from a pew, she had been down front. While it didn't necessarily follow that she would have sat in exactly the same place another time, I thought it was likely. When I enter a church to sit and think, which I do from time to time, I always take an empty spot near the rear and usually on the left-hand side. My vision is pretty good—I don't wear glasses—so from the back I can see the whole church, or chapel, quite clearly. But an elderly woman might choose to be close to the sanctuary so that she could see it and feel a part of it.

I walked down the aisle past the still-magnificent poinsettias and looked inside the row that I guessed was where I had seen her yesterday. Usually, when someone kneels, you can see her back or bent head. Mary Teresa had been totally invisible, meaning she had scrunched down very low, nearly making a ball of herself.

The row was empty, as were the one in front and the one behind. That didn't surprise me. The crime-scene unit would have checked out the whole chapel, taking anything they found, fingerprinting the wood. If she had sat here, there might well be prints on the back of the pew in front. She would certainly have needed the assistance of that pew to raise herself, considering her aches and pains.

I went back out and saw Joseph coming down the path. "I was looking for you," she said. "Would you like to walk?"

"Yes."

We went downhill, away from the buildings of the convent and the college. In summer, this is the most beautiful place in the world and it's not bad in winter, either. I always find walking here exhilarating, renewing, and I was sure Joseph felt the same way. She had spent many more years at St. Stephen's than I had and would doubtlessly remain for the rest of her life. The convent and the college were her sustenance; they kept her nourished both intellectually and spiritually. What had happened here early this morning was surely one of the great tragedies of her life.

"That's where the old orphanage stood," she said, facing a high, flat, treeless area that was well-known to the nuns. "You wouldn't remember it."

"No."

"It burned down the first year I was here, an incredible fire. It was all wood, of course, so once the fire got started, it just took off. People from all the towns around saw it and the police phones rang off their hooks. The papers called it a spectacular fire. I always wondered about that word. A spectacular fire. There hadn't been any orphans in it for several years, of course. They'd been moved to a newer, safer, fireproof building downstate. But it was a beautiful old place with fine floors and the kind of construction you don't find nowadays. Mary Teresa used to tell me stories of the old days, when the orphanage was full and there were a hundred novices or more. She had a sense of history. She wanted people to know what had happened and when." She turned away from the long-gone orphanage. "That's the building where the novices lived, through those trees there. We took that building down before it caught fire. It had a wonderful fireplace, almost like the one in the mother house. You could practically stand up in it. When her memory was still sharp, Mary Teresa wrote her recollections. She'd probably never heard of oral history, but she went around and interviewed the nuns in the villa so that all their recollections would be kept. You probably can't even picture the grounds with those two buildings."

It was true. The raised plateau where the orphanage had stood had long been a place where students sat and studied, sometimes resting against the base of a statue of the Virgin Mary that had been placed there after the building burned down. And the novices' dormitory now had trees growing there, naturally, I had been told, seeds falling from the older trees, maples and oaks, trees that like cold weather. "I've tried to imagine it," I said. "Not very successfully. I've always loved the grounds so much just the way they are."

"I had to call her family," Joseph said. "She had a grand-niece who truly loved her."

"Ann-Marie Jenkins."

"Yes."

"There was a letter from her in Mary Teresa's purse."

"I'm too close to this, Chris. In the past, when you've come to me with questions, I've always been able to look at your conundrum with detachment, to ask salient questions, to see what is obscure to you. Today I feel deep in obscurity myself. Perhaps the police are right and some intruder walking across the campus spied someone outside the chapel. Maybe he thought there would be money in the box and she tried to prevent him from going in."

"You don't believe that."

"She often walked in the evening, especially in the summer. But even in the winter, she liked the fresh air." She looked around at the snow and the sky. "What a nice day this would be if it were not so tragic."

We had reached the first of several benches along the path. The snow had been brushed off, either by a diligent Harold or by a stroller who wanted a place to sit in the sun. We sat down. From the village the sound of churchbells came up the hill. It was Sunday.

"Tell me again what happened yesterday."

"I met Walter Farragut's mother and talked to her, but I got very little from her. The one thing she said that made me take notice was that Julia had a brother named Foster. Angela told me that Julia had said her mother's mental illness began when she lost a son and was told she couldn't have any more children."

"But Grandmother Farragut says there was a son."

"*Is* a son," I said with emphasis. "She said he's nearly thirty now. And that I wouldn't find him very easily. But Jack found him. He's in prison."

"Which makes it equally unlikely that he had anything to do with Hudson's disappearance or Mary Teresa's death."

"But Mary Teresa didn't know Julia had a brother and the name Foster left her confused. When I talked to her yesterday afternoon, her mind wasn't awfully clear."

"That's been happening. But when she was all there, she was her old self."

"She didn't want to talk about the rumors involving Julia and Hudson. She said Sister Clare Angela had said never to discuss it. But it was obvious she had loved Julia. When I saw her the second time in the evening, her mind was sharp. I asked her if she knew Julia had a brother and she said she'd never heard about a brother. When I said his name was Foster, she just seemed confused or agitated, Joseph. We spoke for a few minutes more, but I could see she was edgy. Finally she looked at her watch and said she had to go. That's the last I saw of her."

"Tell me what you think."

"What I think is that the events of yesterday are connected. I spoke to old Mrs. Farragut in the morning and talked about Foster. That night someone killed Mary Teresa."

"Mrs. Farragut called someone to say you were asking questions. Is that what you're saying?"

"But whom?"

"I suppose Walter's the only one."

"Joseph, I have a hard time believing that a man of Walter Farragut's age and position in the community would drive up to a convent, meet an elderly nun, a woman close to his mother's age, outside the chapel, and strangle her to death."

"It is a difficult thing to grasp. And maybe he's not the one. But I believe you're right that there's a connection between your conversation with Mrs. Farragut and what happened here last night."

"It means someone had to call her during the day to set up a meeting at the chapel. When she looked at her watch, she realized it was getting near the time, or that she had to go upstairs and get her coat, or something like that. She may have wanted to spend some time in the chapel before the person she was meeting was scheduled to come."

"There's a chance Angela will remember a phone call. But it's possible the caller only asked for the villa, not for a particular person."

"Then someone in the villa will know. I'll ask around later today. Now I want to get some dinner. I'm meeting Jack at two o'clock at Walter Farragut's house. I don't know if we'll find anything out from him, but I want to look at him, get a sense of the kind of man he is. You've described him as very generous and yet I have the feeling that was a very unhappy family that lived on Hawthorne Street in Riverview. I spoke to the Farraguts' next-door neighbor last evening, a Mrs. Belvedere, and she said as much. If there was unhappiness, there was a cause."

We stood and started back uphill toward the chapel and the mother house. The bare branches were no longer covered with Christmas snow; they had been blown clear or perhaps yesterday's milder temperatures together with the sun had melted the thin white layer. Except perhaps in a black-and-white photograph, there is nothing quite so starkly sad-looking as a bare branch. In May they would come alive again with the fresh, bright green of spring, but today there was no hint of the better days to come.

"There was a son who got into trouble," Joseph said.

"Maybe that's it. Maybe that's why Julia wanted to get out of that house completely."

"Yes, I suppose that's possible. One always hopes a novice will come to us for better reasons."

"She was troubled. Maybe she thought St. Stephen's could help her out of her trouble."

"I wish we had," Joseph said. "I really wish we had."

15

The street was wide, curved, and lined with custom-built houses that shared the image of luxury and nothing else. No two that I could see were in any way similar in design. There were houses of redwood, of brick, and of stone, one story and two story, contemporary, traditional, and Mediterranean. They were spaced far apart, and from what I could see, had deep lots, many with swimming pools, some with tennis courts. Walter Farragut had traded in a hundred-year-old antique for a modern architect's dream.

I had stopped short of the Farraguts' house number. Looking down the block, I now saw that Jack had arrived first, turned around in the cul-de-sac, and parked on the other side, near the far end of the street. He was walking toward me.

We kissed as we met and I turned around as we kept walking.

"Sounds like you're having a rough day."

"Terrible. The nuns are all in shock. Even Joseph isn't faring well." I explained the presumed connection between my visit with Mrs. Farragut and the murder of Sister Mary Teresa.

"How did you introduce yourself to Mrs. Farragut?" Jack asked.

"I said I used to be a teacher at St. Stephen's College."

"And what were you looking into?"

"I was trying to find out what had happened to Hudson and I wanted to know about Julia. Mrs. Farragut is a tough cookie. She didn't let anything slip."

"She told you about the brother."

"I don't think the brother was a family secret. The next-door neighbors to the Farraguts talked to me about him. I

103

think he was Julia's secret. Maybe she was ashamed of his behavior and thought a convent wouldn't want her if they knew about him."

"OK, bottom line—why would Walter Farragut go up to St. Stephen's last night and murder Sister Mary Teresa after his mother calls to say she's been talking to you?"

"Because he knows where Hudson is and Mary Teresa knew something that could put me onto Walter."

"Like what?"

"Jack, I know it's possible that Hudson made a second phone call from the rest stop, but we can't overlook the fact that a man called him at the church in Buffalo that he was visiting and said something very threatening. How did that man know Hudson would be there?"

"You got me."

"Someone told him and the only someone I can think of was Sister Mary Teresa."

"Why would she do that?"

"Because he made her believe he was her friend and Julia's friend. Or that he was Hudson's friend and wanted to surprise him when he came east for the first time in seven years. Every nun at St. Stephen's knew when Hudson was arriving. There are gifts for him under the tree. I'll bet they all knew he was spending a few days in Buffalo first. They probably even know the name of the church or the name of the priest he was visiting."

"You're telling me that someone has been in contact with Sister Mary Teresa for seven years, waiting to get his hands on Father McCormick."

"That's exactly what I'm saying."

"And you think Julia's father may be the person."

"I think Julia's grandmother may be the person."

"Right." He threw an arm around my shoulders. "No one would think twice about a woman calling the convent."

"And no one would recognize her voice."

"OK, let's see where it gets you."

We turned and walked back to my car.

"It's the second house down on this side," he said. "I'll stay here. I think you'll do better alone. Two people at the door can be very intimidating and they'll make me as a cop in two seconds."

"Gee, I thought you were the most uncop cop I'd ever met when I met you."

"That's because you were blinded by the force of my overwhelming personality."

"It was your smile," I said, evoking one as I spoke.

"See you soon." We kissed again and I went down the block to find the Farragut house.

"It's Sunday and my husband is resting."

She was tall with long hair streaked with the color of sand. She was wearing a green velvet jumpsuit with a paler green silk blouse, and to me she looked like every man's second wife, thirties, well shaped, glamorous even on a sleepy Sunday afternoon. And scented. Not like her mother-in-law, who was delicate; this woman reeked of something cloyingly sweet that threatened to make me sneeze.

"It's very important, Mrs. Farragut. I've come down from St. Stephen's convent. A nun who was a friend of Julia Farragut was found dead this morning."

She did something with her mouth as though to say she was tired of the whole thing. Then she said, "I didn't see anything about it in the paper."

"She was found after the papers went to press. I'd just like to talk to him for a minute."

"Come on in."

I walked into a marble foyer with enough mirrors to keep all of St. Stephen's away forever. Just seeing strips of myself wherever I turned made me uncomfortable.

"Stay here," she said. "I'll see if he'll come."

I didn't stay exactly "here," but I remained in the foyer. There was a curved stairway off to my right and doors at the rear of the foyer, probably to closets and a bathroom. The marble floor was so shiny it could almost have been another mirror. And high above me was a skylight bringing the light of day into the windowless room.

"What is it you want?"

I looked around to see the presumed Walter Farragut. He was medium height, silvering hair, wearing a silk-and-velvet smoking jacket in shades of green and black, making me wonder whether he and his wife coordinated their daily wardrobes.

"My name is Christine Bennett. I was a nun at St. Stephen's and a teacher in the college. This morning Sister Mary Teresa was found dead outside the chapel."

"Who is Sister Mary Teresa?"

"She was a friend and mentor of Julia. She was at Julia's funeral."

"Come with me." He turned back and called, "We're fine, Karen," then led the way into a sitting room that had a view of the backyard, although I'm sure he didn't think of it that way. "I don't know any Mary Teresa. I knew a Sister Clare Angela, who was the superior when my daughter was there. She's dead now, I understand."

"Yes, she is. Mary Teresa was a friend of hers and a friend of Julia's. She loved Julia very much."

"So did I. Exactly what do you want from me?"

"I'm looking for Father Hudson McCormick."

"Well, you won't find him here. He left his Jeep in front of my old house in Riverview and took off. How should I know where he is?"

"Because his disappearance is connected to what happened to your daughter seven years ago and to what happened to Sister Mary Teresa today."

"Are you the woman who talked to my mother yesterday?"

"Yes."

"How did you find me? She didn't give you my address."

"I just knew where to look," I said.

He didn't like that. He was a man who was used to controlling situations he was part of and he didn't like someone finding out information that he hadn't disseminated. He answered only those questions that he chose to and changed the subject when it pleased him. "Well, you found me. If I knew where that bad priest was, I'd give him a piece of my mind. But I don't know and I resent your assumption that I do."

"Mr. Farragut, why did Julia keep her brother's existence a secret?"

"Who says she did?"

"Nuns that she was friendly with."

"She was a sick girl. Sometimes she had a hard time telling fact from fantasy."

"Why did you send her to St. Stephen's? Why didn't you keep her at home under the care of a psychiatrist?"

"We did what we thought was best for her." The rancor was gone from his voice now. He sounded resigned, a father who had lost his child.

"Did you know she was suicidal?"

"She wasn't suicidal. Julia had a strong desire to live. Even after her mother . . . passed on, she wanted to make a life for herself. Something happened that day, I don't know what, I'll never know what, and her life came to an end."

"Hudson was gone by then," I said. "He spent that Christmas in the southwest."

"I didn't say he was there or that he had anything directly to do with what happened. Maybe what happened was in her mind. We'll never know."

"If you talk to me about it, Mr. Farragut, maybe we can find some answers. Something was bothering her and she implicated Hudson McCormick, maybe to save herself. I want to clear Father McCormick's name almost as much as I want to find him alive."

"I'm sure he's alive and I'm equally sure he was involved with my daughter in exactly the way she described. May we now put an end to this conversation?"

But I didn't want it to end. "I think she may have killed herself because she was so dreadfully sorry for what she said about him."

"That's what you think. You have a right to your opinion. I have a right to my own."

"What's yours?" I asked.

"Her mother's death destroyed her. She was a fragile child, unready for the world. I'm sure that's why she chose to be cloistered. When her mother died, she blamed herself, which was nonsense, but you can't always get through to someone in the state she was in. She felt that if she'd been home with us, my wife would have survived. The truth is, my wife had lost it long before the day she took her life. She wasn't a well woman."

"Were you at home when Julia died?"

"I was out with friends. It was Christmas Night and I'd been invited. My mother was home with her. This is really very difficult for me to talk about, and all your assumptions are false. You find that missing priest, you'll find the person responsible for my daughter's death."

"We'll still have to find Sister Mary Teresa's killer," I reminded him.

"Why not the priest? He knew the truth about my daughter's problems. Maybe he suspected this nun knew it, too, if she was close to Julia. Once she's out of the way, he's in the clear."

"You're right about one thing. I think Father McCormick does know the truth. But I think it's a truth you're trying to cover up."

I knew I shouldn't have said it, that I was betraying my very unobjective point of view, but sometimes a person says something spontaneously when he's angry that he wouldn't allow himself to say when he's under control. Mr. Farragut wasn't one of those people. He said nothing and I was ushered out very quickly and found myself walking down to the curb.

Jack was standing beside my car and he came over as the door closed behind me. "You got to talk to him."

"Yes, but it didn't amount to much. He admitted his mother had called about my visit, and for a minute I thought he might open up. He came close to being emotional when he talked about Julia, but he caught himself. Then he blamed everything on Hudson."

"So what do you think? He our man?"

"I don't know. He certainly isn't holding Hudson in his house, not with his wife living there."

"He wouldn't keep him there anyway. What's she like?"

"Young, gorgeous, expensively dressed. So is he. Do you have a silk-and-velvet smoking jacket tucked away anywhere?"

"Not lately. That turn you on?"

"Not today."

He pushed my hair off my forehead. "You know, it's so much fun to meet up here, we should think about living together."

"I've been thinking about it a lot."

"Me, too. Soon, huh?"

"Very soon."

"Where to now?"

"I think I want to water some plants."

16

We had a cup of coffee in a pretty place that had a view of the river and then we went our separate ways. I felt pangs of longing as I drove away. Tomorrow Jack would go back to work at the Sixty-fifth Precinct in Brooklyn and it looked as though I would still be here. I was still without answers for Hudson's disappearance, and now the very convent had been invaded.

I thought about what Walter Farragut had said, that Hudson had killed Mary Teresa because he suspected she might know the truth that involved his guilt. Then why hadn't Hudson done it seven years ago? No, I had stirred something up yesterday and someone had decided to silence the poor woman. The question was, was it Walter Farragut?

Over coffee Jack and I talked obliquely about what troubled me: Walter Farragut and his daughter, Julia. I didn't want to think about it, couldn't bring myself to confront it. But it was right there and I couldn't get rid of it.

There was a car in the long driveway next to the Belvederes' house. I parked on the street and walked up to the front door. Marilyn Belvedere answered.

"I heard what happened," she said. "Come in. Were you at the convent when that poor nun was murdered?"

"I've been staying there since Friday. The handyman found her body this morning, lying outside the chapel. I think she'd gone there to pray for Father McCormick." It was probably at least partly true.

"They said on the news it was someone looking for the poor box."

"I don't believe that. Mrs. Belvedere, I need your help. Isn't it time to water the Corcorans' plants?"

She looked undecided for a moment, then said, "I'll get the keys."

She took her coat out of the closet and went somewhere for the keys. When she came back, we went the long way to the house, out the front door, along the street, and up the Corcorans' walk.

"In the summer I go out the side door and cut across, but with all the snow, it's easier this way," she explained. "And you're not wearing boots, are you?"

Neither was she. It took two keys to open the door.

"Did the Farraguts have two locks?"

"No. The Corcorans are a lot more security conscious. Personally, I think they overdo it. You get the occasional burglar out here, but it's really pretty safe. Come to the kitchen with me. I have to fill the watering can."

I followed her through a hall to the back of the house. The kitchen looked completely remodeled, with handsome wood cabinets that might look Victorian to someone living a hundred years later, and plenty of windows facing the back.

"The original kitchen was very small. Housewives didn't do much cooking in a house this size a hundred years ago. They let the servants do that. The Corcorans pushed the kitchen out a little to get room for the island." She turned the water on and filled two cans, one of copper, one of stainless steel. "I'll do the ones here on the window shelves. Would you mind doing the ones in the breakfast room?"

"Not at all." I walked from the kitchen to a charming room with a round wooden table and heavy armchairs. A rubber tree and a large Norfolk Island pine were near the large window. Although light came through it, thin blinds covered it completely. I guessed the Corcorans didn't want people peeping in at them, or at their empty breakfast room. There were some other large, treelike plants that I watered, too, one with a beautiful, variegated leaf. Before returning to the kitchen, I admired the china cabinet and its display of hand-painted plates.

"Beautiful plants," I said as I went back to the kitchen.

"They are. Gail has more than a green thumb. Let's fill up and do the living room and dining room."

We carried our cans to the dining room first. As we were leaving the kitchen the phone rang.

"Don't worry about that. The machine'll answer."

It did. "Gail? This is Sunny. Just wanted to let you know that Miranda had a little girl Thursday night, seven-two, with little wisps of dark hair, an absolute beauty. So she'll get her tax deduction, but she'll miss first baby of the year. Call you when you get home."

"Isn't that nice," Mrs. Belvedere said. "Miranda went to high school with Julia Farragut."

"I guess everybody knows each other here."

"Pretty much."

I watered a crown of thorns and moved on to a group of African violets. "I understand old Mrs. Farragut was home with Julia the night she killed herself."

"I think that's so. I think she called the ambulance."

"Was Walter Farragut home?"

She stopped watering. "He was out. He came home later, after the police arrived."

"Where was Foster?"

"I don't think anyone ever knew where Foster was. Probably out getting himself in trouble." Her voice was tinged with unkindness.

"Then the grandmother was alone with Julia that night."

"I think so. I think she said she went to look in on her, see if she wanted anything, and found her."

We went back for more water. As we entered the kitchen I heard the sound of a piece of machinery turning on. I looked at her.

"Must be the furnace. Gail leaves it at fifty-five or so so the pipes won't freeze."

We refilled and went to the living room. It was an enormous room with a beautiful fireplace. The walls were papered with a tiny floral design that was echoed in the covering on the sofa and two easy chairs. Antique lamps were everywhere, a magnificent collection. I could see the one at the window that I had noticed from outside last evening. Here the shades were down only three quarters of the way, perhaps to allow the plants to soak up the sun. We watered in silence. When we were finished, I paused to admire a tapestry hanging on the wall. Just beneath it was the thermostat. The temperature in the living room read fifty-eight degrees.

"Works fast," I said, meaning the furnace.

"It may have been another zone that went on. The house has several zones. Do you want to go upstairs now?"

"Please."

"We don't need the cans. Gail moves all the plants downstairs when she's away to spare me the trouble. I really shouldn't be doing this."

"I appreciate your help."

There were a lot of bedrooms upstairs, all of them larger than anything in the house I lived in. We looked in on the Corcorans' master bedroom suite with its small adjoining sitting room and full bath, then the children's rooms, which had been decorated with the kinds of colors and furniture and games that I had seen only in magazines in waiting rooms.

"When Gail found out about the suicide, she decided not to use that room for the family. I really can't blame her."

"I understand."

"So it's a guest room now." She opened a door and stood there, not entering.

I went inside. It was a lovely room, larger than the rooms for the Corcorans' children, certainly a room for a favorite child. It was in the corner of the house with windows on two sides. Shades were drawn now, but pulling one aside, I could see the Belvedere house through the trees and behind the one on the other wall the large backyard. It was a much simpler, more natural backyard than the one behind Walter Farragut's new house. Here a swing set stood near a small slide, trees grew, and the edge of a patio was visible. I couldn't see very far to the left because the kitchen extension blocked my view, and what looked like a wooden fire escape also intervened.

A double bed was made up with a colorful quilt and decorative pillows, or perhaps it was a queen dwarfed by the size of the room. A rocking chair had a cushion covered in the same tones as the quilt, and a hooked rug in the center of the room left the old wide floorboards bare, a good touch. There was a dresser with a mirror over it, another wonderful antique lamp on the night table, and a watercolor of a fall scene on one wall. Altogether a very nice room to spend a night in, or to grow up in.

"Do you know where she hanged herself?" I asked.

Mrs. Belvedere had not entered the room. She stood at the doorway as though an invisible barrier kept her from crossing the threshold. "I think the closet," she said uneasily. "I think there was something in there, a bar or something. The ceiling is quite high—maybe it was a shelf." She was plainly nervous.

I opened the closet door and looked inside.

"They changed it," Mrs. Belvedere said. "Gail likes her closets customized."

"They did a beautiful job." There was everything in there you could want, slanted shelves to hold shoes, rods at various heights to accommodate clothes of different lengths, shelves for sweaters, even built-in drawers. Obviously Gail Corcoran used this closet to store her out-of-season wardrobe because it looked like an upscale cruise-wear department.

I backed out and closed the door. "Do you know where the grandmother's room was?"

There was a bang from somewhere in the house and Marilyn Belvedere jumped. "A shutter's loose again," she said. "May we please go?"

"Sure."

"It wasn't a room," she said, answering my question. "She had a separate apartment on the first floor with her own kitchen and even her own living room with a fireplace. It's on the other side of the house. I never saw it, but Serena told me about it. She said it was how they all managed to get along with each other so well."

Then it was true that she could have been in the house and heard nothing. "Do you know which room was Foster's?"

"One of the ones the children have, I'm not sure which. You saw them both. Have you seen enough now?" She was distressed, anxious to leave.

"Yes, I think so." I took one more look around the room and followed her downstairs.

17

I don't know what I expected, but as I drove away I felt disappointed. I had wanted the house to speak to me, to tell me something that I couldn't figure out for myself, and it had not. All that I could see was that Julia had lived in a large, prized room, that if her brother had been home that night and had been in his room, he should have heard something, but if he was out and his grandmother was in her own private quarters, poor Julia could have cried for help and no one would have heard her. Even if Foster were home, if he had been listening to music the way a lot of aficionados do, he would not have heard the noise at the end of the hall.

I left Mrs. Belvedere at the start of the walkway to her house. A second car had joined the first one in her driveway and two men were looking under the hood of the car farther up.

She moaned when she saw them. "My son's been having car trouble since he came home. I hope he gets it taken care of this time."

The second car had MIKE'S AUTO BODY SHOP painted on the side. "I guess this is the season when batteries die," I said.

"That's just what I told him. Well, you can't tell your children anything." She smiled as if we shared a secret, but I was a lot closer to her son's age than to hers.

Now, in the car, I decided to see if Mrs. Farragut would talk to me again. I found the retirement community with no difficulty and parked in the visitors' area. There were children around today, probably because on Sunday Americans visit their families.

Mrs. Farragut answered on the first ring. She looked conflicted about seeing me there, but she hustled me inside. "Do we have anything else to talk about?" she asked.

"One of our nuns was murdered last night."

"I heard about it. Personal safety is a problem everywhere. Even here, we're careful at night."

"The nun was your granddaughter's mentor, her friend, her confidante."

"Then I suppose you'd better look to your missing bad priest."

I was getting a little tired of having Hudson dumped on for everything. "He had no more reason to kill her last night than he had seven years ago."

"Miss Bennett—sit down, sit down, I can't stand having a conversation standing in the middle of the living room—I don't know where your priest is and I don't know how I can help you find him."

"Can you help me find out what drove Julia to take her life?"

"What difference does it make now? It's over. I believe you have to move on in life. It's what I've been trying to do."

"I think she may have been terribly sorry for saying what she did about Father McCormick." I had said the same thing to her son and not gotten very far.

"I'm sure what Julia said was true."

"Did she leave a note?"

"No, she did not." A rapid-fire answer, stated sharply.

I began to detect her scent again, so sweet in contrast to her words and manner. "Can you tell me who was home when she ended her life?"

"I was. I was in my own apartment having a cup of tea and writing thank-you's for Christmas gifts."

"And your son?"

"He was out for the evening."

"Can you remember where?"

"Miss Bennett, it's seven years. I didn't know at the time and I don't know now. Walter was a grown man and led his own life."

"And Foster?"

"He was out, too. Please don't ask me where he was. No

one ever knew where Foster was." She said it sadly, acknowledging failure.

"I know where he is now," I said.

"I beg your pardon?"

"He's in prison. He's been there for the last year and a half."

"You know too much for your own good, young lady." But she didn't usher me out. In some strange way, she was glad to be talking to me about all this.

"Do you have a picture of Julia?" I asked, the thought just occurring to me.

She got up and went to a shelf that had at least a dozen framed pictures and picked up three. "This was the last, when she was at St. Stephen's." In it Julia was wearing the habit of a novice and she stood with each hand hidden in the opposite wide sleeve, but she was smiling. Something about the face gave me a start.

"This was her high-school graduation picture."

There was no doubt now. Even wearing a white cap and gown, Julia and the present Mrs. Walter Farragut looked enough alike to be sisters. I handed the picture back.

"And this was Julia with some friends during her last year in high school. The girl on the left is Billie something and the one on the right is Miranda Gallagher. She's married now," she said sadly.

The name rang a bell. I had overheard a telephone message about a Miranda only an hour ago. The mother's name was ... I couldn't remember. But I would keep Gallagher in mind. A good friend might fit a lot of missing pieces into my holey puzzle.

"She was a beautiful girl," I said, handing the last picture back.

"And kind and sweet and thoughtful and devoted. I will never stop missing her." There was no sharp edge anymore; there was only grief. The lined face had given up the fight to look young and spirited. Slowly, looking at each picture, she replaced them on the shelf and then sat down again. "It was the darkest day of my life."

"I can understand that."

"She had her mother's face. Serena was a beautiful woman."

"I don't pretend to understand why a person, especially a young one, would take her life, but when I spoke to your son this afternoon, he said Julia wasn't suicidal. He said she had a strong will to live. What happened that Christmas, Mrs. Farragut?"

"I'm sure you know that as happy a time as Christmas is for most of us, it is deeply depressing for others. They think of how it used to be, where they were, who they were with, those missing who will never return, and they become unhappy to the point of hurting themselves. I think that's what happened to our Julia."

"What was she doing that evening?"

"Reading. Writing in her diary."

"She was writing in her diary and she didn't leave a note?"

"I told you. There was no note."

"What became of her diary?"

"I don't know."

"Did you show it to the police?"

"I'm sure we must have."

I knew immediately that she was lying. If they had given the diary to the police, she would have said so unequivocally. What she had said was a hedge. "Do you have it here?"

"I do not."

A girl about to take her life is writing in her diary and doesn't leave a note. She doesn't need to because the reason is contained in those pages, maybe in the very last one, maybe in all the pages taken together. "I would like to see it, Mrs. Farragut," I said softly.

"I don't know where it is. It's probably been destroyed."

Hardly. If this woman had possession of it—and she was the person who had found the body, so she must have seen it—she wouldn't have let it go. She certainly wouldn't have destroyed it.

"You know why she killed herself, don't you?" I said, again softly.

"I gave you the reasons. She had lost her mother, she had lost her vocation, she had nearly lost her mind with grief. I shouldn't have left her alone that night. I should have sat with her, talked to her, held her hand, and assured her things would get better because they would have. I am an optimist. You can't reach my age without being one. If I blame anyone for Julia's death, it's myself. I failed her when she needed me most. You must go now, Miss Bennett, and I don't think you should come back. I've told you everything. There isn't any more. You know everything now, including my responsibility in Julia's death. I have nothing more to say." She stood and went to the door. Today she was wearing a blue suit with a white blouse. The jacket was a loose, interesting weave with gold buttons, four pocket flaps, and piping around all the edges and on the hem of the skirt that just covered her knees. A gold choker with a diamond flower was partly visible in the vee of her blouse. She was a well-to-do woman whose money had failed to buy her peace.

I thanked her and said good-bye. I'm not sure she said anything. I think she was glad the interview was over, that she hadn't lost control and spilled the secrets she had kept for so long, not just from me but from the rest of the world, including the police of Riverview, who, I was sure, had never heard of, much less seen, Julia Farragut's diary.

18

I racked my brain all the way back to the convent to think of the name of the woman who had called the Corcorans. Finally I decided it wouldn't make any difference if I remembered it because she was probably listed under her husband's name. I would have to call Mrs. Belvedere or try every Gallagher in Riverview, something I found distasteful. While I'm not exactly a shy person, there are tasks I really don't like to do; calling strangers to find a particular person is one of them. Jack had told me about detectives who sit at a phone and make a case. He laughed and called them telephone detectives, but what a talent.

The nuns were coming out of the chapel after evening prayers as I parked my car in the lot. I waited for the last of them to enter the Mother House and then followed them in. Joseph spied me right away and joined me as the rest of the nuns went into the dining room.

"I know a lot more," I said, "but I don't know where Hudson is and I don't know who's responsible for his disappearance. But I have feelings about things that I didn't have, or didn't have very strongly, before this afternoon."

"Let's get trays and we'll eat and talk in my office."

We went back to the kitchen and filled two trays. It was a Sunday-night pasta supper with a salad of many-colored greens, grapefruit to start with, and a pudding dessert. Jack isn't a pudding man; he's a hard-dessert person who likes to chew, so I enjoyed the chance to eat something I don't make at home anymore.

We carried our trays upstairs as Joseph talked about her afternoon with the nuns in the villa. They were a tough lot, she said, but they were terribly shaken—indeed, everyone was, but she worried about them the most.

In her office, we sat across the long table from each other and I pulled out my notebook, which I had filled with comments after each interview. "Walter Farragut is married to a much younger, very good-looking woman and lives in a modern house that had to cost a fortune," I began. "I really got nothing of substance from him, but later on in the afternoon I talked to his mother again and she let me see pictures of Julia. There's a strong resemblance between her and Walter's new wife."

"I see."

"I can't avoid it, Joseph. I don't want to think it and I don't want to think about it, but I feel something terrible went on in the Farragut house and I keep coming back to the father."

"You think he was abusing her."

"I think it's possible."

"And that's why she came to St. Stephen's." The idea clearly troubled her, both ideas: that he was doing something and that Julia came to the convent to get away from him.

"It makes sense. And I have to believe her mother knew or suspected what was going on. She couldn't handle it and had a nervous breakdown sometime before that last year of her life. Mrs. Belvedere, the neighbor, knew it. Then, seven years ago, she took her life."

"Poor soul. Do you think the grandmother knew what was happening?"

"Maybe not at first. She occupied a separate apartment in the house, about as far, by the way, from Julia's room as she could be. According to the neighbor, she kept to herself much of the time, which gave me the feeling that they were almost two separate families living in different parts of the same house. But she was very fond of Julia. They were both in the house the night Julia killed herself. It was the grandmother that found her and also found the diary she was writing in."

"A diary. Then there is—or was—a document of her feelings. I don't suppose she showed it to you."

"She didn't show it to me and I'm convinced she never showed it to the police. I think she took it out of Julia's room before the police came. When she read it, she may have found out for the first time what was really going on, and once she knew, she couldn't show it to anyone because it would implicate her son in behavior so terrible that making it public would destroy him."

"Without question." She put her fork down. "It makes a kind of poetic sense, too, doesn't it? The natural father does the molesting and the spiritual father is blamed. Which leaves us with one inescapable suspect."

"And that makes me very uneasy," I said. "I just can't come to terms with a man of Walter Farragut's position kidnapping Hudson. What did he do with him? And why would he do it now and not seven years ago?"

"Hudson left very suddenly, before Julia died, remember. If her diary does tell terrible secrets, her father may have felt threatened after he read it."

"But if he was molesting her, he didn't need a diary to tell him what had happened."

"True, but Hudson's return put pressure on him. There was always the possibility that Hudson would somehow let the world know what had happened."

"Or Mrs. Farragut might have felt he was threatened."

"Surely you don't think an elderly woman—"

"I don't, but she's involved in this somehow, Joseph. The telephone call to Sister Mary Teresa."

"I asked the sisters who answered the phone at the villa yesterday if they remembered Mary Teresa receiving a phone call, from anyone, man or woman. No one answered a phone call for her."

The system at the villa was the same as that in the Mother House. When a call was routed there from the main switchboard, the nun assigned to answering the phone would ring bells for the person called. Each nun was assigned a different number of bells.

"And I checked with Angela," she went on, "and she doesn't remember anyone asking for Mary Teresa. So we really don't know any more than we did this morning."

"But we do," I said. "We have a picture of that family now, as they were seven years ago, the grandmother who lives her own life but owns the house and subtly rules the family, the father who has an obscene relationship with his daughter, the son who is forever in trouble—maybe because he knows what's going on between his father and his sister—the mother who knows and can't control it and finally kills herself, and the daughter who loses at every turn, first because she's her father's victim, then because she can't maintain her novitiate, and finally because she loses her mother."

"It's a terrible picture."

"Do you think I'm wrong?"

"I think you're very likely to be right."

"But it doesn't tell us where Hudson is. If Walter Farragut has him, he's put him somewhere where his new wife doesn't know about it."

"He would know the trains, wouldn't he?" Joseph said.

"Of course. He still lives in the Hudson Valley, where they run. He gets rid of Hudson, drives the car to the Corcorans', gets out, and walks down to the station. It's closed for the night, so no one is there to recognize him. When his train comes, he gets on, pays the conductor, and goes home."

"There's one thing we've been neglecting in all this. Assuming Walter Farragut has followed Hudson from Buffalo to the rest stop where the clothing was found, after he and Hudson drive away in Hudson's car, what happens to the car Walter was driving?"

"I'm not sure," I said. "I've thought about it, but I keep turning up in a dead end. It's almost as though there had to be two people involved in the kidnapping so that one could drive the other back to pick up the extra car. I just can't think who that person could be. As much as Mrs. Farragut may want to protect her son, I don't think she would do it. I don't even know if she has a driver's license. And I doubt he would involve his new wife."

"I agree. He wouldn't let her know anything of this sordid past of his."

"So how did he do it?" I said, more to myself than to Joseph.

Joseph got up and went to her desk. She came back with a book that she set down in front of me. It was the Bible I had taken from Sister Mary Teresa's night table.

"Have you looked through it?" I asked.

"Very quickly. It's filled with remembrance cards that go

back over fifty years. There's one for every nun that died at St. Stephen's since she came here and many for people who were probably friends and relatives. There are also scraps of paper with notes on them, although I have to admit I couldn't decipher most of them."

"May I take it with me?"

"I hope you will." She was about to go when the phone on her desk rang. She went over and answered it. "Yes," she said with a smile. "She's right here."

I took the phone and Joseph picked up the trays and left the office. "Jack?"

"You get back all right?"

"Circuitously. We've been having supper off trays and rehashing the day. Have you eaten?"

"Forget food. I've got something for you."

"What?"

"The Oakwood cop who found Walter and Foster Farragut for me through the DMV and some extra digging was intrigued enough to call the prison to check on Foster. He got a Christmas reprieve, Chris. Foster Farragut's been a free man since seven A.M. on Christmas Eve."

19

Everything was now different. Instead of one suspect, there were two. If Foster Farragut had been freed on Christmas Eve, early in the morning on Christmas Eve, he would have had time to track Hudson on Christmas Day, perhaps by driving to Buffalo and waiting outside Hudson's church until he left in his very visible vehicle. A car wouldn't be hard to obtain if his father gave him one, which wouldn't surprise me. It's pretty easy to make a case for needing one; almost anywhere Foster might want to work would require a car if he lived outside a big city. The question of where Hudson was now was still not answered, but Foster would know the Riverview area, and how the trains worked, as well as his father. There was even the possibility that the two men had been in it together. And if they had, the problem of retrieving the second car was neatly solved.

But I had no proof, no evidence, no witnesses, and I didn't know where to find Foster. It was likely, guilty or innocent, that his whereabouts would be known by his father and his grandmother, but I didn't think I had much chance of getting either one to tell me what I wanted to know. Mrs. Farragut had gone further in discussing the events of seven years ago than she had meant to; next time I saw her, she would be on guard. And I had a feeling Walter would throw me out if I turned up at his doorstep again.

I called Mrs. Belvedere to ask her for the name and phone number of Miranda Gallagher's mother, but there was no answer, so I turned to Sister Mary Teresa's Bible. The remembrance cards led me nowhere. They were just dozens of roughly two-and-a-quarter-by-four-inch cards with a picture of Jesus or Mary on one side and the name of the deceased followed by a prayer on the other. The oldest ones intrigued me. The quality of the paper was different, the pictures in black and white or shades of brown instead of in color, the edges occasionally scalloped. Age had given them a delicate fineness; they seemed more than paper cards. Some had a silky finish; some were almost translucent. In the course of forty or fifty years they had become artifacts.

But they were not leads. I turned to the several scraps of paper on which notes were written. Some had names, perhaps the names of new nieces and nephews: Ethan, Erin, Ann-Marie, a name here, a name there. One slip had the name George and an address in New York, but no last name or indication who George might be or when the notation had been made. I set it aside with little hope of figuring out what it meant.

On a page in the Book of John, where the story of Mary Magdalene returning to the tomb occurs, there was a slip of pink paper with a long number written on it, too long for a Social Security number. It looked more like a credit-card number, but that would be impossible for a nun, except perhaps for a superior who might have to charge things for the convent. I didn't think Sister Mary Teresa had ever been in the position of buying in quantity.

I flipped to the pages that are reserved for family entries. Sister Mary Teresa had listed her parents with their birth and death dates, her sisters and brothers, her own name and birth date, and a string of other names that I took to be children of her siblings. There was a page folded into the book with additional entries, several marriages and more names and birth dates. None of them meant anything to me except the names of her Syracuse family. Everything was lettered carefully and, I thought, lovingly.

Finally I closed the book and sat staring at the windows of Joseph's office. There was nothing about Hudson in the Bible, nothing about Julia except for the remembrance card, nothing about Foster or Walter Farragut or about old Mrs. Farragut.

I was sitting there trying to think what to do next when Joseph tapped on the door and came in. I told her about Foster Farragut.

"That does change things," she said. "It gives him the

one thing we thought he didn't have, the opportunity to follow Hudson."

"I'm sure his father and grandmother know where he is."

"And won't tell us." She walked to the window behind her desk and looked out into the dark sky. "I've learned something, Chris. When you've come to me in the past and asked for my help, even though I sympathized with the victims and their families, I was able to look at the facts you brought me with enough detachment that I could ask the right questions and see how pieces of information fit into the puzzle. But now I am utterly unable to look *at* the case because I'm inside it; I'm part of it. Hudson is my brother and my friend, and I feel a sense of panic at what may have happened to him, what may be happening right now. I realize at this moment how much I admire you for the work you've done. You become part of every case you investigate and yet you're able to see facts, to distinguish between important and trivial, and eventually to dig out or uncover or produce the essential piece of evidence that leads to a solution."

I felt embarrassed by her tribute. "We'll do it this time, too, Joseph. And don't forget that when I've done it in the past, it's always been with your help. You've steered me in the right direction and made me see things that were often right in front of me but that were invisible because there's more to vision than a good pair of eyes and a willingness to look."

"We've been friends for a long time, haven't we?" She said it with a half smile.

"We've known each other sixteen years."

"And became friends somewhere along the way in that rather circumscribed manner that nuns have friendships."

"I think we've known each other very well but differently from the way I've come to know some women that I've met over the last year and a half."

"You must talk to them about a whole universe of different things."

"I do. And sometimes I'm surprised at the candidness of what they say—and what they expect me to say. In a way friendship with other nuns was about shared ideas, while friendship with my neighbors is often about shared experiences."

"But it must include ideas, too," Joseph said.

"It does, but the ideas seem to come as an extension of the experiences. The talk about food or gardens or the school system, where to buy a child a certain piece of clothing or what a pediatrician has said, somehow that leads to a discussion of ideas, of styles or medicine or educational philosophy."

"I see what you mean. Our discussions of ideas often led to shared experiences, not the other way around."

"Exactly. And while I know more about some of the women in Oakwood, more, in fact, than I'd like to know," I admitted, "it doesn't mean that I know *them;* I just know about them, a lot of facts that don't always add up to knowing a person. And although there are many things I don't know about you, and never will, I know that we're friends. I trust you the way I trust Jack."

"Yes."

I wondered if she were thinking, as I was now, of Julia Farragut. She was still a stranger to me, a collection of memories and vignettes, of conflicting perceptions, of carefully filtered reports. I needed to know her better. There had to be some essential facts about her that were missing or hidden in the diary, facts crucial to her suicide, facts that would lead us to Hudson McCormick's kidnapper.

"But you've made close friends, Chris. I met one of them."

"Melanie Gross. And it started with a chance meeting during our early-morning walks."

"And led to cooking," Joseph said with a smile.

"And a lot of other things. Gardening. When Jack and I went away on our wedding trip, she watered my vegetable garden." Like Mrs. Belvedere and her next-door neighbor. "She's the first Jewish woman I've ever known well. Her children are really the first ones I've played with as an adult. I've even baby-sat for them when Melanie couldn't find anyone else in an emergency."

"Shared experiences."

"That led to shared ideas."

"Chris, do we know anyone who was a friend of Julia Farragut?"

"I know of one who still lives in Riverview. I think I can get to her tomorrow."

"Perhaps that's what we need, someone who shared experiences with Julia, someone Julia may have confided in or who may have some ideas of her own about what was going on in that house."

"I'll find her," I promised. "First thing tomorrow morning."

I thought a lot that night about our conversation on friendship. I had been a very young fifteen when I came to St. Stephen's, surely much younger than any fifteen-year-old I might run into at the supermarket in Oakwood today, and Joseph had been twice my age or more, a self-possessed young woman who had seemed generations older than I. I had been orphaned and then separated from the only family I knew through circumstances completely beyond their control, and although I had wanted to enter St. Stephen's as a novice, it had all happened in an untimely and unhappy way, with no preparation to speak of, no time to say good-bye to school friends and teachers, to neighbors' dogs, or favorite thinking places. What had eased me into my new life had been Joseph's unfailing gift of herself, her being there, her listening and caring. I attributed my wholeness and well-being, my very sanity, my evolution into the well-adjusted person I believe I am, to her. At some point she had become my spiritual director. Had our friendship preceded or followed that? I wasn't sure, but I knew the watchword as well as anyone else: *Be careful of particular friendships.*

In the secular world there was nothing to worry about. If Melanie Gross and I spent hours together talking or sewing or cooking or shopping or gardening, there would be no eyebrows raised in Oakwood, no talk, no concern that our relationship was anything but "normal." At night Mel would go back to her husband, and I, until a few months ago, to my own house, to a phone call from Jack or a shared weekend. But at a convent such "particular friendships" could not be tolerated. A nun was expected to spread her friendships around lest intimacy take on a dreadful new meaning.

Still, I always considered Joseph to be my best friend, my dearest and closest friend. As I had said to her this evening, there was so much I didn't know about her, the facts of her birth and youth and family, her exact age, the names and addresses of her next of kin, but what did it matter? Our friendship flowed in both directions, although she knew so much more about me than I did about her.

And Jack, my husband of four months. Was he now my new best friend? I sat on the narrow bed, my knees drawn up, a flannel nightgown of a kind I no longer wore at home keeping me warm. I missed him so much I could feel it in my skin and my chest and in that place I had kept quiescent for so many years and that now formed such an essential part of my life, my relationship with my husband.

But were we friends? I wasn't sure. I had heard several women say their husbands were their best friends and I had wondered.

There had to have been someone for Julia. She had been young, a student in the town high school, a child growing into a woman. But she had lived with something unspeakable, and had drawn Hudson into it.

Hudson—was he still alive? The odds were long, the chances slim. I wanted my husband to wrap his arms around me, to make love to me. I wanted Hudson to walk into the Mother House with a smile and a good story.

But I was the only one who could make it happen.

20

My night was far from restful. It was full of images that I sensed were directing me but that dissolved as I reached for them. One that kept coming back was the page in Sister Mary Teresa's Bible where I had found the slip of paper with the string of numbers. What was the significance of the numbers and was there any significance to where I had found them? And most important, did they tie in to the disappearance of Hudson McCormick or the suicide of Julia Farragut?

I woke when I heard the nuns stirring, readying themselves for morning prayers. It was Monday the thirtieth of December. Jack and I had been invited out for New Year's Eve, but the chances of my partying tomorrow night looked rather dim at this moment. I joined the nuns for prayers and then went to mass with them. Afterward Father Kramer stopped me.

"I gather there's no news," he said.

"Nothing to lead us to Father McCormick. Or to Sister Mary Teresa's killer."

"I talked to Detective Lake yesterday. They seem certain she was the victim of an intruder. They said there are several homeless men in the area and that one of them may be deranged."

"What do you think?"

"I think they're grasping at straws." He pulled open the door of the Mother House and followed me inside. "We feed four homeless young men at the church almost every day, and they're about as deranged as you or me."

"I assume the police have questioned them by now. If there'd been an arrest, Sister Joseph would know."

"Well, you'll keep me posted, Chris?" It was a question.

"Of course."

I called Mrs. Belvedere at nine, the earliest I felt was decent. She was out, leaving me without a means to find Julia's friend Miranda.

There had to be some other way. Riverside was a small town and many people would know each other. But I couldn't just walk up to someone on the street and ask what Miranda Gallagher's married name was.

It came to me as I finished my breakfast. The woman in the real-estate office. She had given me Mrs. Farragut's address with relative ease. People in real estate knew everyone in town, as I had learned from someone in Oakwood who remembered with great clarity people long gone, people newly arrived, and the color and design of all their houses.

"Eileen usually takes Monday off." The woman in the real-estate office was tall, with dark hair combed into a chignon. "Weekends are usually busy and Tuesday is our open-house day when we get to view the new listings."

"I'm trying to locate a Riverview woman named Gallagher," I said.

"Gallagher. There are a few Gallaghers in town. I don't really know them."

"She has a daughter named Miranda who's married and has just given birth."

"I haven't lived in town as long as Eileen. I'm afraid the names don't mean anything to me."

"May I have Eileen's home number?" The woman in Oakwood handed out her card with home and office numbers to anyone she met.

"I'll call her for you."

She thinks I'm nuts, I thought. When a police officer shows his badge and asks questions, people generally cooperate unless they have something to hide. When a civilian does the same thing, people think she's nuts.

"I'm afraid she's out. I left a message on her machine. Would you like to give me your name and number?"

I wrote it down, impatient and disgusted. If I'd lied and said I was looking for a house, I would now be in possession of Eileen's last name, her home phone number, and probably a cup of coffee and a Danish. "May I leave a note for her?" I said, sitting down at the empty desk as though I had already been given permission.

"Of course. She'll be in first thing in the morning."

I opened a desk drawer. "She should have paper in here," I said, rummaging.

"I can get you—"

"I've got it, thanks." I took out a memo pad with all of Eileen's personal information printed right on it. I wrote a note, tore off two sheets, and left one on top of the desk. Folded in my hand was all the information I needed.

But Eileen wasn't home. I started back to the convent and made a small detour to Mrs. Farragut's community. When I stopped the car at a curb, I didn't know why I was there. What I wanted from Mrs. Farragut—Julia's diary—I wasn't going to get, not today and not ever. It was even possible that it didn't exist anymore, that she had burned it or shredded it or just tossed it out with the garbage to make sure no one would ever read it, but I had my doubts about that. Julia had been very precious to her grandmother. Diaries and letters probably had great value for the older woman. What, after all, does a person leave behind besides memories? There are photos and snapshots, videos nowadays in some cases, personal belongings like clothes and books. But for many of us, the most cherished items are the writings and drawings and handmade articles, and I could imagine that even if Julia's writings were incriminating of her father, her grandmother might have saved them just because they had been created by Julia.

But there was no way to get access to them. Judges don't issue warrants on the basis of faint possibility, and I am not a second-story man. If the diaries were in the Farragut apartment, they would remain there, unknown to the police and untouchable.

So what was I doing here? Hudson wasn't being hidden here in Mrs. Farragut's apartment and she had said about all she ever would to me. A sudden knock on my window startled me.

A man was standing next to the car. "You can't park here," he called.

I wound the window down. "Sorry. I'm just trying to decide where I'm going."

"Well, you'd better decide somewheres else. This is our main drive and we get deliveries along here."

"OK." I moved forward, toward the visitors' parking area, but I stopped before I got there. Mrs. Farragut was just leaving the front door of her section of the building. It probably didn't matter, but it would be nice to know if she owned and drove a car. I backed up so she wouldn't notice me and bent over. Wherever she was going, I could pick her up in a few seconds. I counted to five with slow determination, then raised my head. She had turned away from my car and was walking toward one of the resident parking lots that were discreetly placed behind the buildings.

And she wasn't alone. A man was walking beside her, not an elderly fellow resident and not her son, someone younger. All I could see were their backs as they turned the corner of the building, but I was willing to bet on his identity. Grandson Foster, newly released from prison, had come home to live with Grandma.

There was only one direction they could turn from the parking lot as this curved section of the drive was one-way. I stayed where I was, waiting tensely. A huge Cadillac pulled into the drive but too soon for it to be Mrs. Farragut's. I took a good look at the driver anyway as he went around the small grassy circle across from where I was sitting. He was gray and full-faced, no one I had ever seen before. It was a minute or two before another car appeared and I knew at first glance that it was the right one. The car was white and medium-sized, the driver a man about my age with a distinct resemblance to Walter Farragut. And sitting beside him was his grandmother.

I waited till they had completed the circle before taking off after them. As I followed at a distance a woman stepped off the curb and I braked to a stop for her just as the Farragut car reached the stop sign at the end of the drive. A right flashing light let me know where they were heading, but the woman crossing in front of me took a long time and I began to fear I would lose them. Prominent signs pegged the speed at ten miles an hour, but I did twice that the second I was able.

At the stop sign I barely slowed, then turned right onto the forty-mile-an-hour black-topped road that led away from the senior community and toward the heart of town. There was a car that might be the Farraguts' down the road and I speeded up to overtake it, hoping to see the license plate so I could identify it accurately. I got close enough to read it and reassure myself that the Farraguts were indeed in the front seat. Then I took my foot off the accelerator and let some space accumulate between us.

There were attractive houses, placed well back from the road, on both sides and a sign pointing to a school. Just as the area began to look more commercial than residential, Foster put his right turn signal on. I slowed down, waited a few seconds, and followed his turn. To my surprise I ended up in a small suburban shopping mall.

At the near end there was a giant supermarket. The Farragut car turned toward it while I hung back. There were a number of other stores there, but on this Monday morning it wasn't particularly busy. I watched the white car circle around a row of parked cars and then disappear. They had found an empty space. I drove to where I could see the entrance and sat watching it until grandmother and grandson went inside. Mrs. Farragut was dressed, as usual, as though she were attending a ladies' tea, in a black coat with a black fur collar around her neck, but her grandson looked appropriately casual. When they were inside, I found their car and parked far enough away that they would not see me. Then I sat and waited.

It seemed like a long time before they came out, Foster pushing a market basket with many bags of groceries, his grandmother walking beside him. They opened the trunk and stashed the bags in there, then got into the car. When they started driving, I managed to put a car between us. The exit they took was on a side road at the far end of the shopping center and Foster took a right toward the rear of the stores. At the road that ran along the back of the mall, he turned right again. He was now heading back toward the apartment on a road parallel to the one he had come on. The trouble was the car in front of me, which was driven by an elderly man who was afraid to turn into the road at the back of the shopping center, or else he was undecided. Several cars passed in both directions as he sat at the corner without moving, and I felt myself becoming increasingly agitated. Please move, I urged him.

Finally he crept forward, looking left and right, trying to get up his nerve to make the plunge. When he did, I was right behind him, slipping into the road ahead of several cars coming from my left. But stretching before me was a long line of cars, and with only one lane in each direction I was unable to pass the slowpoke in front of me. He braked for no reason at the intersection where the supermarket was, then continued on at beginner's speed. He was in no hurry and I was desperate to keep the Farraguts in sight. For all I knew, they were taking provisions to some place where they had Hudson tied up, where they were holding him until he told them the "truth" they wanted to hear. It might seem preposterous to an outsider, but she was a tough old woman whose family came first, and with her grandson to help her, maybe what she was doing was resolving the great tragedy of her life, finding a meaning in the death of her granddaughter.

But at this moment my situation was hopeless. The car ahead of me eventually turned off the road, leaving a half-mile gap of empty blacktop. I tried to make up the distance, but I knew it was futile. The white car was either so far away I would never catch up or it had made a turn somewhere and I couldn't guess at which intersection.

I made my way back to the retirement community and scouted the parking lot behind Mrs. Farragut's building, but the car wasn't there. Had they gone to see Hudson? Or were they filling a refrigerator in Foster's new apartment, somewhere near his grandmother?

Whatever it was, I wasn't going to find out this morning.

I drove back to the shopping mall. The supermarket had a couple of pay phones and I tried Mrs. Belvedere again without reaching her, then dialed the real-estate woman, Eileen Wharton. This time I got a response.

"Of course I remember you. You're looking for that missing priest. Is there any word?"

"Unfortunately not. But I met Mrs. Farragut."

"Isn't she wonderful? If you have to age, that's the way to do it. She's a great lady."

"Eileen, I'm trying to track down a friend of Julia Farragut, a girl she went to school with. I think her maiden name was Miranda Gallagher."

"Oh, the Gallaghers, yes. They live farther up the hill than the Farraguts in a newer house. They're a nice family. I think they have a daughter who got married not too long ago."

"That's the one. Do you know her married name?"

"Oh gosh. Let me think. I should know; they bought a house in town when they got married, or the Gallaghers bought it for them. Who did Miranda marry?" She was asking herself and I hoped her memory was good. "Tony Santiago," she said. "A good-looking boy—I really shouldn't say boy, should I? He's a father now. I just heard that Sunny Gallagher became a grandmother."

"Sunny, that's the name." I could hear the voice on the answering machine delivering her happy news. "Are they listed? The Santiagos?"

"Hold on, I'll get the number." She came back and read off the address and phone number while I struggled to jot it down one-handed. "What does the Gallagher family have to do with your missing priest?"

"I need to know more about Julia. I think Julia may have said things about Father McCormick that she didn't mean because she was protecting someone. If I can talk to a friend of hers, she might know."

"I wish you luck."

"I thank you for your help."

I called the Santiagos' number and a young female voice answered. Although I hate when it's done to me, I hung up without saying anything. Miranda was home and I didn't want to be discouraged from visiting. It couldn't be an easy time for her, a day or two out of the hospital, but I had to do it. It was for Hudson.

21

Miranda and Tony Santiago's home looked like a ginger-bread house with a steep roof and a symmetrical facade that reminded me of every house I had drawn up to the age of eight. When I rang, Miranda herself answered, a pretty, young woman wearing a quilted white robe.

"I'm Christine Bennett, Mrs. Santiago," I said. "I know this is a busy time for you, but I'd like to ask you about Julia Farragut if you could give me a few minutes."

"Julia," she said with surprise. "Can you tell me why?"

I was still standing outside the door. "I think the disappearance of Father Hudson McCormick may be related to her death."

"Come in."

I followed her into a small, pretty living room with a Christmas tree in a corner and a white bassinet as its centerpiece. I could just make out a little head of dark hair under a beautiful comforter.

"Congratulations," I said.

"She's only four days old. Her name's Lisa. I know I should be dressed by now but I didn't get much sleep last night. My mother's coming for lunch, so I'll get a rest later. Can I give you anything? Coffee?"

"No thanks. I'd just like to talk to you about Julia. I know you were friends."

"We were. I couldn't believe it when she—"

"I know."

She had sat down carefully, as though it pained her. Although her dark hair was not well arranged, she was a beautiful young woman. If her tiny daughter looked like her, she would be a beauty.

"You mentioned the priest. That's the one Julia ... the one—"

"He's the one she claimed abused her. I think she may have been wrong."

"She was kind of mixed up at the end."

"Tell me what you think."

A tiny cry escaped from the bassinet and we both looked toward it, but there was no movement. Little Lisa Santiago was still asleep.

"She was having problems. Then her mother died. Do you know about that?"

"Yes."

"It was terrible. She was so devoted to her mother and her mother was just falling apart. Finally, after Julia went into the convent, she was hospitalized, and one day she hanged herself. I think that's when Julia came home."

"I was a nun at St. Stephen's until last year. I knew Father McCormick very well, but the semester that Julia was there, I was studying somewhere else. I didn't know her, but I met her grandmother recently and saw a picture of you and Julia."

"We were together a lot until the end of high school." She had a soft, slow way of speaking, as though there were no hurry, there would never be any hurry.

"Did you know her family?"

"Not too well."

"Why is that?"

"We used to go to my house after school most of the time. When they built the new high school, they located it more centrally than the old one and it was closer to where I lived."

"Were you ever in her house?"

"A few times." She didn't seem to want to elaborate.

"Did you meet her grandmother?"

"Oh yes. She used to take us places sometimes, when we were younger."

"Her mother?"

"I met her. I knew her best when I was younger. She was healthier then, in better shape. Later on—she kind of stayed in her room a lot."

"Julia's father?"

"I used to see him at church, but he wasn't home when I was at their house. He worked in the city or something. I knew him to talk to, but I can't tell you much about him."

"Did Julia talk about him?"

"I don't remember."

"And her brother, Foster?"

"I met him. He was away at school a lot."

"Private school?"

"Yes. Maybe out of state. Foster was . . . I think Foster was a big problem in that family."

"How do you mean?"

"He was trouble in school. I think he may have been seeing a psychiatrist at one time. He was one of those kids who was just, you know, difficult."

"Did Julia talk about him?"

"Sometimes. I think she was happier when he was away. That's the way it seemed to me."

Everything she said was so guarded, so incomplete, as though she were protecting each person she talked about by revealing nothing of importance. She didn't know them well, she couldn't say much about them, she didn't remember. But her face looked strained, her dark eyes haunted.

"Was anyone in that house hurting Julia?" I asked.

Her face crumpled into tears. "I don't know," she sobbed. She dug in the pockets of her robe and pulled out a tissue. "I'm awfully sorry. I didn't know it was going to do this to me. Maybe it's just that I had a tough night and it's hard remembering. It happened at Christmas."

"I know."

"I shouldn't do this in front of the baby."

I kept myself from smiling. Four days after giving birth she was enough of a mother to feel she should watch her behavior before her sleeping infant daughter. There was something wonderful about that.

"She's sleeping," I reassured her.

"Yes."

I didn't want to ask the question again, but I wanted an answer to it and her reaction told me she had some strong feelings on the subject.

"Julia was a reserved person," she said finally, her emotions under control. "She was just as real as anyone else, she had a good time, she slept over at my house, she went to football games, but there was an air of quiet about her. She was the girl everybody's mother loved and it wasn't put on; she was really that way. When she told me she thought she might want to enter St. Stephen's as a novice, I wasn't really surprised."

"Do you remember when she started talking about it?"

"Maybe our junior year. A lot of the girls were making trips to visit colleges that summer and I asked her what she was going to do, and she said she'd been thinking of becoming a nun. It turned out she'd already visited up there, but she'd never told me. She must have gone with her mother or her grandmother, so I guess she'd been thinking about it for a while."

"Did you stay friends during your senior year?"

"Oh yes." She seemed surprised that I might have thought otherwise. "And I don't think she changed much. We still had fun together and went places, but we had this sense—at least I had a sense—that it was all coming to an end, that next year we would go our separate ways. It made me feel sad."

"Was she sad?"

"I don't think so. I think she was really looking forward to entering the convent. She would say, 'Miranda, we'll see each other, I promise.' But I wasn't sure. I know it sounds crazy, but I think I started missing her before she even left." She laughed at herself and her face lighted up. She had unblemished skin, clear of makeup this morning, and it looked the way all the ads want you to believe you'll look if you use their many products.

She hadn't answered my indelicate question yet and I was still afraid to push her, but I wanted an answer before her mother came to visit or the baby woke up.

"It sounds like you had a wonderful friendship," I said.

"We did."

"And you probably knew her better than anyone else."

She nodded, then drew her robe around her as though there were a chill in the room when in fact it was on the warm side. "There was something else. There may have been a boyfriend."

"When?" I asked.

"Just before—the summer before she went into the convent."

"You said 'may have been.' "

"Julia sometimes told stories, fantasies. It took me a while to catch on that they weren't true. She always sounded as if she meant it, but later she would laugh and say forget it, it was just a story."

"What kind of stories?"

"Oh, you know the kind of things kids make up, that they were adopted at birth and it wasn't their real family. Julia said things like that sometimes; it wasn't her real father, it wasn't her real mother. The only one that was really related was her grandmother. That didn't make any sense, of course."

But if her father was doing something terrible to her, that could have been her way of separating herself from him, denying the relationship.

"What about her brother?"

"She didn't talk about him much. Besides, he was away a lot when we were in high school."

"Tell me about the boyfriend."

"Well, that's just it. I don't know whether it was real or one of her fantasy stories."

"You mean a girl getting ready to enter a convent made up a story about a boyfriend?"

"I wish I could tell you for sure that it was or wasn't true. I just don't know."

"And she started talking about him shortly before she entered St. Stephen's."

"That summer. I'm pretty sure."

"What did she say about him?"

"Crazy things. He came to her at night. She met him in the woods. She saw him in her dreams."

Was it her way of describing her father? For the hundredth time I wished I had access to her diary. "Did he have a name?"

"I don't think she ever told me a name. She used to call him her doubter, her sweet doubter, that was it, because he doubted she would go through with her novitiate."

"Then he was waiting for her," I said.

"He may have been. If he existed."

"Miranda, you knew the boys in high school. Could it have been one of them?"

She shook her head slowly. "I would have heard. You can't keep something like that a secret in a town like Riverview."

"Did you ever get the feeling that this relationship was giving her second thoughts about entering the convent?"

"I did, yes. But I think she felt she'd gone too far to turn back, that she'd committed herself and she would have to go through with it."

"All she had to do was say no," I said sadly.

"I told her that. She loved the convent. She said the grounds were beautiful and the buildings were old and solid and the nuns were so nice."

"She was right. Do you remember the last time you saw her?"

"It was before I left for school. I had to go up early for freshman week. Her family invited me for a farewell dinner."

"Who was there?"

"All of them."

"Even the brother?"

"Yes. We ate very formally in the dining room. Her father was in a great mood. They gave me a terrific gift, a piece of luggage to take to school. It was a wonderful night."

"How was her mother?"

"Pretty good. She kept saying how she was going to miss Julia and her husband kept saying, 'We'll see her every weekend, Serena.' I used to hear my mother's friends talk about her sometimes, how she was having problems, going into a hospital, but that night she seemed pretty good." Miranda smiled at me. "You should have heard what my mother was saying about my going away to school. You'd think I was running away forever."

"Did you stay in contact with Julia after that?"

"A little. We wrote a couple of letters. It was really my fault that it petered out." Her voice was filled with remorse. "I was having a great time at school and the work was harder than I expected and I just didn't take the time. I wish I had."

"Do you remember what she wrote about?"

She glanced over at the sleeping infant in the bassinet. "She told me how she spent her days, how early she got up in the morning and how early she went to bed at night. She mentioned one or two girls who were novices that year and talked about a nun who was the novice mistress. That was probably all in the first letter. I know it took me a long time to answer because her letter had been so full of information that I didn't want to just write a few silly lines that didn't say anything; I wanted to write the kind of letter she wrote to me. So it took a while and then she wrote back. I have a feeling that was her last letter."

"Was it the same kind of letter?"

"I guess so." She looked uncertain. "No, I think in the last letter she talked about some of the people at the convent. And her mother. She said her mother wasn't well again."

That would certainly fit with what I knew. "You remember anything else?"

"That must be where she talked about the priest."

I felt a prickle along my skin. "Father McCormick?"

"Hudson River McCormick. That's what she called him. She said she'd been talking to him about her mother. I remember feeling kind of relieved that she was doing that, talking to a professional, I mean. I never dreamed what was really going on."

I let it pass. "Did she mention the boyfriend?"

"I'm not sure. It was a long time ago."

Seven years. "I appreciate your help, Miranda."

"She wrote about someone else," she said as though it had just occurred to her. "A nun that she liked very much, somebody older."

"Would you recognize the name?"

"Possibly."

"Sister Clare Angela?" I said, not wanting to be too direct or suggestive.

"That kind of rings a bell," Miranda said without much conviction.

"Sister Mary Teresa?"

"That sounds more like it. Yes, I think that's the one."

It was nearly noon and I wanted to go before her mother

came. "Miranda, when I asked you a little while ago if someone in the Farragut family may have been hurting Julia, you became very upset. Do you think you could tell me why?"

Her face clouded, but she stayed in control. "She used to say things that didn't make sense, that men were brutes, that they liked to hurt women. I asked her how she knew that and she said she just knew. She wasn't the kind of girl who would read violent books. I think she must have seen something—or experienced it herself. Maybe her father beat her mother, and when the mother was gone he did it to Julia. Maybe her brother lost control. But there was something. Two suicides in two months?"

It was a question neither of us could answer.

"You've been very helpful," I said. "And your baby is very beautiful. I hope you have a wonderful New Year."

"Thank you. I hope you sort everything out. Would you like to see Julia's letters?"

"If you have them." Her offer surprised me.

"I'm sure they're with my college things. My mother can show you where they are. She's just coming up the walk. If you go back with her, it'll give me time to get dressed. She hates to see me like this at lunchtime."

22

Sunny Gallagher was one of those beautiful women who can tramp around in the snow and end up looking like an ad for a fur coat. It was her good looks her daughter had inherited and they had matured well. She took me to her house, which was only a few blocks away from her daughter's but in a more expensive neighborhood. Here the houses had larger plots and two-car garages. Inside she had the evidence of many years of marriage and home ownership, a crowded china cabinet, a living room furnished with traditional pieces, carpeting with a few worn spots. The Christmas tree was soaring, rising into a cathedral ceiling that was hung with evergreen branches. The scent of Christmas was everywhere.

"There's a carton in Miranda's closet that has all her college notebooks and papers," Sunny said. "I can bring it down here if you like."

"Whatever is convenient."

"Why don't you come up with me? I may need some help."

We went to a second floor with greenery on the balcony railing. In Miranda's room, a sweet room with a lot of white and well-taken-care-of furniture, there were candles with lightbulb flames at every window and more greenery on the sills. Sunny went to the closet and hauled out a fair-sized carton.

"This is it. I can get it to the stairs and maybe we can both get it down." She pushed it to the top of the stairs and we bumped it down to the bottom. Then she pushed it into a large, sunny family room at the back of the house.

I thanked her and got to work, first removing a top layer of spiral notebooks, each labeled with the name and number of a course. Not anxious to wear out my welcome, I didn't linger over what I considered irrelevant. Sunny was eager to get back to her daughter's house and oversee the fifth day of her granddaughter's life.

"Did you know Julia?" I asked as I dug deeper in the carton.

"Ever since the girls became friends. Ten years anyway. Maybe more."

"Were you surprised when Julia decided to enter a convent?"

"Not really. Julia was always a quiet child. She didn't seem to have much interest in boys and she liked to help out at the church. And there was the problem with her mother." She said it as though I were already familiar with Serena Farragut's life.

"Did you know Serena?"

"A little."

I had reached a folder of what looked like essays. Miranda had analyzed a Yeats poem, attempted a short story, and described a professor of philosophy in three typewritten pages. But there were no letters, and I laid the folder on the rug near the notebooks and textbooks I had piled on the floor.

"The grandmother was quite a woman," Sunny volunteered. "Mrs. Cornelius Farragut. A very grand lady who was what my father used to call a pillar of the church. She may have been born in that house on Hawthorne Street, I'm not sure, but I know she brought up her son there. That was before my husband and I moved to Riverview."

"But he lived elsewhere for a while, didn't he?" I asked, turning the pages of a scrapbook with pressed flowers and invitations to dances and snapshots of college kids.

"I don't know where he lived before he moved back with her. Her husband had died and she didn't want to give up that big old house, although I once heard what the heating bill was and I don't think we could have afforded it for one winter season."

The scrapbook had nothing I was interested in and I set it aside. "It's a beautiful house," I said, "from the outside. I don't blame her for wanting to keep it."

"Walter's family moved back when Julia was a child,

four or five. She became friends with Miranda in third grade, I think."

"I heard that Foster was a problem."

"There was a streak of violence in him. When children are young, you never know whether it's something they'll outgrow. Of course you hope so and you give children the benefit of the doubt, especially when the parents seem to be sympathetic. But Foster didn't outgrow being a bully and a petty thief. Walter was able to hush things up, to make settlements so people wouldn't press charges."

"So there was never any official record of what he'd done."

"Absolutely nothing. And Julia never talked about him. It was as if she had no brother, as if she just wanted him to go away and not exist anymore."

Her description was chilling. "Do you think he might have hurt Julia?"

"It wouldn't surprise me. But don't expect to get anyone in that family to confirm anything. Walter always looked the other way and old Mrs. Farragut probably thinks to this day that her grandchildren are the world's most perfect people. Personally, although I'm no expert on why people crack up, I always thought Serena couldn't handle that boy, and going off to a nice quiet sanitarium was her way of avoiding the problem."

The letters were in the bottom of the carton, about an inch of them tied with ordinary string. I took them out. "You may be right," I said. "It sounds like an unhappy family."

"I think it was. I think that poor girl did everything she could to separate herself from them, and when the convent failed, she did what her mother had done. It was very tragic."

"Did you go to Julia's funeral?"

"Miranda and I both went. I was surprised only two nuns came."

"The family wanted it that way. They asked that the convent not come out."

Sunny shook her head. "Sad."

"I have the letters." I put everything else back and stood up. There were several letters in the pack, most of them from names I did not know. But the Julia Farragut letters were together at the bottom, the first letters Miranda had received in college. I put the rest of them on top of the carton. "I'll give these back," I promised.

"I hope they tell you what you're looking for. That priest has been missing for days now, hasn't he?"

"Since Christmas Night."

"I don't know why they left her alone that night," she said, as though we were still talking about Julia. "A delicate, disturbed child. Somebody should have been looking after her."

We drove back to Miranda's house and I picked up my car. It was past noon and I wanted a quiet, warm place to read the letters.

I sat in Father Grimes's study and opened the envelope with the earlier date. Father Grimes was out and the housekeeper insisted on making a tray for my lunch, but it hadn't come yet and I wasn't feeling hungry for anything except the contents of Julia's letters.

The paper she had written on was a fine quality white with her monogram on top of the first sheet. The date was late September, the handwriting clear and flourished, as though written by someone with artistic talent. As Miranda had described, the letter detailed the life of a novice at St. Stephen's. Julia's activities were all very familiar to me from the five A. M. rising for morning prayers to the household charges, classes, reading, and early bedtime. She mentioned names that I knew, among them Angela, whom she liked and admired, and Sister Clare Angela, the superior, whom she found somewhat distant. In this first letter there was no mention of Sister Mary Teresa, but "Father Hudson River" earned a few lines indicating her respect for him.

She said her parents and grandmother had been to visit the previous Sunday and how glad she was to see them. In the next sentence she wrote that she had heard nothing from her "Sweet Doubter" but that she hadn't really thought she would.

When she had pretty much covered all aspects of her new life, adequately and rather eloquently, I thought, she asked a bunch of questions for Miranda to answer. What was she studying? What were the professors like? Was she dating as she had said she would or was she sitting in the dorm thinking of Tony? (I assumed that was the Tony Miranda had eventually married.) The tone and the questions were very eighteen-year-oldish. She sounded like a sweet young girl enjoying and sharing a new experience, nothing more or less. From what she said I could not have determined whether she would stick out her novitiate or give it up at the end of a year as some girls did. She certainly didn't seem unhappy or stressed or ill or suicidal.

The second letter was quite different. The first page was a rapturous comment on Miranda's first letter to her. On the second page she returned to life at St. Stephen's, but the tone was more sober. She was starting to become introspective, to ask herself questions, to think about how she fit into the religious community. Father McCormick was helping, and he was helping, too, to work out unspecified problems that she had not felt free to discuss with anyone before. Then there was Sister Mary Teresa,

> *a woman, I suppose, about Grandma's age but whose life could not have been more different. She has taken an interest in me, I'm not sure why, but I am grateful for it. Sometimes when I sit by myself on a bench behind the chapel and think of where I am going, I feel that forty years from now I would like to be like this lovely woman, lending a hand to a novice. And then I laugh because it's so far away and there is so much to come in between and who knows if there will even be novices by then! But I hope so. It's a good life, Miranda.*

But further along her upbeat tone cooled. Grandmother Farragut had told her her mother was not well. The doctor was changing the medication and maybe it would have a good effect; everyone hoped so. Father McCormick was wonderful.

> *I think of him more as the big brother I never had than as the counselor I know he is. And I need a counselor now. I need something to get me through these difficult days. I am so worried about my mother. I should have*

taken her with me to St. Stephen's. She would like it here.
That's silly, isn't it?

There was a break in the letter at that point, and when
Julia picked it up again, she dated it a few days later. The
handwriting was now less perfect. It sprawled as though the
writer were in a great hurry. She mentioned her mother
again, then said she had not been sleeping well, that she
had had disturbing dreams and often woke up confused.
Sister Mary Teresa was there to help and Father Hudson
River had not failed her. She had even received a card from
her "Sweet Doubter" and that had helped to cheer her.

There wasn't much more. I could tell from the date that
the terrible night of Thanksgiving was not far away, that the
worst—or second worst—night of her young life was just
ahead of her.

There was a knock on the door and the housekeeper
came in with my lunch, a bowl of good-smelling soup, a
sandwich, some fruit, cookies, and coffee. Father Grimes
was well taken care of. I thanked her and she left quickly.

As I ate I read the letters a second time. Then I looked
at them page by page, inspecting the handwriting. The de-
terioration was striking. When I compared the first page of
the first letter with the last page of the second letter, I could
hardly believe they had been written by the same person.

I finished my lunch, expressed my thanks, and drove
back to St. Stephen's. Upstairs in the superior's office I
showed the letters to Joseph and told her how I had spent
my morning.

She looked up from the second letter and her face was
masked in sorrow. "What is clear is that she was confused
and she recognized her confusion. This letter may have
been her last or only attempt to get the truth out."

"The truth about her brother," I said.

"And now the brother is out of prison and shopping for
groceries with his grandmother. I wonder how much his
grandmother knows."

"Everything Julia committed to her diary. She knew Julia
had been writing in her diary before she committed suicide.
I'm sure she read those pages after hiding them from the
police."

"We'll never see those pages, Chris. Even if we knew for certain that they existed and that Mrs. Farragut had them, if she's kept them secret this long, she would destroy them before she would let anyone read them. If you saw the two of them together today, it means she's helping her grandson back into society, and I can't fault her for that. It's certainly better than abandoning him. The question is whether he kidnapped Hudson and, if so, what he's done with him."

"And why he may have killed Sister Mary Teresa."

"That may not be too hard to explain. Suppose Foster befriended her after Julia left St. Stephen's, or after Julia died. Only two nuns went to the funeral. They must have been very visible and would surely have spoken to the family and signed the book. Julia may have spoken of Mary Teresa when she was home. From these letters it's clear there was a bond between them. If Foster wanted to keep tabs on the goings-on at St. Stephen's, especially what was happening to Hudson, what better way than to keep in touch with a nun who was fond of Julia and who may well have believed the story about Hudson?"

"I asked her about it," I said, remembering her response. "She said Sister Clare Angela had said it should never be discussed."

"And Mary Teresa would never disobey Sister Clare Angela's caution, not after seven years, not even with a change of circumstance. Let's look further. Whoever was abusing Julia, whether it was the father or the brother, that person knew she had never told anyone. If she had, someone—a friend, a teacher—would have done something about it."

"I agree," I said. "Miranda Gallagher would have told her mother. What Julia did was try to handle it herself by leaving the house. Only it was too late. She'd been hurt too badly to help herself."

"But Foster knows Julia didn't talk about it. If she had told Mary Teresa, Mary Teresa would have brought it to the attention of Sister Clare Angela or the Farraguts. There was no seal of the confessional on her conversations with Julia. Only a confession to a priest is sealed. So Foster feels safe. He stays in touch with Mary Teresa and one day she writes and tells him that Hudson is coming to visit. She also knows, because we all knew, that he was stopping in Buffalo on Christmas Eve to visit friends."

"And he has the good luck to be released from prison that morning."

"Exactly."

"We still have the problem of the extra car at the thruway rest stop."

"True, but that will solve itself when we have the whole picture. What happens next is that after Hudson's car is found in Riverview, you seek out Mrs. Farragut and start asking questions."

"And Foster gets scared. He thinks Sister Mary Teresa put me onto his grandmother, that she's made a connection between Hudson's disappearance and her telling Foster where and when Hudson was arriving." It was plausible; it fitted a lot of what we knew.

"For all we know," Joseph said, "Foster may have been staying with his grandmother and may have heard your conversation. He decides then he'd better speak to Mary Teresa and he makes an appointment to see her that night. Her mind had been undependable lately, sometimes sharp, sometimes very ragged. He may not even have known that before he met her. We'll never know what she said, but he may have felt he had to silence her to protect himself."

For the first time I had the feeling we might be getting somewhere. There were some problems. Sister Mary Teresa would surely not have written to someone in prison, but perhaps she had written to a box number and his grandmother had forwarded his mail. It was a small point. Like the extra car at the rest stop, it would work itself out.

And then it hit me. "Mary Teresa didn't know Julia had a brother," I said. I remembered our conversation very clearly. "I mentioned the name to her and it didn't ring a bell. She had never been to the Farragut house. She didn't know there was a brother."

Unexpectedly, Joseph smiled. "Take a break, Chris. You've learned so much and you've pushed yourself so hard. It will come together when it's ready. If someone has been keeping Hudson alive, they'll do it another day. And if he died on Christmas Night, we will always remember him for what he was."

I picked up the two letters and left her office. I didn't want to think of Hudson as dead, but there had been no ransom request, no phone calls, no sightings, just a vehicle left on the street a healthy walk from a closed train station. Father or son, son or father. I went down to my room and tried to clear my mind.

23

I remember the walk back to the mother house after Jack and I had said our vows. We kissed in the back of the chapel and then went out into the sunshine. I have never felt happier, never felt so surrounded by friends. We stopped about halfway along the path and greeted our guests. There were several I had never met and plenty of nuns that Jack had not yet met, and everyone was smiling. Out of the corner of my eye I saw someone videotaping and someone else taking shots with a camera. I hadn't arranged for any of it; it had just happened.

When our impromptu receiving line had come to an end, we followed the crowd to the Mother House. There we had our wedding feast, laid out in a sumptuous buffet prepared by Jack's sister, Eileen, and supervised by Melanie Gross's mother, who had truly understood that we wanted less than a formal banquet and more than an informal bite to eat. How Marilyn Margulies and Eileen Brooks had managed to work together so well is still a mystery to me but one the international community ought to explore.

The community room had been cleared of its heavy furniture and filled with round tables covered with deep pink damask. Jack and I sat with Sister Joseph, my cousin Gene, the Golds, and Jack's parents, while everyone else was free to sit wherever they wanted. Mrs. Margulies had not really approved of that, but I had insisted. Everywhere I turned there were happy people, including several children dressed so extravagantly that I was surprised they were having such a good time. Jack's mother, who had very much wanted a wedding in New York, seemed to be having the best time of all.

It was everything I had wanted, a day in the country, a

meeting of friends, a good meal, a happy occasion. For the year that I had known Jack I had been tasting his sister's food, leftovers from her catering business or new dishes she was experimenting with. For our wedding everything was perfect, not only in taste but in appearance. It was a far cry from convent fare, not to mention my own cooking. Eileen outdid herself that day, and I think she picked up some future clients.

On that day all the leftovers went to St. Stephen's. The only thing we took for ourselves was the top layer of our wedding cake, which Eileen boxed for us and froze, to be eaten on our first anniversary if Jack doesn't come home famished one night and decide he can't wait.

I closed my eyes and thought of how beautiful that room had been, how sweet the flowers had smelled, how sure I was that I was taking the best step of my life. Joseph was right. It was good to think of something else when you're caught in gridlock.

I must have been asleep because the knock on the door roused me harshly. It took a moment for me to remember where I was, and when. I half expected to see green leaves out the window.

"Chris?"

"Yes, come in." I went to the door, but Angela was already inside.

"Gosh, sorry. I didn't mean to wake you."

"It's OK. I don't have time to waste. Is there a call?"

"Someone's here to see you—Sister Mary Teresa's niece, grandniece actually, I think. She just drove in from Syracuse." For the funeral, although Angela didn't say so. "Joseph thought you would want to talk to her."

"I'll just wash up. I'll be right down." I used cold water and brought myself back to thinking clearly. This would be Ann-Marie, who had written letters to Mary Teresa, a young woman with children, someone who cared about her aunt.

She was sitting near the lighted Christmas tree with the still unclaimed presents in the cotton snow underneath. Joseph was with her and they were both drinking tea, something I thought I would appreciate myself.

"This is Mary Teresa's grandniece Ann-Marie," Joseph said, rising as I approached. "I'll leave you two together. There's a cup for you, Chris. Put some sugar in it. You look like you need some quick energy."

"I didn't know it showed." I turned to the niece and we said hellos. She was a young woman, not very tall, a little busty, a little rounded in the hips. She looked nothing like Mary Teresa. Probably for the benefit of the nuns she was wearing a navy wool skirt and a pink-and-gray-striped cotton shirt. Her face was pale and had only a little lipstick that had mostly worn off and her hair was pulled back, more, it seemed, to keep it out of the way than to make a fashion statement.

"Sister Joseph tells me you think my aunt's death is connected to the death of that novice several years ago," she said when we were sitting down.

I recounted Hudson's disappearance and my conversations with her aunt, telling her I was sure there was a connection.

"I just can't believe she died that way." She had put her cup down and was staring into a place I could not see.

I wanted to say something, but nothing sounded right. She had wanted her aunt to die quietly in her sleep after a long life. "I knew her for a long time and I always liked and respected her. She was kind to newcomers, tolerant of mistakes, helpful, principled. She knew how to laugh."

"Yes, she did." Ann-Marie turned toward me. "And she told a good story."

"A lot of good stories." I sipped my tea. I wanted to ask some questions, but I didn't want to interfere with her grieving, to appear unfeeling. I was almost ready to give up and do it later when she said, "She was my grandmother's sister, you know. She was the last of her generation. When that poor girl died six or seven years ago, my mother came out here to help my aunt get over it. I was twenty-one, I remember. It was before I got married. Aunt Mary never believed that girl killed herself."

"We talked about that, that Julia may have changed her mind at the last minute, when it was too late, when things had gone too far."

"That's not what she meant at all. She thought Julia was murdered. She told me that."

I felt like ice. The Mary Teresa I had known had been a team player. She did not talk behind people's backs; she didn't snipe; she would not have known how to be sarcastic. That she had believed Julia was murdered, that she had said as much to this young grandniece, was a surprise and a shock.

"Would you tell me—do you remember what she said?"

"My mother brought her home after the girl's funeral, to help her get back on her feet. We had a guest room for her. She used to visit us on vacations. I remember my mother tiptoeing around and telling us to be quiet because Aunt Mary was trying to rest, and Aunt Mary came out of her room and said if she rested any more she surely wouldn't be able to sleep at night and what she really wanted was a good stiff drink of Scotch." Ann-Marie laughed. "I'd never heard her say anything like that before."

"Did she get her Scotch?"

"She sure did. My mom poured it for her and I watched her drink it. Then she started to talk."

I was almost holding my breath, waiting for her to go on. She moved in her chair and her elbow touched a branch of the Christmas tree and bells rang softly. Ann-Marie turned toward the tree as she heard them and shook another branch, smiling at the sound. It was distant sleigh bells, children going to grandmother's house. As much as the smell of cookies is Christmas, the sound of those bells is the essence of the holiday.

"She told us this kind of wild story, of a young girl just out of high school entering St. Stephen's as a novice. Aunt Mary said how nice she was, what a fine young person she was, and how something seemed to go wrong after the first month or so. I don't remember all the details, but it sounded like the girl—did you say her name was Julia?"

"Yes. Julia Farragut."

"That Julia had awful problems. Someone in the family was sick, I think."

"Her mother wasn't well."

"OK, her mother. And her mother killed herself, didn't she?"

"On Thanksgiving."

"And then Julia left the convent."

"That's right."

"But there was more to it," Ann-Marie said. "There was someone else, a man—I wish I could remember."

I didn't want to put words in her mouth. "Julia was counseled here before her mother's death," I said.

"Yes, that's the priest who's missing now, isn't it? Sister Joseph was telling me about him before you came down."

"Father McCormick."

"Aunt Mary thought he was a fine person. She really never said anything bad about anyone she knew."

"Do you remember anything she said about why she thought Julia was murdered?"

"She said Julia had a great desire to live and she was a very good Catholic. And she said that Julia was a little wisp of a girl—that's how she put it—and anyone could have killed her and made it look like suicide."

I recalled the snapshot of Julia with Miranda Gallagher. It was true that Julia was slight, but it must be a lot harder to fake a hanging suicide than one with a gun. The story we had been told was that no one was home with Julia except her grandmother. "This man your aunt mentioned, if you think of anything . . ."

"It wasn't someone she knew. It was someone she talked to once, I think. Anyway, she couldn't have known many men at St. Stephen's."

"Did she talk about this again? About Julia and her theory, about anything to do with it?"

"She didn't dwell on it. Sometimes she would say, 'It's this many years since that poor girl died.' That's about all."

"And the man?"

"I don't know."

"What I think, Ann-Marie, is that Mary Teresa kept in touch with someone—or he kept in touch with her—after Julia's death. She may have told this person, whoever he is, that Father McCormick was coming to St. Stephen's on Christmas Night."

"And this man kidnapped the priest?" Her eyes were wide and bright.

"I believe someone who knew Father McCormick was

driving to St. Stephen's was responsible for his disappearance. After the kidnapping, when I started asking questions, he may have arranged to meet Mary Teresa at the convent at night to find out if she was saying things that would incriminate him. It's possible she confronted him with questions he couldn't or didn't want to answer."

"And he killed her."

"If that's what happened, I would say she was an exceptionally brave woman."

"Her mind was going, you know. For the last year, maybe longer. She would ramble. Sometimes she didn't know what year it was." She sounded very sad.

"But not always," I said. "I was with her when she became her old self, when her mind cleared and she spoke with authority."

"It would be nice to think that she died in a battle with evil."

"I believe that she did."

"Sister Clare Angela would be proud of her. They were good friends. Did you know her?"

"Very well. I was a nun here when she was the superior."

"She was a tough old gal, wasn't she? My father used to say she ran a tight ship. It's all different now, isn't it? This Sister Joseph, she's different, she's a different generation. Do you know her well?"

"I think I feel about Sister Joseph the way your aunt felt about Sister Clare Angela."

"You're friends. When did you leave the convent?"

"A year and a half ago."

"A lot of nuns leave now, don't they? I hear about it all the time. Even friends of mine who went in a few years ago are out. It isn't like the old days. Do you think you would have left if Sister Clare Angela was still the superior?"

The question caught me by surprise. I had never thought about it, never considered whether what I wanted to do was a function of a particular time, a prevailing attitude, a certain individual occupying a position of authority. I touched my wedding ring, my husband's gift to me on that beautiful August day, and said, "I don't know." What shocked me was that I really meant it.

* * *

I took Ann-Marie to Sister Mary Teresa's room in the villa. The police had gone through it yesterday morning after her body was found, and after I had finished my quick, surreptitious search. I had not been there since. The police had left the room very much as I remembered it, but then Sister Mary Teresa did not have drawersful of clothes to rummage through, trinkets, jewelry, and such things that you would find in a secular woman's room.

Ann-Marie took a brief look in the closet, opened a few drawers, and touched the papers on the desk.

"The convent will recycle the clothes," I said. "Nothing will be wasted. When the police return her medals, I'm sure you'd like to have them. And Sister Joseph has some of the personal things that I'm sure you'll want to keep, her missal and Bible—"

"Yes, I should take those."

"Let's go to her office."

Joseph had everything in one place. "Was there anything you needed?" she asked me.

I knew she meant the Bible. "I think there was a little scrap of paper," I said, realizing too late that I should never have brought Ann-Marie here until I checked through Mary Teresa's things once again.

Joseph handed me the Bible and I leafed through it. The scrap that I wanted was sticking out, the unattributed number starting with 67-. "Here it is."

And then I did one of the stupidest things I have ever done in my entire life. I pulled it out of the Bible and put it in my purse.

24

I knew instantly what I had done. I had lost the page on which Sister Mary Teresa kept the scrap of paper. If it had been stuck there randomly, nothing was lost, but if there was some mnemonic on one of the facing pages, I had blown a lead. I stood there for a moment, stunned, trying to recover from my blunder. Then I shook hands with Ann-Marie and left her with Joseph.

The kitchen was empty and I used the phone there to call Jack.

"Absence must not be working on your heart," he said cheerily. "It's after two. I thought you'd call earlier."

"Absence is working on my heart and every other organ, including my brain. I've just done something so dumb, so unimaginably stupid—"

"Stop," he ordered. "Knocking yourself will get you nowhere. The difference between you and me is that you admit your mistakes; I keep them secret. You wouldn't want to hear some of the things I've done on the job. During one case—"

"Don't tell me. If you have time, I'd like you to call the Riverview Police Department and ask a few questions about Julia Farragut's suicide. The nun who was murdered yesterday told her grandniece she thought Julia was murdered."

"Hey, you *are* making progress."

"It may be wishful thinking, Jack. Mary Teresa didn't want to believe Julia killed herself. Since no one was home the night she died except her grandmother, I have to wonder about it. But there should have been an autopsy, right?"

"Should have been. But remember, it's a small town where everybody knows everybody else and the police will bend over backward not to hurt the feelings of a suffering family. And you won't have the experienced pathologists you get in New York and other big cities. I doubt you get many suicides or homicides up there. But let me give them a call. You want to know if they ruled out the possibility of homicide, right?"

"Right."

"I'll do what I can."

"You know, I think part of the problem in this case is that there are three different police departments working on various aspects of it. The state police found Hudson's clothes, our local police were called in when Sister Mary Teresa was found dead, and the Riverview police were in charge when Julia died, however that happened."

"They also found Hudson's vehicle in front of the old Farragut house."

"Right, but it's seven years later. I wonder how much continuity there is and whether all these police departments talk to each other very much."

"Hard to say. Let me get on it."

I sat at the long kitchen worktable and reviewed my options. I had talked to just about everybody I could think of except for Foster Farragut, and even if I could find him, if his grandmother allowed me to see him, I couldn't imagine it would be productive. He was now a promising suspect for two or three crimes and would have a cover story that I was sure Mrs. Farragut would support. He would say he wasn't home the night Julia died, he went directly to his grandmother or a new apartment when he was let out of jail, and he was sound asleep when Mary Teresa was murdered. The chances of finding a witness at the thruway rest stop were too small to calculate. If anyone at St. Stephen's had seen or heard anything the night Mary Teresa was murdered, she would have come forward; of that I was absolutely certain. And Mrs. Belvedere's recollections of the night Julia died supported suicide. I took my notebook out of my bag and turned pages, looking for something, anything that would tell me where to go next. Miranda. Miranda Santiago had offered the letters to me and her mother had let me look through the carton myself. I couldn't have asked for more cooperation. If I had learned anything from the letters, it was that Julia, at least when she wrote to her friend, had envisioned a long life.

Then there was the boyfriend, the fantasy boyfriend who doubted she would stick it out as a novice. In a way he had been right, but surely not the way he had expected. Had he hoped she would leave St. Stephen's and fall into his waiting open arms? Did he exist?

And who would know? That was the question. I picked up my things and left word in the switchboard room that I was going to the villa. Joseph had spoken to them and the police had questioned them yesterday morning, but the local police were not interested in the disappearance of Hudson McCormick or a suicide that had taken place in another town seven years ago. I was interested in everything. I believed everything was related.

Every nun now living in the villa had known me since I was fifteen. The group sitting downstairs greeted me and invited me to sit with them. I sensed they had been talking about Mary Teresa.

"We heard Mary Teresa's niece was coming," Sister Dolores said.

"She's here. I talked to her a little while ago."

"She was good to Mary Teresa," Sister Caroline said. "She sent her CARE packages."

"Did the niece call?"

There was general agreement that she did.

"Did any of you ever answer the phone when somebody else called?"

"An old student," one of the nuns said. It went without saying that a student would be female.

"No male callers?"

There were a lot of shrugged shoulders.

"Was anyone here answering on Saturday or Saturday night, the day before we found her?"

"I was," Sister Caroline said. "It was a pretty slow day. She didn't get any calls. I'm sure of that."

At that moment a nun stuck her head around a corner into the room and asked for me. "Telephone," she said. "Want me to ring some bells?"

"No, thanks." I ran, laughing, to an old black phone on a table just outside the community room and picked it up.

"Glad they found you," Jack said.

"That was fast."

"Tells you how long and detailed my conversation was. You're not gonna love the Riverview Police Department the way you love NYPD. I got a lieutenant who's old enough to remember the Julia Farragut suicide and enough of an old boy that he won't talk about it."

"You got nothing out of him?"

"Very little. The family asked that it not be discussed to spare their feelings. I gather Walter wanted the records sealed, which he couldn't really do, but the police do their best when a citizen makes a request. It's not as if they were legally sealed by a court. You just can't get anyone to tell you anything."

"Sounds like he wielded a lot of power."

"Who knows what was going on? I did get him to say there had not been a full autopsy because it wasn't indicated. Julia had been disturbed, she had lost her mother a little while before, and it looked like the Christmas blues got her down."

"He said that?"

"Almost in those words."

"What you're telling me is that some professional looked at her body, decided she'd died by hanging, and let it go at that."

"I'd guess that's pretty much what happened. Don't even think about exhuming the body. There isn't a chance in hell of getting that."

"I know."

"I asked if there was anything new about Father McCormick. He said there was nothing, that they were keeping the vehicle in case the priest turned up and wanted it back. The feeling I got was they'd sock him with a big fat storage fee."

"I feel stonewalled," I said.

"I can see why. You gonna let this go for a while and come home to someone who loves you?"

"I can't, Jack. We've lost a nun and we don't have Hudson back and I've got to do something because the police won't."

"Like what?"

"Like I'm just going to have to start at the beginning

again. And I'll have to be smarter and tougher the second
time around."

"Smarter I can probably live with. Do you think you
could go easy on tough?"

"For you, my love, anything."

"Just not tonight."

"Maybe tomorrow. If I'm lucky."

I went back to the nuns. They were in better spirits now.
We talked for a little while, exchanging anecdotes about
Mary Teresa. Then I went back to the Mother House.

They had given Ann-Marie an empty room to stay in till
Mary Teresa's funeral. Her aunt would be buried with other
nuns in the St. Stephen's cemetery as soon as the body was
released.

I found Ann-Marie in her room. "I have to ask you
something," I said, hoping she wouldn't think I was crazy.
"Is it possible your aunt had a credit card?"

She laughed. "Aunt Mary? Aunt Mary hardly knew what
money was. She had no use for it. The convent took care
of her needs and I sent her little things after my mom
passed away. What would she want with a credit card?"

"I don't know. I found a scrap of paper in her room yesterday with a long number on it."

"Could it be a telephone number?"

"It's much too long for that. And it doesn't look like a
phone number."

"I wouldn't know."

I thanked her and went to Joseph's office. "Do you have
a credit card?" I asked her.

"Still thinking about that number?"

"Yes. Maybe someone gave her a credit card to thank her
for keeping in touch about Hudson." I didn't believe it, but
I had to try everything.

"I have one for the convent. It helps to keep our accounts
straight." She got it out for me and put it on the table.

It had thirteen digits. Mary Teresa's number had fifteen.
Joseph picked up the phone and called someone. "How
many digits does your American Express card have?" she
asked. She listened and said, "Thank you." She hung up.
"Fifteen."

"That could be it."

Joseph picked up the phone and did some calling. Finally she said, "This is Sister Joseph, General Superior at St. Stephen's Convent. One of our members, Sister Mary Teresa Williams, died yesterday. I want to know if there is an unpaid balance on her account." She read off the number on my scrap of paper. "She's checking," she said to me.

I waited tensely. If we could find out who was paying her bills . . .

"Yes, I am." She listened. "You're certain about that? . . . Well, thank you very much." She hung up. "The number isn't one of theirs and Sister Mary Teresa Williams has no account with them."

"I should have known it was too easy. Maybe it's one issued by another company."

"Chris, your friend Melanie. She must have some cards."

"I guess so. We don't shop together much, but . . . Let me call her."

Mel was there and I asked her the crucial question.

"I have every card you could ever want. Saks? Bloomie's? Lord and Taylor? I even have Neiman Marcus, if you feel like splurging."

"It's not for me, Mel. I'm trying to identify a number I found scribbled on a piece of paper. What I really want to know is how many digits your cards have to give me some idea of the source of this number."

"I'll count." She had a Visa card with sixteen, which was three more than Joseph's Visa card, two gasoline credit cards with eleven each, and eight digits for the department-store cards. Not one number had the fifteen digits of Mary Teresa's. "How'm I doing?" she asked after the last count.

"You're doing fine. I'm not. Maybe it doesn't mean anything."

"I talked to Jack last night. Poor guy's lonely, Chris."

"So am I."

"He's coming to dinner tonight."

"Oh thanks, Mel."

"Shall I tell you what we're having?"

"Please don't. I don't think I can bear it."

"Come home soon."

I promised her I would and hung up.

"Sounds like you didn't find a match."

"It's amazing, isn't it? There must have been ten numbers and not one was fifteen digits long."

"We'll figure it out, Chris. I got a call from Detective Lake a little while ago. The autopsy has been completed. Mary Teresa wasn't strangled, as we thought. She was suffocated and suffered a heart attack."

"Suffocated?"

"Her attacker probably tried to keep her from screaming and clamped his hand over her mouth and nose. She put up a struggle."

"I never thought otherwise," I said. "I'm going back to Hawthorne Street, Joseph. That's where Julia died, that's where someone left Hudson's car. I think the answers are there if I can just think of the right questions to ask."

"Why are the answers there?"

I wasn't really sure. It was something about the house. I kept feeling the house was trying to tell me something. "It's the source," I said. "It's where the trouble started and ended. It's a feeling, Joseph, and I'm at the point where all I have is a feeling."

"You have much more than that."

"But I can't put it together." I put my bag on my shoulder. "See you later," I said.

I stopped at Ann-Marie's room on my way out. "I know it's hard to tell with numbers," I said, "but do you think your aunt wrote this?" I showed her the strip of paper I had found in the Bible.

She looked at it carefully. Then she took an envelope out of her bag and put the strip under the street address. "Aunt Mary had a very old-fashioned way of writing numbers, kind of schoolteacherish, like the numbers you see on the wall in the first grade. These don't look like that. They're much rounder. Look at the difference in the twos."

She was right. The two in the address made an angle at the line. The two on the strip of paper was looped. Someone else had written the numbers on the strip and given them to her.

"Thank you, Ann-Marie. You're absolutely right." I had finally asked a good question.

25

I sat across the street from number 211 and watched the house. Around four-thirty lights went on in the front window of the living room. A few minutes later lights went on upstairs, then again in another room. The house now had a comfortable, lived-in look. Next door in the Belvederes' house lights were going on at almost the same time. This late winter afternoon their driveway was empty. Either the family was out and their lights were also going on automatically or the cars were put away in the garage at the end of the long drive. Maybe their son had gone back to wherever he lived now that Christmas was over. Tomorrow evening he would probably be celebrating New Year's Eve with his friends as I would like to be doing.

When I got cold enough, I got out of the car and crossed the street. I was wearing snow boots, but I didn't need them for the sidewalk, which was clean in both directions, or for the front walk to the porch or for the driveway. Instead I walked around the right side of the house, through still-undisturbed snow, leaving prints as I went.

Just even with the ground were basement windows. I knelt and looked inside one, then another. At this hour there wasn't enough natural light to let me see very much. I continued to the back. It was a deep house from front to back and, like many Victorians, had many protuberances, small extensions of rooms. One near the back was off the kitchen. I skirted it and came to the rear.

It was dark now and I took my handy flashlight out of my bag. It was small and lightweight and produced only a narrow beam of light, but it was enough to let me see flower beds and keep from tripping.

Along the back of the house I could see the windowed

extension to the kitchen the Corcorans had built. And between that and the corner of the house where I was standing was an old outside staircase that led to the third floor, where a door opened off a small landing, perhaps the entrance to the servants' quarters from a time when a staff lived upstairs but didn't mingle with the family. From Julia's window yesterday, I had mistaken these stairs for a fire escape.

I put my foot on the first step to see if it was icy. It wasn't. The sun had done its work today. Holding the light in my hand, I went cautiously up the stairs.

"Who's that?" a man's voice called from below, stopping me dead and frightening me.

I turned around carefully. "My name's Christine Bennett," I called down into the darkness. "I mean no harm."

"Come down here."

I descended, feeling very scared. He had not identified himself and no one could see us from the street. "Who are you?" I said, reaching bottom and stopping more than an arm's length away. The man was carrying a more powerful flashlight than mine, which he turned on me as I stood there.

"I'm Warren Belvedere. I live next door. My wife saw a light back here. Want to tell me what you're doing?"

Not an easy question to answer, but I felt a little less afraid. "I'm trying to figure out what happened to the missing priest."

"Well, you're looking in the wrong place, and if you aren't careful, you'll get yourself—"

"Warren?" a woman called. "Are you all right, Warren?" It was Marilyn Belvedere, holding a coat together as she lifted her feet awkwardly to tramp across the snow.

"It's Chris Bennett, Mrs. Belvedere," I called.

"My Lord! What are you doing back here with a flashlight?"

"I just wanted to see the house."

"Why don't you both come inside? It's freezing out here."

Her husband waited till I had walked past him before he followed us, as though to ensure that I not spend another minute looking around. We went inside through a door along the side of the house that led to a small room off the kitchen, where we took our boots off and carried them through the house to the front door. Warren Belvedere took my coat and hung it in the closet along with his and his wife's. Then we went back to the room where she and I had talked on my visit on Saturday.

"Tea?" she asked with a smile.

"I'm going upstairs," her husband said irritably. "I'm tired of this whole business. The priest isn't here. The Farraguts haven't lived here for years. I'm sorry the girl killed herself, but if I'd been brought up in that family, I probably would've considered it myself."

"Why?" I asked.

"Because everyone there was nuts," he said angrily. "The mother—"

"Warren," his wife said.

"The son, the father who paid off the whole police department to keep his son out of trouble—"

"Warren, you don't know that's true."

"Don't I? You mean *you* don't know that's true because you don't want to believe it. He destroyed property, he was a common thief, he put his hands where they didn't belong."

"Go upstairs, Warren, and leave us alone."

"Don't rush me. I just want this to be over. The Farraguts are gone, the girl is dead, and no one in this town left that damn Jeep out there. I don't know who you are"—he faced me—"but if I catch you around here again sneaking around with a flashlight, I'll call the police first and tell them there's a prowler. Is that clear?"

"Very clear, Mr. Belvedere."

"Enjoy your tea," he said bitterly, and left the room.

"Warren's just a little edgy," his wife said nervously. "I'll be right back with the tea."

"I don't need tea. I just want a little information."

She sat down, looking wilted.

"The house next door has an outside entrance to the third floor," I said.

"I think Mrs. Farragut rented it out for a while after her husband died. She didn't like being alone and she didn't want to give up the house. It used to be the maids' quarters in bygone days."

"Did the Farraguts use it for anything?"

"They had a live-in maid sometimes, kind of on and off. There wasn't any maid that Christmas," she added as though she sensed where I was going.

"The night Julia committed suicide, when did you know something was wrong?"

She looked around as though to assure herself that her husband was out of earshot. "I heard sirens and then an ambulance pulled up and a police car; I really can't tell you which came first. But those flashing lights were on for a long time, I remember that."

"And who was home at the Farraguts' that night?"

"As far as I know, only Julia and her grandmother."

"You told me you saw Walter Farragut come home after the police had been called."

"That's right."

"I wonder how you could have seen him. Wouldn't he normally have driven up the driveway on the far side of the house and gone inside through the side door?"

She thought about it for a moment. "Normally, yes. But I'm sure I saw him rush up the front walk. He must have seen the ambulance and parked his car on the street. Yes, that's what happened. The ambulance was in the driveway when he came home."

"And the police car?"

"Out front. I'm sure of that because I could see it through the front windows."

It made sense. The other possibility was that Walter had left the house when the body was discovered and made a conspicuous return when the police and the ambulance attendants could see him. "What about Foster?"

"I didn't really see him come home. I wasn't watching for anyone. I was concerned about what was happening. To be honest, I thought at first that old Mrs. Farragut had had a heart attack. I had no idea it was Julia."

"Did you go over to see what was happening?"

She didn't answer right away. Her face was tight, her forehead pinched. "Warren did," she said.

The way she said it, the way she looked when she said

it, made me wonder. I took a calculated risk. "I heard a rumor that Julia was murdered," I said.

Her hand moved spasmodically, pushing a small dish harmlessly to the carpeted floor. "I never heard that. Who told you that?"

"The nun who was murdered yesterday morning."

"I can't imagine—what would make her think such a thing?"

"She knew Julia well. Julia had a great desire to live. She was also a devout Catholic."

"The police said it was suicide."

"Your husband mentioned that Walter Farragut had bought off the Riverview Police Department."

"Warren's just upset. He says things he doesn't mean. No one was home that night except the grandmother. You can't believe that an old woman . . . And she loved Julia. She adored her."

"She loved her grandson, too, didn't she?"

"Of course. What does that have to do with anything?"

It might have a lot to do with her motive to protect either him or his father, but I didn't want to discuss it with her. "I'm not sure," I said evasively. "I was curious about something else. The grandson—was Foster Serena's maiden name?"

"Foster was his mother's maiden name."

I looked at her. "You mean he wasn't Serena's son?"

"Oh no. I thought you knew that, but I suppose not many people did. Walter had a son by his first wife. After she died, he married Serena. Foster must have been four or five when they married. Old Mrs. Farragut always attributed his problems to losing his mother when he was so young."

A line in one of the letters to Miranda came back to me. *The brother I never had.* She had never thought of him as her brother. It cast a new light on what Julia had told Angela about her mother losing a baby boy. "So Foster and Julia were half brother and sister."

"That's right. But no one talked about it. As far as the Farraguts were concerned, they were a family."

But not to Serena, I thought. Serena had taken on the task of raising another woman's son, a boy she could not control, in the home of a mother-in-law who loved him and probably excused much of his behavior, and with a husband willing to pay off the police to keep the son on the street and his record, not to mention the Farragut name, clean. It occurred to me that the offense that had finally put him behind bars had very likely occurred in another jurisdiction, where Walter had carried no influence.

My heart ached for both of them, mother and daughter, Serena and Julia. What a mess Julia had been born into. No wonder she had lived for the day when she could escape. What had she written to Miranda? She wished her mother could have come to St. Stephen's with her.

"Thank you, Mrs. Belvedere," I said.

"If I knew where your priest was, I would tell you."

"I'm sure you would." I meant it. "Did anyone in that house ever talk about him?"

"Never. But we heard about it. It's hard to keep things like that a secret. Serena never said anything. By the time Julia went to the convent, Serena was spending most of her time at home. I went over once in a while to talk to her, to sit with her, but it wasn't the same."

It hardly could be. The grandmother would be there, depriving Serena of privacy.

"I watched her decline," Marilyn Belvedere said sadly. "I watched her slip away." She looked at her watch. "I'm afraid I must ask you to leave. It's nearly dinnertime now and Warren doesn't like his dinner late."

I wasn't surprised. I thanked her again, got my coat and boots at the front door, and walked down to the street. The old Farragut house was alive with light. Only the third-floor windows were entirely dark.

I crossed the street and got into my car. I wanted to complete my circle of the house, but I was afraid to agitate Warren Belvedere. For all I knew he was peering out of an upstairs window, watching me. I wasn't ready to call his bluff about the police, not now, not in this town.

But there was something about the house, something I knew or almost knew, as though a fact had already registered in my brain and I had failed to recognize it. That empty house with its windows all lit up was trying to tell me something.

I had no idea what. I started the motor and made a

U-turn, driving slowly toward the center of Riverview. I needed a warm place to think and I didn't want to return to the convent. Threats or not, I was going to have to go back to the Farragut house again and shake loose what my mind was concealing from me.

26

I ended up back at Father Grimes's rectory. He gave me his living room and promised no one would bother me. Then he went upstairs.

I took out my notebook and looked over what I had just learned from Marilyn Belvedere. No one else had even hinted at the relationships in the Farragut family. If the Farraguts had moved to 211 Hawthorne Street with a ready-made family of one son and one daughter, it was easy to see why no one would suspect that the children were born of two marriages. And since there seemed no limit to the lengths Walter would go to protect his son, one could only wonder whether that included harming his daughter as well.

Backward and forward, backward and forward. I flipped back to where I had copied Sister Mary Teresa's long number onto a line on my page. Someone had written it for her, someone who wanted to make sure it would not be easily identified because it gave access to something. Not a locker or a post office box, not any credit card that I had been able to dig up, not a phone number, because it was too long and the first three numbers were not an area code and the dashes were in all the wrong places.

What happened next was like standing in a museum looking at a painting that was only pieces of color, and then seeing it again from a certain distance or in a certain light and the pieces come together and take on a form. My mind was still thinking about backward and forward and I started to read the number from the right instead of the left. It ended with -50. If you started with the zero, you had 05-1837-. And suddenly there it was. The dashes were meant to confuse, not to aid: 518 was the area code for Albany and the upper Hudson Valley! I stood up and ran to the kitchen, where the housekeeper was putting the finishing touches on Father Grimes's dinner.

"May I use your phone?" I asked breathlessly.

"Right over there, dear. Is something wrong?"

"No. I've just never seen a phone number this long or one that starts with a zero."

"You dial the zero first if you need the operator."

"Why would she need the operator?"

"Who?"

"The person making the call."

"My grandchildren call home with a special number that makes it collect. My son told me about it. They can call from anywhere in the country, any phone at all, and they don't have to pay for it."

No one had called Mary Teresa two nights ago. She had made the call herself and it would never appear on the convent's bill. I dialed the long number and heard a ring. I had no idea what I would say if someone answered.

After the third ring, I heard a pickup. Then a strange, genderless, robotic sounding voice said, "Leave your name and number. I'll get back to you."

I hung up, then dialed St. Stephen's. They found Joseph for me and I told her what had happened.

"You mean Mary Teresa could have telephoned this person every day and we'd never see it on our bill?"

"That's right. Something in this number must tell the telephone company it's collect. And since she could dial it without going through an operator, whoever was on the switchboard wouldn't even know she made a call."

"And you have no idea who the person is?"

"I don't even know whether it's a man or a woman. It sounds like one of those computer voices and it doesn't identify itself."

"We'll have to find out who that number belongs to."

I looked at my watch. "It's too late for me to get Jack. He's on his way home now. But this has to be our killer."

"It's hard to believe that a prison inmate could have a telephone and answering machine in his cell."

"Which means we're back to Walter. Or old Mrs. Farragut. Maybe she took the messages."

"Let's give it some thought, Chris."

"I'll see you later. I still have some things to clear up in Riverview."

The housekeeper got a hug from me and I accepted a cookie from her to tide me over till I had time for dinner. Then Father Grimes came down and I had to rebuff his invitation to stay for dinner. I was too keyed up to eat and I wanted to get back to the Farragut house to see if I could figure out what it was that I almost knew.

I retrieved my coat from the living room and put my notebook back in my bag. As Father Grimes helped me on with my coat, I heard the furnace kick on under the floor I was standing on. The whole downstairs was pleasantly overheated and I couldn't quite see why more was needed.

"Is that the furnace?" I asked him.

"Probably not to heat the rectory. The rectory and the church are one building with one furnace and several heating zones. We have to make sure the pipes don't freeze in the church basement, so we've got a zone down there that we keep warmer than the rest of the church overnight."

"I see," I said. "Thank you, Father." I buttoned my coat as I ran.

This time I didn't park on the street. I drove up the driveway and shut my lights off as soon as I had a good look at where the garage was. Then I inched my way forward, past the side door where the drive was canopied and on to the back of the house. There I turned off the motor and got out of the car as quietly as possible. The house to the left was some distance away, but I didn't want to alert those people any more than I wanted Warren Belvedere after me.

This would be the side of the house where Mrs. Cornelius Farragut's private apartment had been. I pointed my flashlight through each window along the back section of the driveway but saw little. Shades were drawn over some and curtains over others. I turned the light off and continued cautiously to the back of the house.

The garage, when I reached it, looked more like a small barn than a place to keep a car, but this house had been built before the days of automobiles and the little barn made a perfect home for two cars. I looked through a window on the left side and saw one car and space enough for more than one more.

I turned the light off and made my way carefully along the back of the house, circling a small shed built off the end of the kitchen, to the wooden staircase where Warren Belvedere had caught me earlier, keeping an eye on the side of the Belvedere house. With luck they were still having dinner and the dining room had no windows facing this direction.

Holding the railing tightly, I climbed the stairs. It was miserably cold and a light wind made it worse. When I reached the landing at the top, I cupped my hands around my flashlight and pointed it through the window on the upper half of the door. I couldn't see much beyond the wide painted boards of the floor. Turning off the light, I turned the door handle just on a whim. Incredibly, the door opened.

I let myself in and closed the door behind me, my heart pounding crazily. I was standing on the old softwood floor of a bedroom, surrounded by cartons and old furniture. The Corcorans obviously used this little apartment as an attic. I felt my way to the open door.

The only direction to go from there was to the right. Feeling safe, I turned on my flashlight. On the left was a staircase going down to a closed door. I had probably walked right by it on my visit with Marilyn. I went down the stairs and tried it, but it was locked and I went back up. On my right was a small bathroom, then another room. I pointed the flashlight inside.

A mattress was stretched across the floor and near it was the residue of a meal, a square pizza box and two paper cups. One of the cups was empty, but the other still had a spoonful of light coffee in the bottom. A couple of feet away from the mattress was an old chair. I ran the light over it, finding a couple of coins. Someone had sat here and coins had fallen from his pocket.

I went out into the hall and ran my light along it. There were no other doors. I called, "Hudson?" but there was no answer, no sound of movement. But he had been here; I was sure of that. I remembered the bang of the shutter when Marilyn and I were in Julia's room. Had it been a shutter or had Hudson heard voices and tried to signal us?

I went back to the room with the mattress and ran the light along the wall. Near the door was a thermostat. Tonight it was set at fifty. But yesterday it had been set at a livable temperature. Someone had taken Hudson out of here last night and turned the heat down.

What had they done with him? I went back to the first bedroom and let myself out. In the dark, I went down to the ground. I had looked in the garage and no one was there. I walked along the back of the house to the potting shed that seemed stuck onto it. There was a window on each side and a padlocked door on the side facing the backyard. I held my flashlight against the window on the Belvederes' side and looked in. I could see a worktable with garden tools and ceramic pots, a pair of heavy gloves, a watering can. I moved the light, straining to see. The floor, a dirt floor, seemed so far away, but there was something there, something that looked like a blue-jeaned leg.

I tapped on the window. "Hudson," I called. "Hudson, it's Chris. Are you all right?"

There was no movement, not a twitch. I could feel tears welling. I wasn't even certain it was Hudson, but everything inside me told me it had to be. I tapped again, holding the flashlight on what I was fairly sure was a denim-clad leg. It didn't move.

I ran across the snow to the Belvederes'. On the front porch I pressed the doorbell twice in my agitation. The musical chimes began a concert that was interrupted when Marilyn Belvedere opened the door.

"Miss Bennett," she said, clearly surprised.

"Please call the police," I said breathlessly. "There's a man—a body—in the Corcorans' potting shed behind the house."

"A what?"

"Please!" I said, stepping inside, stamping the snow off my feet on her little mat.

"Warren?" she called. "Warren?" She went toward the living room and met him about halfway. "I think we have to call the police." The tone of her voice implied she did not want the decision to be hers.

He saw me and his face turned furious.

"Call the police," I said more calmly than I felt. "Right now. Right this minute."

"I'll do it," his wife said.

27

The whole area around number 211 was alive with lights. It took a call to the police chief to get permission to batter in the door of the shed, the services of a locksmith deemed too time-consuming. It was the first time I had ever seen a police officer put his shoulder to a door outside of television, where, Jack had frequently reminded me, all is fiction. Doors to New York City apartments are steel clad and succumb to the shoulder only on the screen.

I stayed back, fighting panic, hoping it was Hudson and that he was still alive. After the police broke in, the medics followed with a stretcher. I could hear male voices, commenting on the smell, the debris, the whole scene.

"He's alive," a police officer said, coming out of the little building. "But just barely. He may not make it."

"May I see him?" I asked.

"You don't want to and they gotta get him to the hospital pretty quick. It's gonna be touch and go. He's half-frozen and there's no sign he ate anything. How'd you know to look for him in there?"

"His car was left on the street in front of the house. Whoever kidnapped him must have driven the vehicle into the garage and hidden it there for a day or so." I didn't mention the third-floor apartment. That would come later. "He was probably trying to get Father McCormick to tell him things that a priest can't disclose."

"You mean he'd die instead of telling?"

"I'm sure he didn't think he'd die. He believed someone would find him. He was right."

"You got a lot of faith, ma'am."

Not as much as I'd like to have, I thought. "He had the faith," I said. "Will you see to it that he's guarded in the hospital? Whoever left him there expected him to die. If the kidnapper thinks Father McCormick can identify him—"

"I'll take care of it."

The medics were carrying him out now. Watching, I could not keep my tears from spilling over. He was wrapped in blankets, belted down on the stretcher, his face partly covered. To be truthful, I didn't really recognize him, but I knew it had to be Hudson. They took him around the side of the house to where the ambulance had pulled up the driveway, just as it had on Christmas Night seven years ago for Julia Farragut.

I got the address of the hospital they were taking Hudson to and started down the drive to my car, which I had reparked on the street after the Belvederes called the police.

"Miss Bennett! Christine!"

I turned around and saw Marilyn Belvedere coming across the front lawn of the Corcoran house, where the snow was now trampled flat.

"How on earth did you think to look there?" she asked as she reached me.

I said something sketchy about the ATV and the house.

"Well, I'm glad it's over. You were right all along, weren't you?"

I wasn't sure what she thought I was right about. "I believed he was alive. I'm thankful he is. I hope he survives."

"Well, if there's anything we can do . . ."

"Thank you. Not right now." I wished her a good night and went down the block to my car.

I called Joseph from the rectory, where Father Grimes was elated at the news.

Joseph was almost in tears. "We'll have Christmas again," she said.

"He's in very bad shape, Joseph. He's dehydrated and he may not have had anything to eat for several days, I think, possibly since Christmas Night. And he's suffering from exposure. There was no heat at all in that shed and it was in the teens last night."

"We're all behind him. We won't let him down. Chris, I almost forgot, you got a phone call a little while ago."

"From Jack?"

"From a woman. She sounded very hesitant and wouldn't leave any kind of message. I spoke to her myself. She sounded almost relieved that you weren't here."

"I wonder if it was Marilyn Belvedere. She stopped me as I was leaving the house on Hawthorne Street. I had a feeling she might want to say something but couldn't put it in words."

"Then maybe that's who it was. Come home as soon as you can, Chris. We've got a lovely dinner for you."

"Don't worry about me. It's Hudson we've got to think about."

"We'll get to that right away."

I knew she meant that the nuns would pray for him. A few might go to the hospital and wait for him to revive. I wanted to be at the hospital myself, but I knew I was close now, close enough that I had a chance of bagging a killer. First I called Melanie to see if Jack was there. He wasn't.

"He called and said he'd be late. I guess he's out on a case. I'm holding dinner for him, although he said he'd find some scraps at home."

I laughed. "Is that what he said? Scraps?"

"His word exactly. I'll make sure he's well fed, Chris. Can I pass along a message?"

"Just tell him we've found Father McCormick alive."

"That's wonderful."

"It is." I described the situation.

"That's murder," Mel said.

"Let's hope it's only attempted murder. Thanks for looking after Jack."

I was pretty sure the discovery of Hudson would draw out his kidnapper, especially if the kidnapper thought Hudson was alive and could identify him. Trusting that there would, indeed, be a police guard at the hospital, I dialed Mrs. Farragut's number. There was no answer. I let it ring several times, but neither she nor a machine picked up. I took another cookie, said my good-byes, and left, my thoughts turning to Marilyn Belvedere. What could she want to tell me that she hadn't had the nerve to say earlier? I drove over to find out.

She seemed nervously unhappy to see me. "This has all been so upsetting," she said as we stood in the foyer. "Warren and I just wanted a quiet evening. Is there something I can do for you?"

There was a fresh scent in the air and I realized I was standing under a piece of mistletoe hanging from a red ribbon. "I understand you called me at the convent."

"When?"

"A little while ago. After I left here."

"I'm afraid you've got the wrong person. Why would I call the convent?"

"I'm sorry," I said, embarrassed at my mistake. "The person who called didn't leave a name and I thought . . . I'm really very sorry."

She smiled. "That's all right. We're a little discombobulated tonight. Was there anything else?"

Aware that I was being ushered out, I shook my head. "Enjoy your evening."

Dumb, I told myself, walking down to the street. But if it wasn't Marilyn Belvedere, who was it? Mrs. Farragut? Had she tried to call me before leaving the house, possibly after hearing the news from her friends at the police department or from her son? Did she even know Hudson had been found?

I got into the car, trying to sort out what I knew. Someone had left Hudson to die in that little shed, because once he knew his kidnapper, he could not be allowed to live whether he gave up secrets or not. So what had happened? The kidnapper or Hudson with a gun on him had driven from the thruway rest stop to 211 Hawthorne Street and into the garage, the kidnapper having found out in advance that the Corcorans would be away for the holidays. Hudson was then taken to the third-floor apartment, where he was fed at least once and questioned about his relationship to Julia Farragut. Then what? Then he was tied up and left in the shed, but not before the heat was turned down on the third floor. Had one of the Farraguts kept the key to that door, hoping the Corcorans would not change the lock?

I was sure the transfer to the shed had happened last night, after I had gone through the Corcoran house with Marilyn Belvedere and heard the furnace kick on. The cold of the shed would assure both that Hudson would die and that the smell of death would be minimal. Perhaps the killer intended to come back and get rid of the body before the Corcorans returned; perhaps he intended to let the Corcorans discover it on the first day of spring planting. Any of the Farraguts would have known exactly where to leave the car, where to leave Hudson. They might even have prepared in advance by removing the Corcorans' padlock, if there was any, and getting a new one. But which of the Farraguts?

And who had called me at the convent? Mrs. Farragut? Who else could it have been? But if it had been Mrs. Farragut, wouldn't Joseph have said it was an older voice? All she had said was that it was a woman. I started the car. Two police vehicles were still parked in front of 211, a car and a station wagon, which I guessed was a crime-scene crew shared by the local towns. They would be looking for fingerprints and other evidence in the shed and might be there for hours. I drove to the center of town.

I wanted to try that phone number again, but I didn't want to bother Father Grimes. There was a diner near the main street of Riverview with a parking lot outside and several cars in it. I went inside and found the phones. I dialed the long number and waited for the brief mechanical message. Then, altering my voice, I said, "This is Sister Mary Teresa. I have a message for you. A little while ago—"

The phone was lifted and a man's voice interrupted. "Hello? Who is this?"

"This is Sister Mary Teresa," I said again, slowly and carefully. It didn't really matter whether he thought it was she or not. The fact that someone had connected him with her would be enough to shock him.

"Sister who?"

"Sister Mary Teresa from St. Stephen's Convent." I kept my voice flat.

"Why are you calling me?" Did I detect a note of panic?

"I have to tell you something about Father Hudson McCormick."

"I think you must have the wrong number." Definitely not calm.

"Father McCormick was found alive a little while ago in

the old shed behind the house that the Farraguts used to live in in Riverview."

"Who is this?" he said loudly.

"This is Sister Mary Teresa," I said in an almost mechanical voice. "I thought you should know that Father McCormick was found alive a little while ago. He was in an old shed—"

The phone at the other end was hung up with a bang. I replaced the receiver in the pay phone in front of me, feeling very satisfied. I hadn't recognized the voice, but he was clearly rattled. I was pretty sure I hadn't been speaking to Walter Farragut. The voice was younger, although voices can be deceptive. But I had scared someone, and with luck, I had gotten him moving. The question was, where would he go? To the hospital, to the old Farragut house, or to a family member? With luck we would find out soon. Putting a quarter into the slot, I tried Mrs. Farragut's number again, but there was still no answer.

The counter was L-shaped and I sat on a stool on the small leg. Three men sat along the long side, all eating hefty meals. I asked for a cup of hot chocolate and watched as the counterman whipped it up for me. A man and woman came in, bringing with them a gust of cold air that blew directly at me. I clutched my coat, shivering at the blast. The couple sat at one of the plastic-topped tables near my stool after wishing a loud Happy New Year to the man behind the counter, who waved and responded as he carried my whipped-cream-topped chocolate to me.

I sipped it slowly, relishing its warmth. One of the men eating dinner said something and the one next to him laughed loudly. I let my eyes pass over the three. The one nearest me looked vaguely familiar, which probably meant he was wearing something trendy that I had seen on someone else. I finished my chocolate before anyone else finished eating, paid up, and went outside.

The couple had driven a large Lincoln, which now stood just to the right of the door to the diner. Next to it were a tow truck, a van, and my car. I slowed to look at the tow truck, then got in my car to avoid the wind.

The question I was worrying was who had called me at St. Stephen's. I wasn't convinced that it wasn't Marilyn

Belvedere. Perhaps there was something she wanted to tell me that she felt she couldn't say in front of her husband, who had very likely been sitting in the living room when I came in. That meant she wouldn't speak to me unless he wasn't around. Mrs. Farragut, a slimmer possibility, didn't strike me as a hesitant person. She was pretty forceful, and I suspected she didn't consider the possibility that she might be wrong. If she had decided to divulge information to me, she wouldn't tremble at the brink.

What other women had I spoken to? There was Eileen at the real-estate office, but that didn't seem promising. Miranda Santiago's voice sounded more girlish than womanly, and her mother had been so forthcoming it was hard to believe there was anything else she could tell me. I had gone through that carton myself without any interference and I really didn't think I had missed anything. But who else was there? I had talked to the housekeepers in two rectories and had actually gotten some interesting facts from Mrs. Pfeiffer at Visitation, but that had been a dead end. OK, Kix, I said to myself silently, narrow it down. How would Jack do it? She's local, she's interested or involved, and it's a short list. Don't discard any possibility. It can't be any of them, but it has to be one of them.

The diner door opened and two men walked out, one of them getting into the tow truck after calling his good-bye to the other. I watched it back out, then turn left into the street. Something about it, something about the driver.

"OK," I said aloud. "Let's try Sunny Gallagher."

The counterman gave me a battered phone book and I looked up Gallagher. There were several listed, but I recognized Sunny's street name. She answered on the second ring.

"Mrs. Gallagher, this is Chris Bennett."

"Yes, hello."

"I understand you called me this evening at St. Stephen's."

She said nothing. Then: "I—yes, I did. How did you know?"

When you can't answer a question, ask another, one of Arnold Gold's golden rules. "Do you have something to tell me?"

It was obviously very difficult for her, but I had expected that from Joseph's description of the call. "There is something, yes."

"Please tell me."

"I've been thinking about it all day." Her voice had none of the strength and energy of this morning. "There's something I didn't tell you." Another pause and then it came. "There was a third letter."

28

She ushered me into the house with a face that belied her name.

"It came in December of that year. Serena Farragut died around Thanksgiving and Miranda went back to school that Sunday. The funeral was the day after, I think, and the Farraguts let it be known that it would be private. I sent a basket of flowers, but I didn't visit the family. Julia came home when her mother died and she never went back to the convent. She wrote to Miranda after she came home and addressed the letter here. I can't really explain why I opened it. It's not the sort of thing I do, but I think I wanted to protect my daughter from the pain her friend was suffering."

We had walked into the family room where I had gone through the carton early this afternoon. A fire was burning in the fireplace and I sat near it. Sunny sat in a chair across from me so that we shared the warmth.

"I have some conditions you will have to agree to," she said.

"What kind of conditions?"

"I will read the letter to you. I will not give it to you. I do not want my daughter to know this letter ever arrived and I want you to promise you won't tell her."

"I promise."

"This is a personal letter. It's not evidence and I won't turn it over to the police. I can't explain why I've kept it all these years, but I have. Maybe there really is such a thing as destiny and this letter has been waiting all this time for someone to come along and look into what happened in that family. If so, then I'm glad I kept it. You seem the right person to be doing it. I think you genuinely care about what happened to Julia and you don't seem to have an ax to grind. But my daughter must never know of the existence of this letter."

"She will never know it from me."

Sunny pulled the letter out of the envelope. " 'Dear Miranda,' " she read. " 'I'm sure you have heard that my mother is gone. Of all the people I have ever known, I have loved her the most. I don't know how to live with her loss, but I know that I have to. I know she only wanted the best for me and I will accomplish that best in her memory.

" 'I wanted so much to see you while you were home, but it was impossible. Daddy wanted as little display as possible, so we kept to ourselves and mourned together.

" 'I will not be returning to St. Stephen's. My life there was the best I have ever had but I've been confused— maybe even a little mad—and I've done some awful things. If I write them down, perhaps they will make sense to me. You've been such a good friend for so long, maybe you'll know what I should do to right my wrongs.

" 'I'm sure I wrote you about the priest I call Hudson River McCormick. He is a truly wonderful person and he's helped me more than I can describe. But I had bad dreams and I made accusations—I don't even remember what they were—that weren't true. Well, maybe I do remember. Maybe it was confusion. The accusations were true, but they were made against the wrong person.' " Sunny looked up. "This is very painful," she said.

"I know it is."

She looked back at the page. " 'I have a brother who really isn't my brother—well, maybe he is. He is a sad, confused person and we have all tried our best to make him happy. Maybe I didn't try hard enough, but I know that I have been happiest when he was away. I think that's true of my mother, too. He has hurt me on many occasions, Miranda. I have not wanted to complain. Sometimes I've thought it might have been my fault, that something I was doing was wrong, that I was encouraging him. My mother, who was the only person I could talk to, said that wasn't true. She said I shouldn't blame myself. Now that she's gone, I feel I have no one to turn to, no one to take her place and keep me going. I want to live a happy and productive life, but how can I do it in this house? But I know I must. It's what my mother wanted for me, what Hudson River wants for me, and what I want for myself.' Her handwriting becomes hard to read here," Sunny said. "As if she's disintegrating as she writes."

"It happened in the second letter, too."

" 'I have decided to write a long letter to my mother, a diary letter, to tell her everything I have been unable to say out loud. Maybe that will help me. I know my mother will read what I write and forgive me. She always did.

" 'And then, of course, there is my Sweet Doubter. In the end, it looks as though he was right. I could not finish my novitiate. I have not seen him for some time, but I still have deep feelings for him. He will come back, I'm sure of it. We will see each other at Christmas and that will be a happy time but also a sad one, without my mother. I'll see you, too, then, Miranda. This is a terrible burden I have shared with you, but I know you won't let me down.

" 'I have somehow mislaid your college address, the box number and all that, so I'll mail this to your house and have your mother forward it. Do well in your exams. I hope to go away to college myself when things get straightened out, maybe even the spring semester if we can arrange it.

" 'See you at Christmas. Lots of love, Julia.' " Sunny folded the sheets and put them back in the envelope.

"It doesn't sound like a girl who's giving up on life," I said.

"No." She took her glasses off and laid them on the table next to her chair, but she held on to the letter as though I might grab it and run with it. "Once I read it, I couldn't send it on to Miranda," she explained, her guilt spilling over. "Miranda was only eighteen herself. She was much too young to involve herself in such a terrible situation. I felt for Julia, I really did. I called her after the letter came and asked her how things were going. She said she missed her mother, but she was looking ahead. She asked if the letter had arrived and I said it had and that I would give it to Miranda when she came home for Christmas. Maybe I thought I would at that point. Maybe I thought Miranda and I would try to do something together for Julia."

"You opened it when it came," I said.

"Almost immediately. I had that sense of foreboding when I saw it. I told myself I would just read it and then tell Miranda I had opened it by mistake. I was making excuses from the first moment, but after I read it, I knew I couldn't let my daughter get involved in this. I couldn't let her go to that house with that monster. I know I should have gone to the police or to Father Grimes or—"

"I'm not judging you, Sunny. I'm very grateful that you read the letter to me."

"What do you think? Do you think Foster kidnapped the priest?"

"It certainly looks that way. We found Father McCormick a couple of hours ago in a shed behind the Corcoran house."

"Is he alive?"

"Yes, he is. I'm hoping—we're all hoping—he'll be able to identify the person that left him there to die."

"I hope so, too. I mean that."

I knew she did. I understood that in protecting her child she did not mean to harm Julia, but I could not help wondering how different things might be if the Gallaghers had invited Julia to go away for Christmas, to have a good time with her friend. But realistically, it might not have worked. Julia was a religious girl who might have chosen to be home for the holiday, to go to her own church, see her own priest, be with her father and grandmother.

Sometimes you dream about things you can't change, but tonight I had no time for dreams. I had to catch a killer.

This time I found an open pharmacy for my phone call. I'm not sure why I didn't want to go back to the diner, but something about it made me feel creepy. The pharmacy had a pay phone in a less open place and I didn't have the feeling that everyone around me was listening to my conversation. Angela must have closed the switchboard because Joseph answered on the first ring. When the switchboard is closed, all incoming calls go directly to her room.

I told her about Sunny Gallagher's letter.

"I guess that answers our questions," she said.

"Only some of them. There are still a lot of things that aren't clear to me, things that aren't consistent."

"Maybe our numbers are wrong, Chris."

I waited for her to amplify, but she didn't. "You're being a sphinx again," I said with a laugh.

"You know those jokes about how many people it takes to change a lightbulb?"

"Most of the answers are insensitive or politically incorrect."

"True, but I've been thinking, perhaps we should be asking how many people it takes to change two lightbulbs. That may simplify the problem for us."

"Joseph," I said, feeling a sense of excitement building, "you may have it. A couple of things happened tonight—I don't have time to tell you about them. I wish I could remember what page of the Bible Sister Mary Teresa left that scrap of paper in."

"It will come to you. And I'm right here. All night."

"I'll talk to you again soon."

I tried Mrs. Farragut again, and this time she answered.

"It's Christine Bennett," I said. "I thought you'd like to know that Father McCormick has been found alive."

"That's certainly good news. You've been successful."

"Yes. We're all very relieved, not just that he's all right, but that he'll be able to name his kidnapper."

"Then that should put an end to your little investigation."

"I think so. Everything seems to be falling into place. By the way, he was left in the shed behind 211 Hawthorne Street."

There was a pause. "How unfortunate for the new family."

"But fortunate for the investigation. It links his kidnapper to your granddaughter's death."

"Whatever pleases you, Miss Bennett. If you'll excuse me, I'll say good night."

"Good night, Mrs. Farragut."

Had she been a little anxious to get off the phone?

As I drove back to Hawthorne Street all kinds of things started to make sense. Little bits of conversation with people I had interviewed came back to me, this time with new meaning. Things I had seen and ignored because they struck me as irrelevant now took on great import. Even the mistletoe I had stood under earlier in the evening had a message for me.

The scent I had detected as I stood in the foyer had not come from Christmas greenery; it had been Mrs. Farragut's own fragrance. That was why I had not been invited in; she had been there, discussing who knew what with the Belvederes, who had told me they hadn't kept in touch with her. They had done more than keep in touch. They had been part of a conspiracy. I wasn't sure exactly how it worked, but I sensed I was about to find out.

I turned into Hawthorne Street and parked the car on the opposite side from number 211 and before I reached it so that the Belvedere house was farther down the block. A lone police car stood in front of the Corcorans', which meant the crime-scene people had done their job and gone on their way. I got out of my car and crossed over, then walked up the driveway to the back of the house. As expected, one policeman was standing near the shed, just outside the yellow-and-black crime-scene tape, which was stiff from the cold. This was a routine procedure, guarding the crime scene to make certain nothing was disturbed in case the crime-scene people needed to come back for further evidence.

I called, "Hello," and he came to attention.

"Who's there?"

"I'm Chris Bennett. I found Father McCormick in the shed."

"Right. I recognize your name."

He looked young enough that he might not have been on the Riverview police force seven years ago, might feel no obligation to the Farragut family.

"How long have you been on the police force here?"

"Three years. Three and a half. Spend most of my time riding around in my car. On patrol, you know?"

"I was so shaken up when I talked to the police before, I forgot to mention something. Whoever kidnapped Father McCormick kept him in that third-floor apartment for a while." I pointed to the stairs.

"How'd you get in there?"

"The door was open. The kidnapper probably forgot to lock it when he took Father McCormick down the stairs last night. There's a mattress up there and some coffee cups. Your crime-scene people will want to look it over."

"Can I ask you how you came to try that door?"

"I think someone who had access to this house, maybe when the Farraguts lived here, had a key."

"I'll call it in," he said. "Have a good night."

I wished him the same and went back to my car. Then I waited. I turned on the radio to help stay awake. Two men and a woman were talking about some topic that I never quite got straight. It had something to do with Christmas and something to do with women. I didn't really listen; I thought about Hudson, Sister Mary Teresa, and Julia. I put together what I knew and what I thought was likely and I kept my eyes open. If I had laid a trap, someone might take the bait.

It took half an hour. The woman on the radio was talking about the portrayal of women in the New Testament. "After all," she said, "it was Mary Magdalene who carried the word to the disciples, 'I have seen the Lord; and these things He said to me.'"

The page in Sister Mary Teresa's New Testament! I almost started the car to find a telephone when I saw headlights, a car coming toward me, slowing as it approached. As I watched, it turned into the driveway. The trap had sprung.

29

A second police car pulled up in front of 211, then turned into the driveway. That would be in response to the first officer's call about the third floor. I crossed the street and joined both men behind the house.

"Someone may try to get into that third-floor area," I said. "To clean it up."

"We'll look out for him."

"He may try the front door. I think he has a key."

"Why don't you go around front, Bud?" the one who had just arrived said. "I'll go look at the upstairs."

I walked back down the driveway with Bud.

"Someone's at the front door now," he said in a low voice, reaching for his gun. "Stand back."

I watched him step carefully through the snow as the person at the door fumbled with a key. The crunch of the surface ice seemed very loud. As he went forward he moved into a crouch.

"Police," Bud called in a loud voice. "Don't move." The order was loud and direct. And ignored.

I watched as the figure turned, as the frightened face was revealed by the porch light. It was Warren Belvedere.

There was a light on at Mike's Auto Body Shop. I tapped the dirty glass in the door and went inside.

"Help you?" he said. It was the man I had seen at the diner. He was sitting at a lighted table, papers spread out from end to end.

"I need to make a phone call. I wondered if I could use yours."

"Sure thing. There's a pay phone in the work area. Turn left."

I dialed the convent and Joseph answered on the first ring.

"It's Chris. The page in the Bible is where Mary Magdalene goes to the tomb after the resurrection."

"That story is in all the Gospels. Do you remember which one?"

"John, I'm sure of it. It was near the middle of the book. John ends around the middle."

"Let me find it." She was gone a short time and I looked around the body shop. A crushed and mangled car was about ten feet from me, minus a lot of necessary parts, not that it would ever ride the road again. I wondered if the occupants had survived the crash. "Here it is. Shall I read it to you?"

"Tell me what follows. I don't think the Mary Magdalene story is what matters."

"The next thing is that Jesus comes and speaks to the disciples."

"OK. And then what?"

"And then there's the discussion of the disciple Thomas."

"Thomas," I repeated. "Doubting Thomas."

"The very same."

"I think we've got him, Joseph."

"Got whom?"

"Sister Mary Teresa's killer."

"Be careful, Chris."

"I will."

I hung up and went back to where Mike was sitting at a table working with papers. "You're Tom Belvedere's friend, aren't you?" I asked.

"Yeah, that's right. We've been friends since kindergarten."

"He borrowed your car last week, didn't he? When he had car trouble."

"How'd you know about that?"

"I saw you working on his car the other day," I said, not exactly answering his question. "Thanks very much for the telephone. I'd better be going now."

"Good night."

I waved and left him at his table, looking a little puzzled.

* * *

I was pretty sure you couldn't use a private tow truck on the thruway, but I've seen cars pulling a second car as if it were a trailer. It wouldn't have taken much to prepare for that kind of tow if Tom Belvedere, Julia's Sweet Doubter, had intended to follow Hudson and waylay him at a rest stop. It's a pretty sure thing that on a trip of that length, about three hundred miles, you'll make at least one stop. All Tom Belvedere had to do was ask his friend for the use of the car I had seen in the Belvederes' driveway. It had MIKE'S AUTO BODY SHOP on the side, but it was a regular sedan, not a forbidden tow truck.

When I had left the Corcoran house a little while ago, Warren Belvedere was trying to explain to Bud that he was just going inside to water the plants, as his wife had forgotten to do it for several days, something I knew firsthand was a lie. As I saw it, Tom, after hearing my Mary Teresa impersonation, had come home to clean up the third floor before the police nailed him for kidnapping Hudson. He must have told his parents about it and his father decided he would enter through the front, where he might avoid being seen by the police guard in the rear. Fortunately, we had caught him.

And with Mike of the auto body shop, I now knew how Tom's car had been retrieved from the rest stop. All Tom had to do after securing Hudson in the third-floor apartment was drive back, attach one car to another, and continue home. If the toll collector complained that his ticket didn't mention a trailer, he could easily say it hadn't been noticed when he got on in Buffalo and simply pay the difference.

I drove back for what I hoped would be my last visit to Hawthorne Street. There was still one police car in front of 211 and one in the driveway. I walked to the back of the house, where I ran into the second officer.

"Bud's next door with the guy who was trying to get in the front way," he said in answer to my question. "There was a lot of screaming and yelling. We'll have to see if he left any prints on the third floor, where it looks like he kept the priest for a while."

"It's his son," I said. "The father was just coming over to clean up for his son."

"You know what he did it for?"

"Love. What else?"

Bud let me in the Belvedere house. Marilyn Belvedere was crying; Warren was trying to explain that he had nothing to do with Father McCormick's kidnapping, that all he wanted to do was water some plants and he wouldn't say anything else till his lawyer came.

"He didn't do it, Bud," I said. "It was his son."

"You folks have a son?" Bud said, turning to them.

They looked at each other as though they weren't sure.

"He's probably upstairs. He came home about half an hour ago, just before you found Mr. Belvedere at the front door."

"You want to call him down, ma'am?"

Marilyn got up, dabbing at her eyes, and went to the foot of the stairs as her husband watched speechlessly. She looked up for a long moment before she called, "Tom? You want to come down, Tom?"

There was a muffled answer and a door closed. I looked at him closely as he came down the stairs, a tall, handsome man in his late twenties or early thirties, four or five years older than Julia. He stopped when he saw the uniform.

"Is something wrong, Officer?" he asked politely.

"I just have a few questions to ask you," Bud answered, equally politely.

"Don't say anything, Tom," Warren called. "Don't say a word."

"Can you tell me what this is about?"

"This lady thinks you were responsible for kidnapping Father McCormick."

"I don't even know who he is," Tom said quietly.

"He was Julia Farragut's friend and confessor at St. Stephen's Convent," I said.

"I hardly knew Julia. That was a long time ago."

"You not only knew her, you were in love with her. She gave you the key to the third-floor apartment and you used to go over there to see her and let yourself in."

"Where did you get this crazy story from?"

"She talked about you to friends. She wrote letters. I

read some of them this afternoon." I didn't elaborate. It was enough that he knew I knew the truth.

He looked a little less sanguine. Bud had taken out a small notebook and flipped it open.

"Tom, you shouldn't be saying anything," Marilyn said.

"I haven't said anything, Mother. This woman is doing all the talking."

And Bud was writing. I wanted to give him enough that he could get a search warrant to look for the key to the third-floor apartment. I was pretty sure Tom hadn't used the downstairs key because the door at the bottom of the third-floor stairs had been locked. He had come and gone through the door on the third floor.

"You must have met Sister Mary Teresa when Julia died," I went on. "And you gave her that collect number to your apartment so you could keep in touch with her. You wanted information on Father McCormick and she could give it to you. You found out from Mary Teresa that he was coming east for Christmas and she also told you where he would be the night before. You followed him on the thruway till he stopped to change his clothes and you kidnapped him."

"This is ridiculous," he said.

"Your friend Mike at Mike's Auto Body Shop lent you his car so you could retrieve your own car at the rest stop because you drove Father McCormick's ATV to Riverview."

"Where he left it at the curb," Bud said, "so we'd think the priest was giving us some kind of message."

"But he didn't leave it on the street till the night after Christmas. Maybe he thought he'd let Father McCormick go if he cooperated. Maybe he just hadn't thought the whole plan through to the end. But the first night he must have parked the vehicle in the garage, where no one could see it. He knew how much time he had to work with because his parents were friends of the Corcorans and knew when they were returning from their vacation."

"Who is this Sister Mary Teresa?" Bud asked.

"She was an older nun at St. Stephen's Convent. She was murdered between Saturday night and Sunday morning. She must have realized that the man she talked to on the telephone from time to time, the man she had given all that information about Father McCormick, was the one who made him disappear. So she called and left a message." I turned to Tom. "Did you have the call forwarded to this number or did you check your answering machine?"

"This is all a fabrication," Tom said, but he had lost his cool. "You can't prove any of this."

"The telephone company will have a record of every collect call from the St. Stephen's number to yours. She was such a lovely, caring old woman. I don't know why you had to kill her." I said it with the full force of my grief.

"I didn't kill her," he said, his voice breaking. "I was just trying to keep her quiet. She started shouting and screaming and I covered her face to shut her up and suddenly she slumped. She just fell through my hands."

"Tom," his mother wailed.

"Tom," I echoed. "How long have you been talking to Mary Teresa?"

"I met her at the funeral. I told her I was Julia's cousin. I let her in on some details so she would trust me and we wrote to each other sometimes. A few years ago I gave her the free number to the phone in my apartment. She would call me every couple of weeks and we'd talk. She liked to talk to me and she would tell me little things about Father McCormick when she heard them. I told her I wanted to meet him if he came back to visit, and finally it paid off. A couple of months ago she called and said he was coming for Christmas."

"But you didn't just want to have a conversation with him," I said.

"I knew about the charges against him and I wanted him to tell me if they were true. I wanted to know what the hell had gone on between him and Julia, if he was hurting her because he had control over her. I wanted to know if she'd told him about Foster and, if she did, why the hell he didn't do anything about it. I hated him for that, that he knew and didn't do anything."

"I think he was trying very hard to help her," I said. "It wasn't his decision to send her away from St. Stephen's. It was someone else's. And he couldn't disclose to you or anyone else what she told him in the privacy of the confessional. Even her death doesn't change that. I think it's your-self you're angry at, Tom. You're the one who could have helped her. You're the one who could have blown the whistle. Instead you took it all out on a priest who really tried and a nun who loved her selflessly. Why did you meet her that night?"

"She called and said she had to see me," he said, his voice low now, resigned. "She didn't exactly threaten me, but I knew if I didn't show up, there'd be trouble. She'd put together the priest's disappearance and her telling me when he was coming. Then she just went crazy. She started accusing me of killing Julia. She said she would go to the police and tell them it was me. I was scared. She was a sweet old nun, she was believable. Who was I? I was already in trouble with the priest, who wouldn't tell me a damn thing, and if this nun went to the police, the Farraguts would—"

"Tom!" Marilyn was on her feet.

"What would the Farraguts do?" I asked, addressing all of them. "You told me you'd lost contact with them, but Mrs. Farragut was here tonight, just an hour or so ago." I looked at my watch, surprised at how late it had become. "She was here when I was here."

There was a lot of silence, but I could almost hear the deafening roar underneath it. Something had gone on between the Belvederes and the Farraguts, and these three people knew what it was and were all part of it.

Tom broke the silence, a silence that was seven years old. "I'm not going to jail for something I didn't do. I don't care what that old woman says."

"I think I should advise you of your rights," Bud said, and I wondered whether, in this small, quiet town, it was the first time in his three years in the police department that he had said it.

"Hang my rights," Tom retorted. "Foster Farragut killed his sister seven years ago and those people have been pro-tecting him since it happened."

"Tom," Marilyn said, "I beg you."

"If we'd spoken up then, we'd all be better off."

I wasn't sure he was right, but at least he was finally ac-cepting responsibility. "Did you see him do it?" I asked.

"I saw them through the window of her bedroom. I was coming up the stairs to see her. He had the rope in his hand, behind his back, and he was shouting at her. He was a crazy son of a bitch and he'd been jealous of her all her life. I ran up to the third floor and got my key out to open the door, but it was so damn cold, I dropped it and it went through the boards down into the snow. I ran down and found it and raced back up, got inside, and went down to her room on the second floor. She was hanging from the rope." He stopped, his face contorted as the pain the memory had brought to the surface hit him. "I grabbed her and tried to lift her, to get the pressure off her throat, but I could see it was too late. It was too late. I was too late to save her." He wept into his hands.

"What happened then, Tom?" I asked gently.

"I got the rope untied. I laid her on the bed and tried mouth-to-mouth. There was nothing I could do to help her. I ran to find the grandmother. I said, 'Foster killed Julia.' I'll never forget her reaction. Her eyes opened wide and she said, 'That's nonsense. Foster isn't even home.' I've never seen such cold-blooded presence of mind. We ran up to Julia's room and she called the police and asked for an ambulance. She said her granddaughter had attempted suicide."

"Where was Foster?"

"He sure as hell wasn't in the house. He came back later, a lot later."

"Did Mrs. Farragut take anything out of Julia's room?" I asked.

"How did you know?"

"What did she take?"

"The papers on Julia's desk. She just grabbed them and took them away. And she said to me, 'Young man, I know what was going on between you and my granddaughter. If you make any accusations, I will see to it that you are charged with her murder. You and that priest both defiled her.' I remember she used that word, *defiled*. I didn't defile Julia, I loved her."

I turned to Bud. "If you can keep this quiet, you may be able to get a warrant to search Mrs. Farragut's apartment for the diary. Julia wrote it as though it was a letter to her dead mother, telling her the truth of how her brother abused her. But if Mrs. Farragut gets word that you're after it, she may destroy it to protect her grandson."

"How do you know she still has it?"

"She talked to me about it. From what she said, I had a strong feeling she had kept it."

He unsnapped the leather loop on his belt, unlatched the handcuffs it held, and said to Tom, "I'm going to have to take you in, sir. I'm arresting you for the kidnapping of Father McCormick. You have the right to remain silent. You have the right . . ."

The wail from Marilyn Belvedere drowned out the rest of the Miranda warning.

30

I went to the hospital to see how Hudson was doing. Four of the nuns from St. Stephen's were there, including Angela.

"The doctor said he hadn't eaten for several days, hadn't had much to drink. He's very dehydrated and he spent the last twenty-four hours in that beastly-cold shed without warm clothing. And because he was tied up, he couldn't move around much. He was very near death, Chris." She said this last in a low voice, as though speaking such words softly might prevent them from becoming true.

"I know. I wish I had put it all together sooner."

"You found him. No one else was even looking for him."

I went over and talked to the other three nuns. They would spend the night here, hoping for good news to telephone to Joseph. I longed to get into that room, to see if he looked better than when they had taken him from the shed, but no one was allowed in on orders of the doctor. I was relieved to see a police guard posted outside the door. Foster had not yet been arrested, but the Riverview police assured me they were working with the local police in Mrs. Farragut's town. It was a messy, complicated case and there was still plenty of resistance in the Riverview Police Department against reopening the suicide of Julia Farragut. But if there is such a thing as resting in peace, I felt that Julia and her mother now had that chance. I went back to St. Stephen's.

Joseph was waiting up and we sat together with a pot of hot tea.

"Jack called at some point," she said, as though time had become a variable. "He was out on a case that took hours."

"A lot of them do."

"Look how long this one took. Another day and we would have lost Hudson."

"Tom Belvedere's first mistake was leaving Hudson's car in front of 211 Hawthorne. It drew me to the house. It made me feel the house was the place to look for answers."

"Your instincts are good. Even when you're personally involved, you don't sacrifice your good sense."

"If I had only realized there were two killers."

"We weren't even sure how many crimes there were, Chris."

"Too many as it turned out. And poor Mary Teresa got herself in the middle. Tom told her he was a relative of Julia and he wanted to talk to Hudson if he came east. When she put things together, she must have been mortified to think she had unwittingly become part of his kidnapping. I have to admit she was pretty gutsy to meet him alone at night, especially when she suspected he was also guilty of murdering Julia."

"The villa's full of tough old women," Joseph said. "You know that."

"I do know that. I'm very proud of it."

"So am I. Go to bed, Chris. We have a big day tomorrow."

We buried Sister Mary Teresa in St. Stephen's churchyard the next morning. The sun was out and the snow glistened on top of the tombstones. Generations of St. Stephen's nuns were buried here, some of them people I had known during my fifteen-year tenure, all of them strong and memorable women. Mary Teresa would be in good company.

Detective Lake was waiting in the Mother House when we came back from the cemetery to give a formal report to Joseph. Tom Belvedere had been arrested for the murder of Sister Mary Teresa and the kidnapping of Father Hudson McCormick and was being held in the county jail. A search warrant had been executed and Mrs. Farragut's apartment had been searched. This was in still another town, Detective Lake pointed out, but the various departments were working together. For a change, I thought with some bitterness. Papers had been found in her apartment that might shed light on the apparent suicide of Julia Farragut seven years ago. So they had found the diary. And not unexpectedly, Tom Belvedere's lawyer was looking to make a deal with the district attorney. Tom had some evidence he wanted to give on the death of Julia Farragut and the involvement of her half brother, Foster. It would take time to make sense of the whole case.

The word from the hospital was noncommittal. Hudson had not yet regained consciousness and his condition was described as critical. It looked as though he might lose several toes and possibly some fingers to frostbite, but it was still too soon to tell if he would pull through.

It was New Year's Eve and I had finished my work. I took Joseph's advice and went home. I was so exhausted, I took my clothes off and went to bed. We were expected at a party at the Grosses', and I remembered, from what seemed half a lifetime ago, I had promised to help get things together. But I had had very little sleep and the pressure of the last days all crashed down on me as I reached home. I slept.

My wonderful husband, fresh from the outdoors, woke me when he sat down on the bed and kissed me.

"Oh Jack," I said, "have I missed you."

"It's only six o'clock. We could make up for it."

"That would be good." I pulled him down, feeling his cold cheek against my very warm one.

"I'm still dressed," he said.

"I don't remember that was ever a problem. For long."

"Not for long." He kissed me. "Boy, have I missed you, sweetheart."

I unbuttoned his shirt and moved my face against his chest. "I'm glad to be home."

The party was terrific. We met a lot of Oakwood people and a lot of people the Grosses knew from other places. And the food was the best I'd eaten in ages. Melanie had been cooking and freezing for weeks—how had she ever managed to take time off to help bake Christmas cookies?—and everything was superlative. At midnight we had champagne and more food and sang "Auld Lang

Syne," which I have always felt was a very necessary element on New Year's Eve.

At one-thirty we walked down Pine Brook Road with our neighbors, the McDonalds. We were all feeling good, and Midge and I were giggling like children. At our house, we called a lot of good nights and Happy New Years and Jack and I went inside. Our Christmas tree was still fragrant in the living room and the fireplace had that after-fire smell that I like so much, smoke and burned wood; let no one dare tell me they're a hazard to my health.

"Great party," Jack said.

I was about to agree with him in decisive but tipsy terms when we heard the phone ring. "Hudson," I said, my heart doing terrible flips. I dashed for the kitchen and answered.

"I have a collect call for anyone from Sister Dolores in Riverview," the operator said. "Will you pay for the call?"

Not surprising. Sister Dolores wasn't likely to have more than fifty cents or a dollar with her and she might already have spent it for coffee to stay awake. "Yes, I will," I said, fear clawing at me.

"Chris," Sister Dolores said loudly, "I've been trying you all evening. He's awake! He's talking!" I could hear the excitement in her voice, the exuberance.

"Thank God," I responded, turning to Jack and making a circle of my thumb and forefinger, then brushing my eyes.

"It's still touch and go. The doctor doesn't want us to be too optimistic, but who listens to doctors at my age?"

"Dolores, I'm so happy. I'm just so happy. What did he say?"

"What else? Merry Christmas."

31

The Saturday after New Year's we all got together at St. Stephen's to visit with Hudson. It was a second Christmas and a celebration of his return to the living. He still looked frail and there were bandages on his hands and feet and a pair of crutches resting against the stone fireplace near where he was sitting, but it was the old Hudson smile and his eyes were bright.

We had introductions to make and catching up to do before anyone ventured to talk about the events of the last two weeks and those of seven years ago. Arnold and Harriet Gold had joined us for the day and Arnold and Hudson had plenty to talk about.

"I don't know, Chrissie," Arnold said, turning to me. "This is the first case you didn't ask for my good counsel. I must be getting old and useless."

"Two words no one will ever apply to you, Arnold," I countered.

"She didn't even ask me for much," Jack agreed. "And when I could have been helpful, looking up that collect phone number, I was away from the station house and she had to do it all herself."

"We Franciscans are pretty resourceful," Joseph said. "If I do say so myself."

"Say it all you want," Hudson said. "If not for Chris, I wouldn't be here."

"How did Tom Belvedere get you to Riverview?" I asked.

"I gather he knew where I was staying in Buffalo and followed me on the thruway. I don't know why he didn't take me when I called from Albany. Maybe he lost his nerve; maybe I was parked too close to a lot of other people. He couldn't count on my stopping again, but I did, to change my clothes, and that time I parked farther from the building and took my clothes with me so I could change."

"We had dogs in the parking lot, Hudson. They made it look as though you'd walked in a circle."

"Sort of a circle. I started for the building with my suit over my arm and I heard someone call my name. There was a guy there wearing a ski mask or half a mask. I asked him who he was and he said he wanted to talk to me about Julia Farragut. I was feeling kind of confused. I didn't like the ski mask, although it was cold enough to wear one, but it didn't occur to me he'd been following me. I thought it was a chance meeting, and not a very auspicious one. I said why didn't we go inside and have a cup of coffee and he said he had a better idea, and I could tell from the way he said it, it wasn't going to be better for me. I asked him if he was Foster Farragut and he said it didn't matter who he was, so I assumed I had guessed right. It never entered my mind that he was Tom Belvedere. Julia had talked about him as the sweetest person she'd ever met and this man was anything but sweet. He was angry and determined and he had a gun."

"Did you see it?" Jack asked.

"I felt it in my side and I didn't want to call his bluff, in case it wasn't a bluff, and it wasn't. I saw it later. It wasn't very big as guns go, but he was very close. We were walking along the side of the building—he'd said not to go inside—and when we got to the back, I just kept walking onto the snow behind the building and the parking lot. He started asking me about my relationship with Julia, what I knew about her brother, and I said there were a lot of things I couldn't answer, but I could assure him I had been a priest and a friend to her and that was it. That wasn't the answer he wanted. He wanted an admission of intimacy and I couldn't give him that. We went back to my car, but I managed to drop some of what I was carrying, just to leave a trail. I didn't know what he had in mind, but I knew he was dangerous. When we got back to my car, he made me lie down on the floor in the back and he tied me up and covered me with a blanket."

"Had he come prepared for that?" Joseph asked.

"He had rope in a duffel bag he was carrying and a knife that looked like it could cut through steel. Even if I thought he might not use the gun in a public area, the knife looked pretty lethal."

"So he drove," I said.

"He drove and I lay in the back of what has to be the most uncomfortable vehicle I've ever been in—my own."

We laughed.

"For what it cost, you'd think they'd do something about that backseat floor."

"And then when he took you out, you were at 211 Hawthorne Street."

"In the garage. We went up some stairs outside the house to the top floor and we spent a long, unpleasant night together up there."

"More than one," I said.

"Pretty near a week. He kept me hungry and thirstier than I've ever been and about as dirty as I ever want to be, but I don't think he really set out to kill me. I think he thought I'd tell him what he wanted to hear and he'd let me go. But after a couple of days he seemed to change his mind. When he threw me in that shed, I began to lose hope."

"Did you think he was Foster the whole time?" I asked.

"After a while I stopped thinking straight about anything," he said, coming close to admitting despair. "But since I was in the Farragut house, it seemed logical to assume that. But the questions didn't all make sense. He asked me about Julia's suicide and I couldn't tell him anything. Sister Clare Angela never told me about it. It was Joseph who wrote. Whatever my thoughts, it truly didn't occur to me that she had been murdered."

"She was going to expose Foster," I said. "I haven't seen her diary, but Jack's been in touch with the Riverview police and they told him it was very revealing."

"I'm not surprised," Hudson said.

We will never know what she confessed to him, but I am sure he must have tried mightily to get her to speak up about what was happening in that house.

We celebrated Christmas again that day, opening the wonderful, handmade gifts Hudson had carried with him from Wyoming. My gift was a pair of dolls dressed as bride and groom. I will treasure them forever.

We were about to leave when Angela came to me and said someone was waiting to talk to me. I went to the door of the Mother House and saw Marilyn Belvedere standing in a fur coat and boots.

She gave me a tentative smile. "They told me you would be here today. I wanted to explain some things to you."

I found a quiet place for us and she folded her coat over another chair and sat. She was dressed in a dark suit adorned with a diamond brooch and she looked uncomfortable, as though she didn't know how to behave in a convent.

"I wanted you to know why I didn't tell you the whole truth," she said.

"I understand. It was your son."

"It was fear. After Julia's death, Mrs. Cornelius Farragut came over one day and said the night Julia died Tom had been ranting about her being murdered. She knew that that wasn't true, she said, and she knew there had been a relationship between Tom and Julia that might have led to bloodshed. She said she had proof of that, although she never showed us any. She said if Tom went to the police or ever told anyone anything foolish about what happened in her house on Christmas Night, she would have him arrested for Julia's murder."

"And you believed her."

"We couldn't take a chance. He's our son."

"So she protected her grandson, whom she must have suspected was a killer."

"Don't you see? Those two children were her only grandchildren, the only children of her only son. She wanted the Farragut line to continue. Seven years ago it looked like it was ending. She was willing to forgive Foster for killing Julia so that Foster would continue the family."

"Did Walter Farragut know what was going on in that house?"

"I don't think so," Marilyn said. "I think Serena knew and didn't tell him. He should have sensed it, but it wasn't the first time a parent looked the other way. And I'm sure

Mrs. Farragut knew. There wasn't anything that happened in that house that she didn't know."

"I'm sorry about your son. He got caught up in something that led him down two terrible paths."

"I know. He never meant to hurt anyone." Her voice wavered.

"But he did, Marilyn."

"He loved Julia. He couldn't bear to think she had been hurt."

There had been a lot of preparation in Tom Belvedere's kidnapping of Hudson, years of preparation, including the special phone number he gave to Mary Teresa. "The only people who hurt her were in her family," I said, "and old Mrs. Farragut more than any of the others. If she knew and did nothing, she's partly responsible for Julia's death. It was a terrible waste of a young life."

Marilyn put her coat on. "I wish I could have told you," she said. "Perhaps that nun would still be alive. That was an accidental death, you know. She died of a heart attack."

I didn't say anything. She had just admitted being part of a conspiracy to withhold information on a capital crime, and now she had made a second homicide into a death by natural causes. Perhaps when she and her husband were done, they would convince themselves that Hudson had tied himself up and locked himself in the shed to die.

I walked her to the door and said good-bye.

"He's as good as you promised," Jack said as we drove south after Sister Dolores's second Christmas dinner and Hudson's first.

"I didn't know how much I'd missed him till I saw him today. Arnold had a lot to talk to him about, didn't he?"

"About law on the reservations. I thought Arnold was going to offer to go back to Wyoming with him and set up shop there. If he wants to work for nothing, he can probably be employed for the rest of his life."

"He does that here," I said wryly.

"I'll tell you, being around all those nuns really brings back my misspent childhood. When I talk to you, I can believe all nuns are sweet old ladies like Sister Dolores. Twenty, twenty-five years ago, man, that was a different story. We had one nun at my church we used to call Sister Merciless."

"Jack," I objected.

"I can still feel the back of her hand. Didn't you ever notice that scar on my—"

"Jack!" I was giggling in a most undignified manner.

"All I did was—"

"What? What could you have done to deserve the back of her hand?"

"She asked me a question and I forgot and said, 'Yes, Sister Merciless.' "

"You didn't."

"A momentary lapse. Hey, am I perfect? Are you perfect? Who on this earth is perfect?"

"I guess that's it," I said. "Tom wasn't. Sister Mary Teresa wasn't. Old Mrs. Farragut wasn't."

"That's why there was a Christmas Night murder."

"But that heating system. That was pretty close to perfect."

"That's why there weren't two."

now. We had one out of ten (there was not so far Sister Mercies."

"Yes, I helped."

"I am still in the eye of her head. Today you can see her that easy enough—"

"Yes?" I was sitting in a most depraved manner.

"All I do was—"

"What?" She could not bear time to reverse the bed for her head."

She put on a question, and I forgot and said, "Yes, Sister Mercies."

"You didn't?"

"No, not this time. No, and I put out the way I feel."

"I guess that's it. I said, what wasn't I, Sister, with these words. Oh Mrs. Burger, wasn't?"

"This we think was a Christmas Night murder."

"Yet, that during all with what was pretty close ropes."

"No?"

"That's why they would find."